North of the Heart

North of the Heart

By

Julie McDonald

For Gunda, with the good wishes of the author,

Julie McDonald

ISBN 1-58500-586-X

ABOUT THE BOOK

North of the Heart is the story of Alexandra Lund, a young Danish woman who is enjoying the bohemian life in Copenhagen at the dawn of the Roaring Twenties when she attends a press conference with a journalist friend and meets Stig Brand, a Polar adventurer who has come home to celebrate the proclamation of Greenland as Danish territory. They fall in love, he proposes, and although her family objects, she sails for Greenland with him three days after their meeting. They are married by the ship's captain.

Before they can head for his home far to the north, he must guide an American film crew on an expedition to make a documentary, and Alexandra goes along. A young man in the American party falls into a crevasse, and Stig rescues him, but he later dies of pneumonia. Because there are no embalmers in Greenland, the body is shipped home in a cask of imiak (Eskimo beer), which is a preservative.

This is just one example of the culture shock Alexandra experiences. In this remote land where the mail comes once a year children play the "breathless game" and sometimes strangle themselves with the cords of their parkas, chanting shamans called angagoks go into trances and discover hidden secrets, the perpetual darkness of winter can cause a condition of raging despair called perlerorneq, and a favorite dessert is cloudberries in a mixture of seal oil and chewed caribou tallow beaten like whipped cream.

This icy and primitive land challenges the passion Alexandra feels for her husband, and she sometimes wonders if this cold and dangerous place is north of the heart, but she fights the temptation to believe it. Stig injures his arm first and then his leg, and they return to Denmark to seek medical help. After the amputation of his leg, Stig is resigned to staying in Denmark, but Alexandra now feels the pull of Greenland, and they return to a place which they know is not north of the heart.

I

I have always hated the cold. When the short Danish summer signalled its end with sleet-like spray from the Kattegat, I was the first to say, "Let's go home!" Not that my family listened to me--my brother Frederik is a crazy Viking who likes to swim among bobbing ice floes, and he always begged to postpone the return to Aalborg. I walked the beach shivering, longing for our snug, stuccoed house under the huge horse chestnut trees.

Even on a bright day in May, remembering the cold wind cutting under the door of the beach house made me shiver, and I looked at Stig Brand with utter disbelief. This man had spent years in the Polar Arctic by choice, and he had survived to lend glamour to this historic occasion, the proclamation of Greenland as Danish territory on May 10, 1921.

Stig Brand was tall and dark-bearded. His face looked weathered, and the blue of his eyes seemed faded. He didn't seem to be entirely present, and his gaze was fixed on a distant point until someone spoke his name to claim his attention.

Then he was looking at me--really seeing me, Alexandra Lund. I caught my breath and felt the blood rush to my face. I was embarrassed and furious, thinking this was no way for a New Woman to react to a man's appraisal, even if he *was* famous.

"Get ready," Leif whispered.

I tried to look severe in my masquerade as a journalist, positioning my pencil above the small notebook Leif had lent me.

Leif Skovgaard was a reporter for *Folkebladet.* We met at a poetry reading in someone's apartment two weeks earlier, and he had been trying to "emancipate" me with "real life" experiences like this press conference.

"I can get you in," he said. "I'll just borrow Inger Kaarup's credentials. Luckily, she's at home recovering from an appendectomy."

That's how I turned up in this *Rigsdag* chamber as a fake journalist using someone else's name.

"I won't have to ask any questions, will I?" I had asked Leif.

He shrugged and said, "It's up to you."

I listened and took notes as the legislators and Brand answered questions other reporters asked about policy, trade, and effects on the homeland.

Then Leif said, "*Hr.* Brand, we know that you have a special feeling for the native population of Greenland. Will you elaborate?"

Brand looked down at his boots, then raised his eyes and shook his head slightly, as if dismissing a presence that kept him from the moment.

"As you may know, I lost my wife, Naika, to the Spanish influenza three years ago. That contagion was brought to Greenland by foreign ships, and I believe that we must close Greenland to immigration to save the Polar Eskimo."

A widower, I thought. *How sad.*

Then he looked at me again. Flustered, I tried to formulate a question and blurted out, "If Greenland is, as you said, seven-eighths buried under ice and snow, it surely can't be green. Why do they call it that?"

Everyone in the room laughed, it seemed to me. All but Brand, who answered seriously, "Eric the Red gave the world's largest island that name to attract settlers, but it wasn't the name that attracted me."

I wanted to creep away and hide, but I knew he was trying to rescue me. I forced myself to ask, "What was it, then?"

He looked at me with those faded blue eyes, and I thought my heart would stop. Then he shifted his gaze to the brightness beyond the tall, arched windows of the chamber and spoke.

"All who love Greenland are lost. The dream of it is in your blood--the call and the longing last as long as you live."

The press corps stopped smirking and picked up the quote.

The press conference ended, and Leif grabbed my elbow. He said, "You're pretty clever about when to play dumb, aren't you? Thanks for the lead!"

We parted in the street, as Leif needed to write his story, and I hailed a carriage to take me to the *Strøget*. Leif always insisted upon an Austin Seven for the sake of speed, but I had plenty of time--too much time. Once more I would look for a job in some shop. If I didn't find one soon, I would have to go home to Aalborg. My parents had given me three months in Copenhagen to establish myself, and if I couldn't manage that, I'd have to give up and work for my father at the bank.

"Those who love Greenland are lost. The call and the longing last as long as you live." Brand's words echoed in my head. So did the way he pronounced a dead woman's name. "Naika," spoken passionately and hopelessly. Suddenly, I wanted him to say "Alexandra," passionately but not hopelessly. Why couldn't it be?

Because of the cold--the deep, dreadful, never-ending hell that was his unforgettable Greenland. For him, it was always the barren season when Persephone joined her husband in the Underworld, but apparently, he didn't mind this. No matter where he was in the world, part of him would be on that God-forsaken island that I couldn't bear thinking about.

I might as well forget about Stig Brand, I thought, and the press conference had made one thing very clear to me--I had no wish to be a journalist. I told the driver to let me out at a Georg Jensen silver shop and paid him, noticing that my folded wad of *kroner* seemed alarmingly thin.

I scarcely recognized my own reflection in the shop window, as I was wearing what amounted to the national uniform--Chanel's beige cashmere jersey dress. My corset was deep in a drawer in my room at *Frue* Steinsen's house, and I knew my mother would be shocked at this display of my natural contours, but in Copenhagen they scarcely attracted a glance.

Stig Brand had glanced. The memory heated my cheeks, and I forcibly pushed it from my mind as I approached a supercilious-looking man with a carnation in the buttonhole of his dark suit.

"Good morning," I said, trying for the authoritative tone of my grandmother, wife of the *amtmand* in the seaside town of Nordhav.

With a languid gesture toward the gleaming silver, he said,

3

"How may I serve you?"

"I am seeking employment."

He appraised my rings, shoes and gown with one quick sweep and said, "I shouldn't think that you'd had experience in this line."

"And I should think it would be more civil for you to ask than to assume."

His eyebrows shot up. "Well, *have* you had?"

"No," I tried to keep my voice cool, "but I appreciate beautiful things, and I'm very quick to learn."

One of his eyebrows descended and the other stayed high. "We'll see. Step behind the counter and see what you can do with those women who just came in."

For the second time in one day, I was trying to do something I'd never done before. I quickly stepped behind the glass counter, removed my hat with a single motion, and eyed the rings, pins and bracelets in the case. Where were the prices?

Hr. Supercilious volunteered no help, and the women were upon me--a mother and daughter, apparently. I smiled at them encouragingly, asking if I could help.

"We're looking for a silver bracelet for Kaja, here," the older woman said. "The trouble is, they all seem to look alike."

"Well," I shrugged in what I hoped was a charming manner, "elegant design calls for certain basic elements, but perhaps we can find some unique detailing that will please you."

The bracelet I reached for had a circling relief of sleek seals. As I placed it on the black velvet for their inspection, I had to laugh at myself for thinking I could dismiss Stig Brand so easily. From the way the girl's eyes lighted, I could tell that he was rescuing me again by making me choose the seals.

I slipped the band over her hand and said, "This design is particularly appropriate today. Stig Brand, the Polar adventurer, is in Copenhagen to celebrate the recognition of Greenland as Danish territory."

"Is that so?" the woman said. "Never heard of him."

Kaja stopped admiring her wrist long enough to say, "If it's

4

nothing but ice and snow, why do they call it Greenland?"

I laughed and said, "That's exactly what I asked, and *Hr.* Brandt told me Eric the Red called it that to attract settlers. And he said, `The dream of Greenland is in your blood.' You'd think that big island was a woman he loved!"

Kaja looked at the bracelet again, then stared through the window into the milling crowd of pedestrians in the *Strøget.* Obviously, the romance of Ultima Thule was working on her.

"Well?" said her mother, who obviously had not buried her corset in a drawer. It pressed her ample bosom upward into a massive shelf.

"Yes, I think I'll have the sweet, little seals," Kaja said.

I was overjoyed but also faced with two problems. I didn't know the price, and I had no idea where to find the materials to make a parcel.

Hr. Supercilious was lurking nearby, and I raised my voice just slightly to communicate with him. "Excuse me, Sir, but I have not seen the latest price list."

He approached languidly, reaching into a drawer for a black leather folder. With the other hand, he retrieved a black plush box for me and indicated the spool of silver cord I was to use.

I found the description and price, placed the seal bracelet in its box and tied it with a flourish. Making change from a large note flustered me a bit, but I tried not to let it show. Kaja and her mother departed, seemingly satisfied customers.

"Well?" I said to *Hr.* Supercilious.

"When would you like to start?"

"Now."

"What is your name?"

"Alexandra Lund."

"Well, Alexandra Lund, I am Anton Hertz. I did not intend to hire you, but since I have, please adorn yourself with some of the merchandise. I think you'll show it off nicely."

"Anything in particular?"

"There's a seal necklace in the next case down. You seem to

5

favor that design."

As I fastened the clasp of the heavy circlet around my neck, I shivered--for joy, I thought--but I would look back on that moment and wonder.

II

I was born in Aalborg in the last year of the century and grew up behind a neat picket fence that protected me from everything but myself.

My father, Jacob Lund, was a banker, and he came from a distinguished family, according to the estimate of the Lunds. His own father was the *amtmand* in Nordhav, a regional administrator appointed by King Christian IX. His mother, my grandmother, was equally proud of her station in life. Her father had been a diplomat, representing King Christian in the court of the Czar.

My mother, Thea, was the child of a pastor in a small village parish, rescued by her exceptional beauty from the rigorous life of the New Missioners.

My parents met on the shore of the North Sea, and they liked to tell the story of *Mor* looking at the sky and *Far* looking at the sea and how it was all the same thing.

"Before you even come to the sea, the sky tells you of it," my mother would say. "Streaks of dark clouds hang at an angle at the horizon, the twins of ocean currents."

And my father would add, "Ah, but the blue water, the white caps, the breakers roaring like artillery!"

And then, because the familiar telling made me impatient, I would say, "So you were looking out and she was looking up, and you bumped into each other!"

Both would look at me, bemused. I had jarred them from their mutual memory with a bald summary. I would climb into one lap or the other and burrow lovingly into a parental neck by way of apology. Like a chair built to fit into a corner, the three of us were securely placed and sheltered.

Then Frederik was born. You know how men are about their sons. Before the child could even speak, *Far* carried him off to the outdoor tables at Kilden to show him off to his friends, leaving me at home with *Mor*.

I remembered the pre-Frederik days when *Far* had taken me to Skovbakken hill to look out over the Limfjord and the cement factories with their huge chimneys. On gray days, the fjord, also gray, seemed to swell beyond its banks, and when the sun shone, the green-coated copper spire of St. Budolfi Church looked like an exotic plant sprouting from the city.

Why is it that a hotel in the city where you live seems so much more exciting than a hotel in a strange place where you actually book a room? Aalborg's big, white Hotel Royal fascinated me, and I begged my mother to let me stay there.

"You have your own very nice bed," she told me.

"Why can't I try one of theirs?"

"Because it would look very strange. People know we live here and don't need a bed at the Royal."

Her face was a dull rose shade, the same as it had been when we took a wrong turn one day and saw some women standing outside the shops on a street near Budolfi Church. They had painted faces and smoked little cigars.

"*Mor*," I said in my piercing, little voice, "those ladies are going to freeze their bosoms. Why don't they get their shawls?"

"Hush, Alexandra!" she hissed, dragging me up the street while I swiveled my head to stare at the women.

She never missed an opportunity to tell me that I had been named for a queen, and I must behave with decorum. She mentioned it again as my feet went one way and my eyes went another.

As always, I asked, "Queen of what?", and she patiently answered, "Queen of the United Kingdom of Great Britain and Ireland."

Princess Alexandra, the eldest daughter of our King Christian IX, married Albert Edward, Prince of Wales, and she didn't get to be a queen until she was really old. She wasn't a queen yet when *Mor* gave me her name, but *Mor* didn't realize I knew that. I had seen pictures of a young Alexandra, and I admired the beautiful lady with the slender neck banded with a jeweled ribbon to hide a scar of some kind, but I surely wouldn't want to marry some prince with a walrus mustache, even if he turned into a king pretty soon. I didn't want to be like her. I wanted to be like me.

Who was I? The process of finding out was both exciting and painful. When I was nine, I dragged the small boat propped up near the beach house to the Kattegat, climbed in and rowed to find the horizon. Eventually, I grew tired and stopped rowing, thinking the waves would bring me back to shore. The currents carried me farther away, and suddenly I was frightened. The red tile roof of the beach house was no more than a ruddy dot along the shore, and I was no closer to finding the seam between sea and sky than I ever had been.

"Oh God, save me!" I whimpered.

The answer to that prayer was not immediate, but it came. As I strained my eyes toward the shore, I saw a dark dot on the waves. In what seemed like an eternity, it grew larger and became recognizeable as *Far* in the neighbors' boat. He rowed hard, but the currents carried me away from him.

"Alex!" he shouted, "Use your oars!"

I tried, but I lost one oar to the waves and winced to hear his curse. Another eternity passed before my red-faced, panting father extended one of his oars and yelled, "Catch hold, and don't let go!"

There we were, a two-boat butterfly on the waves, together but not safely joined. Soaked and shivering, I clung to the oar while *Far* maneuvered close enough to throw a coil of rope into my boat.

"Run the end through the ring on the prow and throw it back!" he shouted.

Clumsily I threaded the rope through the ring, but my arm was not strong enough for the throw. The rope swam like a snake on the water just out of *Far's* reach and started to pull from the ring.

He swore and said, "You'll kill us both! Keep it in the ring!"

I flung myself headlong toward the prow and caught it just in time, hanging on for dear life as I rolled in the water that sloshed in the bottom of the boat. Then I felt the jolt of *Far's* boat hitting

9

mine. His hands grabbed the rope, pulling it burningly from mine, and when he had lashed the boats together, he lifted me into his boat. Clasped between his thighs as he rowed, I watched the red roof of the beach house enlarge. If one never could arrive at the joining of sea and sky on the outward journey, it seemed that inbound one could arrive at home.

I was punished, of course. When my parents took Frederik to the amusement park the next day, an outing I had greatly anticipated, I was made to stay home with Anna, the village girl who came to clean.

"Why did you do that?" *Mor* asked me.

"I wanted to see what was out there," I said.

"You must never do anything like that again!"

I promised, perfectly willing to give up heading for the North Sea in a rowboat, but "anything like that" covered much more. I still wanted to know what was out there.

That's why I made a middle school friend who was unacceptable to my parents and was forced to see her on the sly.

Dorte looked like a Gypsy with her dark hair and Tartar-slanted eyes. She smoked Elephant cigarettes and was allowed to go to the music hall on Fredrikstorv. She had even been to Enighedslund, the dance hall where women bared their legs to the knees and seamen roared and knocked their glasses over.

Dorte's father was engaged in the canning business, and during the war, he made a huge profit selling a disgusting tinned stew to the Germans.

Yes, I wanted to know what was out there, and Dorte told me the facts of life according to her lights. The experience I gained through her was all vicarious, and when she failed to pass her middle school exam, I went on to grammar school without her. We grew apart.

When I met Anders, I was swept away by his burning belief in the Communist Manifesto. Anders had watched his father sicken and die from a lung disease contracted in the cement factory where he worked fourteen-hour shifts.

"They won't exploit me like that!" he said, "I'll be educated--able to defend myself until the workers win."

I pondered what he said, "from each according to his means to each according to his need," and said, "Isn't that what they did in the early Christian church?"

"Don't bring God into it! Sometimes I wonder why I waste time on a bourgeois like you!"

A bourgeois like me had a distinct sense of personal property, which Anders might have shared if he possessed anything, I thought. He wore the same threadbare suit constantly, and his collar and cuffs were none too clean, but he was tall and broad-shouldered, and he moved gracefully. His eyes were hooded, his nose was sharply-chiseled, and his lips were narrow but surprisingly warm and encompassing in a kiss.

I brought him home one night, and while *Far* and *Mor* treated him with great courtesy, serving us coffee, cakes and *snaps* in the parlor, the occasion was uncomfortable.

"Bankers have nice houses," he said bluntly.

My mother thanked him for the compliment and urged him to have more apple cake.

"No, thank you," he said. "Despite my lowly estate, I manage to get my nourishment."

Far cleared his throat loudly and said, "We try to offer our guests pleasure, not charity."

"I wish I could do the same!" said Anders, setting his Royal Copenhagen cup and saucer down so hard that *Mor* winced.

That's when my brother made his usual crashing entrance.

"Hey, Alex! Where did you get *him*?"

"We met at school," I said. "Anders Hagen, this is my brother, Frederik."

Frederik held out his hand, and Anders grasped it hard enough to inflict pain.

The visit limped on for what seemed like a very long time. Anders scorned small talk, and my parents were not about to discuss Marx and Engels. Frederik just sat there and stared at Anders, whistling under his breath. At long last, Anders stood and said he must go home and study.

"Alexandra will see you out," *Mor* said. "Good night."

Far offered his hand in farewell, but Anders ignored it.

At the front door, Anders pulled me out into the night.

"Come home with me!"

"I thought you had to study."

"That can wait. I have to break you out of your bourgeois mold!"

"How?"

"Like this!" He seized me and kissed me, grabbing my breasts.

I twisted away, startled by the violence of his touch. The few kisses we had shared before had been tender explorations, but this was something else. He seemed to want to bring me down, to punish me for my privileges.

"Good night, Anders."

"You won't come?"

"No," I said shortly.

He turned and started away with an angry stride. He had miles to walk and stoke his fury, and I wondered if I should be afraid of him the next time we met. There was no next time, but I heard about him when he led a syndicalist strike a few years later.

Then came the war that brought prosperity at first but later began to hurt us. By 1917, rationing was in effect. Restaurants and theaters closed early to save energy. We boiled our food and put the pots in hay boxes to hold the heat. We read by stinking carbide lamps.

I read poetry and stories filled with violence, terror and power. I looked at paintings that didn't seem to be anything but feelings laid out in line and color. In other words, I entered the Twentieth Century, better late than never.

Aalborg began to seem provincial to me, and I wanted to experience life in the real city--Copenhagen. My parents were reluctant to let me go, mentioning my unfortunate attraction to unsuitable companions (like Dorte and Anders), but I persuaded

12

them to give me a three-month trial. They insisted that I stay with *Frue* Jacobine Steinsen, a friend of *Mor's* family from the old days. Fortunately, *Frue* Steinsen remembered how it was to be young.

Not that I was all *that* young. I was twenty-two, and Frederik teased me about being a spinster. I'd had at least one offer of marriage which I refused, to the regret of my parents. His name was Ivar, and his father was a count.

After my breach with Anders, I found myself included in the parties at Ivar's country manor house. We played drawing room games and danced, and when most of the crowd disappeared into the long bedroom corridors, Ivar and I sat beside the fire and talked.

"Alexandra--" he spoke my name with such urgency that I looked up in surprise.

"Yes?"

"Would you be at all interested in marrying me?"

"Good heavens, Ivar, we're good friends, but--"

"But you don't feel that way about me."

"I guess that's it. I'm sorry."

"Damn!" he said, getting up to poke at the fire. "My family looks upon all this as a kind of horse breeding. They want me to find somebody healthy and intelligent to carry on the line, and I thought maybe you--"

I laughed and said, "Thanks for the compliment to my health and intelligence, but I'm afraid I'm not the mare for the job!"

Then he laughed, too. We shook hands and promised to be friends for life. When I told my parents about refusing the proposal, their attitude showed how far our country was from the classless society Anders yearned to achieve. They were devastated.

Frue Steinsen introduced me to some young people in Copenhagen, and one acquaintance led to another until I met Leif Skovgaard at that poetry reading in an apartment on Vestergade. If not love at first sight, it was at least deep liking at first sight. We met for a drink, a meal or to attend a performance almost every day. Either I owe everything to Leif or I can blame him for everything.

14

III

I put in a full day at the silver shop, and my feet hurt from standing behind the gleaming counter for so many hours, but I was exhilarated. I had a job, and I wouldn't have to go home and work for *Far,* counting out money from a barred cage in the *Folkebank.*

Hr. Hertz asked me to fill out some forms, which I did, and he named a salary that disappointed me, but I didn't protest. I could manage, I thought, and it meant everything to me to stay in Copenhagen.

"I think we'll get on very well together, *Frøken* Lund," he said.

I smiled and asked permission to use the telephone. *Hr.* Hertz gestured toward the instrument with the grace of a dancer and discreetly disappeared.

Fortunately, I knew the *Folkebladet*'s number, because the directory was nowhere in sight. Leif was a long time coming to the phone, and he said "hello" breathlessly.

"It's Alexandra. I have a job!"

"Wonderful! You caught me as I was going out the door. *Frue* Steinsen said you hadn't been home, and I was just leaving to look for you. Did you read my story?"

"No, I've been working all day. I hope no one is looking for *my* story."

Leif laughed. "They might be. The rest of the reporters were wondering about you, and I wouldn't tell them a thing. Let them find their own pretty girls!"

"You're too kind!" I said with the ironic tone that kept Leif in line.

"Where are you working? Where are you now?"

"The answer to both questions is--the Georg Jensen shop at the top of the *Strøget.*"

Leif's whistle shrilled through the phone, and I said, "Ouch!"

"Stay put. I'll pick you up, and we'll go somewhere to celebrate."

"Terrific! And bring your story about Stig Brand. I want to read it."

"Will you be admiring me or him?"

"Both, I would imagine."

We went to Tivoli's wine bar, where we could hear the shrieks from the roller coaster and watch the fireworks.

Raising his glass of burgundy and touching it to mine, Leif said, "To the saleswoman supreme!"

"Thank you. Did you bring the story?"

He pulled the cutting from his breast pocket and handed it to me, trying to look nonchalant while I read it.

"'The dream of Greenland is in your blood,' says Stig Brand, the Arctic explorer, and today that dream is in the blood of Denmark with the proclamation of the world's largest island as Danish territory.

"The bearded explorer seemed larger than life in the confines of the *Rigsdag* chamber where he spoke this morning, advocating that Greenland be closed to immigration to save the Polar Eskimo.

"Brandt's Eskimo wife, Naika, died from the Spanish influenza three years ago, and he says the contagion was brought to Greenland by foreign ships.

"Brandt helped establish the trading post of Thule in the extreme north of the island, and he has participated in the rescue of numerous explorers and whalers who have come to grief in these inhospitable climes."

I looked up from the columns and said, "This could have been more personal if you had spoken with him alone, don't you think?"

Leif was stung by that remark, and I was sorry that I'd made it. I quickly added, "I don't mean to be critical--"

"I suppose you think I should have put in that stuff about the call and the longing?"

"You know your business better than I do, Leif." I returned to the story, finding it more impersonal as it went along.

He sat opposite me, blowing smoke rings and tapping his pack of Players on the table top. He finished his wine and shoved the glass away.

"Drink up," he said. "Not much excitement around here tonight."

I hadn't eaten lunch, not to mention dinner, and if I drank up as he suggested, I'd be dizzy, at the very least. I offered my glass to him, and he upended it.

"Let's get out of here," he said.

Leif had borrowed a car from a friend, and he drove to the waterfront. A fog had rolled in to dampen the cobblestones and make them shine in the pale yellow light from the windows of the workers' cafe that seemed to be our destination.

We took a seat near the windows to enjoy the view--coal bunkers and the lights on an overhead crane. The place was full of sailors, some of them with over-painted girls.

Leif ordered *smørrebrød* and beer and said in a low voice, "See that fellow over there? The one with the knit cap?"

"He looks like a criminal," I said.

"He's a damned good poet."

"He could be both, I suppose."

"The *Folkebladet* refused to review his book because he's such an anarchist, but some of the poems were really powerful. I'm glad he doesn't know me on sight, because I'm sure he blames me. After all, he sent the book to me."

"He does *look* dangerous. I'll try to avoid saying your name and putting you at risk. What's his name?"

"Anker Klage. He chose that surname for himself because Jensen was too common."

"But it means 'complaint'," I said.

"What could be better for a man like him? He despises the way things are and wants everything changed."

The sawdust dumped on the floor to absorb spills had worked its way into my shoes, and I reached down to remedy the situation. As I straightened, I saw him coming through the door. Stig Brand.

Leif jumped up and went to him. "*Hr.* Brand, please join us."

I had removed the silver seals from around my throat and put

17

them back in their case before I left the shop, but at the sight of Stig Brand, it seemed that I still wore them. I could feel their cool weight just above my collar bone.

"We meet again," he said, pulling a chair from another table and seating himself between me and Leif.

"Give him my story, Alexandra," Leif said. "Perhaps he hasn't seen it."

Our fingers touched in the transfer, and I was startled that his were so warm. I watched him read, better able to get a grip on myself when those faded blue eyes were hooded by his lids. His reading speed was greater than I would have expected from a rugged outdoorsman.

"An excellent account, *Hr.* Skovgaard."

"Thank you, Sir!"

"And your story, *Froken*? I don't believe I heard your name this morning."

Leif laughed and said, "If you had, it would have been the wrong name!"

Brand looked directly at me and said, "I don't quite understand."

I could feel the hot color in my face, and that in itself embarrassed me more. His name, Brand, meant fire, and that was the effect he had on me.

Leif seemed hugely amused as he jumped in to explain. "She had fake credentials. She's no more a reporter than I'm an opera singer!"

Brand still looked at me. "Your questions got to the heart of the matter, did they not?"

I said, "At least I remember the answers. My name is Alexandra Lund--truly!"

The waitress was slow in attending to the newcomer, and I offered him my beer, also the *smørrebrød.* He drank deeply, wiped his mouth with the back of his hand, and returned the glass to me. I surreptitously held it up to the light to find the print of his lips, and while he was talking with Leif, I drank from that rim.

"I never expected to see you on your own in Copenhagen," Leif was saying. "Why aren't you off at some fine dinner or reception?"

Brand fingered his beard and said, "I was invited to both, but I wanted to revisit the scenes of my youth, I guess."

"Surely your youth is still in effect?" I said.

"Be careful--you'll turn my head completely. When you live among the Eskimos, you never hear a flattering word, and you are expected to devalue yourself as much as possible."

"Why?" Leif asked.

"So the people around you will deny that you're ugly, incompetent, or foolish. There's your compliment, and it's hard-won."

"You'll never catch Leif Skovgaard bad-mouthing himself," Leif said with a sharp laugh. "What about you, Alexandra? Would you say terrible things about yourself to get someone to deny them?"

I lowered my eyes and said, "I don't know how you gentlemen can allow yourselves to be seen in public with a woman as unattractive as I--someone with such pitiful manners and behaviour." I was struggling to keep from smiling.

Brand leaned close to me and said, "Perhaps the lady's mirror is defective. It certainly must be if it shows her anything other than beauty. As for her manners and behaviour, they are as mellow and lovely as the amber gown that matches her amber hair."

"Pure poetry!" Leif said, not altogether admiringly.

Then a dark form blocked the lamplight, and we looked up into the face of Anker Klage. He folded his arms and glared at Leif.

"So you're Skovgaard."

"I am."

"Your words are better-looking than your face."

Leif laughed uneasily. "I choose my words, but I didn't choose my face."

"You received my book for review?"

"I did, but my editor took exception to your political views. What could I do?"

"Have the courage to defend your own views, for one thing."

"Well, I did tell him that 'Bleeding Dawn' was a fine poem. He didn't want to discuss it. *Hr.* Klage, allow me to present you to *Frøken* Lund and *Hr.* Brand."

I tried to smile, and Brand stood, holding out his hand, which Klage ignored. "The fewer capitalist pigs I come to know, the better," he said with a sneer.

Brand rolled his eyes and sat down, but Leif remained on his feet, leaning into Klage's face to scold him.

"Your behavior toward this lady is inexcusable, and if you haven't been living in a sealed room somewhere, you should know who this gentleman is!"

Klage's fist shot forward so fast that I saw it in a blur, and then Leif went down with his face in the *smørrebrød* plate.

"Where's your coat, *Frøken* Lund?" Brandt said.

"I didn't bring one."

"Do you have a car outside?"

"Yes, but it's locked, and Leif has the keys in his pocket."

Brand picked Leif's pocket neatly and hurried me outside.

"What about Leif?" I asked as he put me into the car.

"I'm going after him right now," he said. "Keep the car door locked until you see us. This is a bad neighborhood, as they say."

I tried to see through the windows of the cafe, but they were too dirty. The noise grew louder with shouts and blows. Anker Klage was dragged into the street, supported by two of his friends, and they disappeared into the darkness. What seemed like a long time later, Brand emerged, holding up a semi-conscious Leif. I quickly unlocked the car door, and Leif was dumped into the back seat like a rag doll.

"Is he going to be all right?" I asked.

"He'll have a bad-looking eye for a few days, that's all. Where does he live? We'll put him to bed."

I told him the address, and the police were just coming as we drove away.

"Why are they still fighting?" I asked. "The man who started it all is long gone."

20

Brand shrugged and chuckled. "That's how it is in these civilized countries. One thing leads to another."

I waited in the car while Brand took Leif to his apartment and put him to bed. Then he came back to drive me to *Frue* Steinsen's house. He said he'd return the car to Leif's place and take a cab to his hotel.

He walked me to the door, and having said nothing about seeing me ever again, said, "Good night, amber lady."

How sorry I was that I was living with a friend of the family, who undoubtedly was peering at us from behind her lace curtains at this very moment. I was surprised that she didn't have an old-fashioned gossip mirror to keep her current on the doings of a larger circle.

"We scarcely had a chance to talk," I said.

He smiled. "That's the way it is in Nyhavn. Plenty of action but very few words. I take it that you prefer words?"

"That depends," I said, holding out my hand to say good-night.

He took my hand and pulled me close, brushing my lips with his ever so lightly. He whistled a jazz tune as he walked away from me. Fresh from Greenland, where could he have learned a thing like that?

IV

I had left a scrawled note on *Frue* Steinsen's kitchen table, "I have a job! A.", and in the morning I found a parcel beside my coffee cup with a note that read, "*smørrebrød* for lunch to save money! T.S."

The strong coffee cut through the exhaustion of too much excitement and too little sleep, and I wrote "*Tak!*" at the bottom of her note before hurrying out to catch the trolley.

How grand it was to have purpose, a place to go, a job to do. I scrutinized the other passengers and wondered what they did for a living. Although it seemed early to me, the hour was too late for factory workers. The men were better dressed than the few women on the trolley. Most wore dark suits, velour hats and flowers in their buttonholes and read tightly-folded copies of the *Folkebladet*. I could make out Leif's by-line, but I couldn't determine what he had written without becoming a contortionist. The women's aprons marked them as maids or waitresses, and a few of the men wore light-colored suits and looked about them with the darting gaze that signified American go-ahead. They were new-style salesmen--the type who would not be tolerated in *Hr.* Hertz's domain.

I turned from the passengers and looked out the window just as the trolley passed the Hotel Opera, white as a frosted cake in the early sun. A bearded man wearing a cap and a seaman's jacket appeared at the entrance, nearly stopping my heart. It could have been Stig Brand or someone who looked like him. The moment passed too quickly for me to tell, and I was left with that nightmare sense of loss--the train missed, the outstretched hand that can't quite touch, the gift snatched away.

I realized then that I had been deliberately suppressing all thoughts of Brand. I had no reason to believe I would ever see him again, and I was determined not to grieve over that state of affairs. Why should I care about him? I was young and alive in the center

23

of things, and this peacetime world of ours offered every possibility. Who needed Stig Brand? Not I!

The *Strøget* already had its share of pedestrians, many of them pausing for coffee at sidewalk cafes before the shops opened. Buying three red tulips from a flower vendor, I smiled at everyone in general on the way to my shop. At the door I pulled on one glove to tap on the glass for admission, not wanting to smudge that sparkling expanse.

Marie, the girl who worked at the counter next to mine, let me in and whispered, "You had a phone call, and *Hr.* Hertz doesn't allow that sort of thing."

Hertz was advancing on me with a deadly, measured tread. I stepped behind my counter and found a vase for the tulips. When they were arranged to my satisfaction, I looked up and smiled at him. "Good morning, *Hr.* Hertz."

"*Frøken* Lund, you have a great deal to learn about this establishment."

"Oh, I certainly realize that, Sir."

"You will instruct your friends not to telephone you here."

"I can't think who would have done that, Sir."

"It was a man."

"Ah," I said, surmising that it would be better for me to have one possibility than several. "I will attend to it."

Somehow the morning passed. As I polished and arranged displays and waited on a few customers, I was agitated by the possibility that the caller had been Stig Brand.

I moved close to Marie's post and whispered, "Did you take my call?"

She shook her head and pointed silently to *Hr.* Hertz, who stood with his back to us. No chance of asking him what the voice was like.

Although it was only eleven, Marie told me to go to the back room to eat my *smørrebrød* and then out into the May sunshine for a brief stroll in search of a cup of coffee. *Hr.* Hertz did not approve of what he called "domestic arrangements" on the premises of

24

Georg Jensen.

I sat at a table next to two old ladies who were enjoying their small cigars and heard their comments on the cigarettes of "modern girls."

"*Helvede!*" said one, "Little white sticks!"

"*Ja,*" said her companion, "anemic!"

The *Strøget* seemed peppered with beige Chanel dresses. I couldn't help wondering if Stig Brand might look at a woman wearing one and expect her to be me.

The thought of him pained me, and I quickly finished my coffee and hurried back to the shop.

At noon, Leif came into the shop and headed straight for my counter. His right eye was framed with livid, plum-colored bruises.

"I called to invite you to lunch," he said. "Have you been too busy to let me know?"

"So you're the one!" What a letdown, I thought.

He laughed, then winced, touching his cheekbone ruefully. "I suppose six fellows ask you to lunch daily?"

Hr. Hertz was watching with an expression that resembled a gathering storm.

"I am not permitted to take calls here," I said coldly. "In fact, the manager is looking at us right now."

"Then I'll pretend to be a customer while we arrange lunch, and we can leave separately."

"I've had lunch."

Leif studied the objects in the case intently and said, "Please show me that silver hand mirror."

I pushed the sliding panel and reached for it, placing it on a square of black velvet.

He picked it up and inspected his bruises, saying, "I've invited Brand to the poetry reading at Claudine's tonight."

"Did he say he'd come?"

"He didn't say he wouldn't."

"That might be a bit tame for a man of action."

Leif laughed again. "Action? As soon as the action started last

25

night, you two ran out on me."

"But he came back in and rescued you," I defended.

"That may be. It's all a blur in my memory."

"When did you invite him to Claudine's?"

"I called his hotel this morning."

Hr. Hertz was looking at us again, and he caught my eye significantly.

"Well, Sir," I said to Leif, "do you like this design, or shall we look at something else?"

He picked up the mirror, turned the glass toward me, and said, "I like the design you're looking at right now."

"I'm not sure that one is available."

"Then order it for me. See you tonight."

When he had gone, Marie began to arrange merchandise in the case closest to me and spoke without looking at me.

"That fellow is crazy about you, isn't he?"

"He's just a friend."

"Oh, go on!" she said.

Leif certainly had been a friend to me, showing me the city and introducing me to exciting people, making me part of his own elite group. He thought my conventionality stood between us, that my banker's daughter code kept us from intimacy, and that he could break down these barriers, given time.

Given eternity, he couldn't, I thought.

I didn't want to arrive at Claudine's apartment early or even on time and be forced into a *tete-a-tete* with some bore. I arrived thirty minutes after the stated hour and found a cushion to throw on the floor for a seat. Low-hanging curtains of cigarette smoke and dim light from two small, opaque-shaded lamps made it hard to recognize the other floor sitters.

Although I wished to enhance my "amber lady" look, I didn't want to wear the dress Brand had seen. I considered long and hard, deciding to dress in black. Who stands out in a crowded room? A nun. I wore the necklace of fish scale amber beads *Tante* Kamille had given me for confirmation and twisted my hair in a Psyche knot.

Somebody handed me a glass of unidentified liquid, and when I took a sip, I choked. "What is it?"

"That's Babette's American bourbon," Leif spoke close to my ear. "If you don't like it, give it to me. It's hot stuff!"

I passed him my glass, and another glass--red wine--was placed in my hand.

Claudine was dressing in her bedroom, late as usual, and carrying on a shouted conversation with one of the women in the living room.

"So Anker Klage pasted Leif in the eye?" Claudine yelled.

"Yes, in Nyhavn."

"Leif was slumming again, eh?"

Leif jumped up and shouted through Claudine's closed door, "Slumming, hell! I was seeking the common man in his favorite haunts. And besides, the food is cheaper!"

Claudine emerged with a Gypsy scarf tied around her hips. Those hips swayed as she took Leif's face between her hands and kissed him on the lips. Then she caught sight of me and gave him a playful shove that knocked him down and into my lap.

"Give us a kiss," he pled, looking up into my face.

"I thought this was a literary group," I said, reaching into my bosom for a handkerchief to mop up the wine spilled on my sleeve. I was glad I'd worn black.

The wine bottle tilted, was emptied and was replaced before Claudine clapped her hands for attention and positioned Holger Petersen in the doorway between living room and kitchen to read his epic poem.

"What's it about?" I whispered to Leif.

"Greenland. That's why I asked Brand, but I guess he isn't going to show up."

"I guess not," I said, experiencing the dropping-away sensation that always came with deep disappointment.

The poem started badly, and it didn't get any better. Lines like "Where glaciers creep and icebergs roar" and "The silent, white abyss of chilled and sterile wilderness" occasioned some eye-rolling among the listeners.

The final words were, "Where daring Danes can still explore." As the poet read them, I saw the shadow of a bearded figure on the foyer wall. Brand!

A long silence followed the poet's reading, broken finally by Leif.

"Holger, *nobody* rhymes anymore. Why do *you* insist upon it?"

Petersen shrugged his massive shoulders. "It just comes natural to me."

"What do you know about Greenland, anyhow?" somebody else asked.

Brand stepped into view, and Claudine undulated forward to welcome him. She untied the scarf from her hips and threw it around his neck, pulling him toward her. And he was looking at me.

Leif jumped to his feet and said, "Let's have three cheers for the great Arctic explorer, Stig Brand!"

Everyone cheered but me. My eyes were still locked with Brand's, and I was truly speechless.

Holger Petersen's poem was forgotten as people clustered around Brand, asking him questions, telling him about themselves.

Finally he broke away and came to Holger. "You had some good lines in that poem," he said.

"Oh, thank you! You don't know what that means to me--such words from a person like yourself!"

"Of course, I didn't hear it all."

"I could do it again," Petersen said eagerly.

"Oh no, you couldn't!" Leif protested. He grabbed the sheaf of pages from Holger and held them out to Brand. "He can read it for himself."

"That--that's my only copy, but I could make another and send it to you, *Hr.* Brand."

"Sending things to me is easier said than done. We have only one mail delivery a year at Thule."

"Why, that's impossible!" Claudine said.

As people moved around to find more drink and pick up

crackers loaded with Limfjord mussels, Brand approached me and said, "Let's get out of here and go somewhere to talk."

"All right, but I'll just say thanks to Claudine--"

"Don't do that. It will break up the party. Eskimos never say good-bye, and I think they have the right idea."

I let myself out first, and then he came. We met in the downstairs entry hall and went into the cool night to look for a cab. The sounds of the party were loud from Claudine's open windows on the third floor until we were several blocks away.

He took me to a plush, little hole-in-the wall on Alfarvej, where we shared a bottle of Burgundy. At first, the waiter was insulting, scorning Brand's seaman's attire, but the command in the voice straightened him out immediately.

Brand asked me about myself, and I told him about my parents and Frederik, about the summers at the shore.

"I can see you strolling on the sands like the ladies in long gowns that Kroyer painted."

I laughed and said, "My gowns usually were knotted above my knees, and once I got into a boat and tried to row to the place where land and water meet. My father had to rescue me."

"Adventuresome, are you?"

"Oh, yes! Right now, I'm trying to be a New Woman."

"And what might that be?"

"I want to be free and intelligent and independent."

"So do we all," he said. "My wife Naika was all those things. In addition, she could open a tin can with her teeth, drive a team of sled dogs, and go to a dance a few hours after giving birth."

My eyes widened, and I didn't know what to say. I felt like a silly school girl.

Then his hand found mine on the table top, and he said, "The best thing for a man and a woman is to be interdependent. We were, and that's why I'm so lost now."

I squeezed his hand in sympathy, feeling the scars that laced it.

"I left our daughter Nauja in Greenland. She's staying with the trading post manager and his Eskimo wife while I'm away. I doubt

29

that she remembers her mother. She was only a year old when Naika died."

"How old is she now?" I asked.

"Four. A real enchantress."

It was getting late, and I had to work the next day, but I didn't want to leave Stig Brand.

We finished the wine. Then we sat in silence for what seemed like a long time. The waiter watched from a distance but did not bother us about replenishment or payment.

Finally, Brand said, "I have seen you three times in two days by some happy accident, and that has the look of fate to me. I believe that I must court you, *Froken* Lund. Is that agreeable?"

I nodded wordlessly. How could one argue with fate?

"Come," he said, rising and holding out his hand. "I will take you home."

I stifled a sigh, not really daring to protest the tempo of the promised courtship.

The kiss at *Frue* Steinsen's door was longer and deeper, and like the Eskimos, we did not say good-bye.

V

We strolled on the Langelinie along the harbor and stopped to gaze at the Little Mermaid, that shy little figure lonely on her rock. The evening was balmy, and I didn't have to worry about her freezing, as I often had in my childhood.

Visits to the Glyptothek with Leif had accustomed me to viewing nudes in male company, enabling me to present a worldly-wise personna to Stig Brand. I even ventured, "I'll bet you never see that much bare flesh in Greenland."

He laughed with a big, bass sound that turned the heads of passers-by.

"On the contrary," he said. "When the Polar Eskimos are at home in their winter houses, they strip. Of course, the women may keep their foxskin panties on, but most of the clothes are tied in a bundle and hung from a hook in the ceiling to keep the lice out of them."

I shuddered with double revulsion for cold and vermin, and Stig laughed again.

"Are you really so delicate?" he said.

"I'm not sure," I said in all honesty. "I've never been put to the test."

"We can do something about that. Marry me--and Greenland."

The words I had wanted to hear had been uttered, and now I was both gratified and panicked. I gazed beyond the Little Mermaid to the shipyard of Burmeister and Wain and struggled to form an answer.

If he had said, "Marry me, and we'll live in Denmark," I would have agreed instantly. I loved the sound of his voice, the way he looked at me, the way he looked, the way I felt when we kissed. I loved the way he protected me from myself when I wanted much more than kisses. But his proposal included Greenland, that alien place which he described in the tones a man would use in speaking of his mistress. In short, I was jealous. I loved him for the dangers he had passed, but I was afraid to face new dangers with him.

"You haven't answered," he said softly, tracing the curve of my cheek with one finger.

"We haven't known each other long--"

"I feel that my heart has always known you."

That melted me, and we kissed, holding each other tight beside the Little Mermaid.

"Is it yes, then?"

"As long as you love me better than Greenland," I said with a pout.

"A bird will sit on that lower lip," he said with a chuckle.

"Come home with me to Aalborg and meet my parents."

"There's no time. The Hekla sails in two days, and I want you on her with me."

"But that's impossible! We can't be married that soon!"

"Come away with me. The captain can marry us at sea."

He put his arm around me and pulled me along to a snug, dim cafe, where he ordered coffee.

I was too stunned to speak. My mind was racing in all directions--how to tell my parents, what I would need to survive that icy wilderness, how angry *Hr.* Hertz would be when I told him I was leaving. *Mor* had been planning my church wedding since I was a little girl, and she would be devastated.

"So many shadows flitting across your lovely face," Stig said. "Have I made your life so difficult?"

I nodded, laughing a little. "Even so, I can no longer imagine my life without you."

"Good! Tomorrow, we'll go shopping for your Arctic gear, and that may be difficult in Copenhagen in May."

I reached for his hand across the table and said, "Oh Stig, I'm afraid--"

"You were brave enough to row to the horizon."

"And terrified when I lost the shore!"

Both of his hands closed over mine, and he said, "Dear

Alexandra, you must learn to live like the Greenlanders--one day at a time. No single day can hold too much difficulty to handle. Just say *ayorama* and get on with it."

"What does that mean?"

"That's how it goes." He rose and gestured for me to precede him to the door.

A few people in the cafe obviously recognized him, pointing and whispering behind their hands. I was proud to be with him and knew my pride would increase when I was his wife.

The telephone connection to Aalborg was bad. I could scarcely hear *Mor*, and even *Far's* booming voice was muffled.

"You're *what*?" he shouted.

"I'm getting married--on the way to Greenland--to Stig Brand!" I yelled.

"Who?"

"The Arctic explorer. I love him. He loves me."

"Let me get your brother. His ears are better than mine."

I could hear *Far* shouting for Frederik and *Mor's* anxious voice making indistinguishable sounds. If only I could see them--explain face to face. *Frue* Steinsen had left the room discreetly when I made connection, and now she looked in fleetingly and withdrew again.

"Alex!" Frederik boomed, "Are you in trouble?"

"No, I'm in love!"

"Do tell! And you had to scare the pants off of everybody to tell us that?"

"I'm going to marry Stig Brand. We're leaving in two days--"

"Who?"

"The Arctic explorer," I screamed in exasperation. "We're going to Greenland."

"Hey, can I come along?"

"No! Put *Mor* back on."

The crackling on the line subsided, and I could hear my mother much better. I knew that she was crying.

"Don't cry, *Mor!* I love him. He's a wonderful man--strong and gentle at the same time--"

"How long have you known him, Alex?"

"Three days."

"Is that enough for making a decision to last all your life?"

"You knew right away when you met *Far* at the shore! I've heard you say so a million times."

"But he wasn't taking me away to the ends of the earth!"

"He took you away from the New Missioners."

She fell silent and put *Far* back on the line.

"Alexandra, I forbid you to marry this stranger!"

"*Far*," I adopted the sweet wheedling tone that never failed to move him, "he's no stranger to me, and I'm a grown woman who can't be forbidden to do anything. Please be happy for me!"

But his anger crackled through the line all the way from Aalborg, even as he said, "Alex, I only want the best for you--you're my only daughter--"

Frederik grabbed the phone and said, "Take me along!"

"Not on your life! This will be my honeymoon."

"*Far* wants to know if he has any means."

"Just like a banker! Tell him I didn't ask for a financial statement, but I'm sure Stig can take care of me. One can live rather cheaply in Greenland, I should think."

Then *Mor* spoke again. "When will we see you again, Alex?"

"I really don't know, but I do know the mail comes just once a year to the place where he lives."

"Dear God," Mor quavered, "this is what we get for letting you go to Copenhagen!"

"I love you, *Mor*, please give me your blessing. I won't let you go until you do!"

"Like Jacob wrestling with the angel," she said. "Well, I guess we must trust you to decide. God bless you, Alexandra. I'll be praying for you."

Far shouted in the background, and I could just make out a few words, "This time--too far--after you in a rowboat!"

As I hung up the phone, I remembered the safety of being clasped between my father's thighs as he rowed me home. It would

34

not be safety that I would seek between the thighs of my lover, and I would have to make a new home in a dangerous and desolate place.

Frue Steinsen entered the room silently and placed a cup of coffee before me. "*Tillykke!*" she said, "Congratulations!"

Exhaling shakily, I thanked her and thought of the next hurdle to be cleared--*Hr.* Hertz.

Stig came for me in a cab in the morning, and *Frue* Steinsen was thrilled to meet him, having seen his photograph in the newspaper and read of his exploits. She wanted him to sit down for coffee and pastry, but he declined graciously and hurried me to the cab. Once settled in the back seat, we engaged in a long kiss that had the driver tapping his steering wheel.

"I must go to the shop first thing, Stig," I said. "I feel terrible about leaving *Hr.* Hertz without notice like this!"

"As I understand it, you came to him without notice, so you might as well leave the same way. Are you afraid of him?"

"Not really--"

"In other words, the answer is yes. I'll go in with you and browse while you talk with him. If you need me, just call my name." He leaned forward and directed the driver to take us to the *Strøget.*

As I used my key to let us into the shop, Marie looked at us with unconcealed curiosity.

"Good morning, Marie," I said, "is *Hr.* Hertz in yet?"

"Of course he's in. I think he sleeps here."

"I'll go back and have a word with him, then." I quickly introduced Stig to her without clarifying our relationship and went to rap on the manager's office door.

"Enter!" It was a command, not an invitation.

I opened the door cautiously and saw him at his desk, raising one eyebrow in inquiry. His coat was on the back of his chair, and he reached for it as if by reflex.

"Please, don't put on your coat for me," I said. "I'll only take a moment of your time."

He pulled the watch from his vest pocket to time that moment and waited.

"*Hr.* Hertz, it's this way--much as I appreciate the job you gave me just a few days ago, I must give it up. I'm to be married."

"Why didn't you tell me that when I hired you?" he asked icily.

"I didn't know it then. I scarcely knew the man then. We had just seen each other for the first time."

"Are you out of your mind?"

"Very possibly. Maybe Stig Brand has stolen my wits as well as my heart."

Hr. Hertz steepled his fingers. "Stig Brand, eh? *The* Stig Brand?"

"Yes, the Arctic one."

Hr. Hertz sighed and shook his head. "What can I say? I've dreamed of such adventure myself, but here I stay--in the silver shop."

He stood and held out his hand. "I regret losing you, *Frøken* Lund, but I wish you well."

I shook his hand firmly, thanked him and turned to go. This encounter hadn't been anything to fear, but I didn't know that in advance. Perhaps experiencing Greenland would be that way, too.

Stig was idly looking at hollow ware when I rejoined him, and Marie was rearranging her counter display.

"Good-bye, Marie," I said, holding out my hand to her. "I have enjoyed our brief friendship."

"You're leaving?"

"Yes, I'm to be married--to *Hr.* Brand."

"Wh-what about the--" she began and stopped abruptly.

Undoubtedly she failed to recognize Stig and wanted to know what I'd done with Leif but didn't want to cause me any trouble.

We had left the shop and started down the walking street when I realized that I really should telephone Leif. If I were simply to disappear the day after tomorrow, heaven knew what he would think.

Finding a public telephone was not easy, and Stig suggested that we take a cab to the *Folkebladet* and tell Leif our news

36

personally.

"But don't go into detail," he warned. "We have a lot of shopping to do."

"I don't *know* any details!" I said. "I'm simply jumping off a cliff into my future."

"I'll catch you. Trust me."

I caught his hand and kissed it.

Somehow we got the same cab. The driver must have been watching for us, theorizing that lovers were heavy tippers. This time, he was quite patient during our backseat kiss.

Leif was rushing out of the building as we drove up, and when I hailed him, he said, "I'm on my way to a fire--literally!"

"Then jump in," Stig said. "We'll take you there."

"What's burning?" I asked.

"A little building not far from the stock exchange. They're afraid it may spread." He leaned forward to give the address to the driver, then sat back and said, "What are you two up to?"

"We're getting the lady outfitted to go to Greenland," Stig said, "and we haven't much time, but she insisted upon seeing you."

"Yes, Leif, it all happened because of you, and I wanted to thank you--"

"Now wait a minute. What all happened because of me?"

"Stig and I are sailing for Greenland on the Hekla, and the captain will marry us on the way."

"The sooner, the better!" Stig said, putting his arm around me and pulling me closer.

"Well, I'll be damned!"

"Aren't you going to wish us happiness?" I said, "Even journalists have been known to have a *few* manners."

But Leif was scribbling madly in his notebook. We'd just given him a scoop.

We let him out at his fire, which was by now producing sullen puffs of smoke but no flames, and then Stig gave the driver the address of a store where seamen bought their warm clothes for North Sea duty.

37

We found an anorak meant for a small sailor that fit me fairly well, and Stig pulled a parcel from his own inside pocket. He shook out a strip of fox fur soft as a breath and the color of fog and asked the clerk to frame the hood with it. While we waited for that, he chose trousers and heavy mittens for me.

"I haven't worn that many clothes since I went sledding in Aalborg as a child," I said. "Where did you get that beautiful fur?"

"Trapped it myself."

"And you just happened to have it along today?"

He shrugged. "Deep down, I must have known I would meet the woman destined for me."

"Am I a fool to fall for such pretty speeches?"

"Not unless I'm a fool to make them."

When the fur was sewn to the anorak hood, I tried the parka on and gazed at my reflection thoughtfully. Did Stig look at me and see the face of Naika framed by that cloud of fox fur? Realizing the hopelessness of getting an answer to that question, I resolved never to ask it or any other like it.

We made another stop to buy some costume jewelry, which I thought might appeal to the Greenlanders. I wanted to be liked in my husband's chosen territory, and a small gift here and there couldn't hurt.

Finally, we stopped for lunch--open-faced sandwiches and beer--and as we sat at the table in a sidewalk cafe with the shadows of beech leaves dappling our faces, Stig reached into another inner pocket. The box he drew out was from Georg Jensen.

"While you were talking to *Hr.* Hertz, I chose a small engagement gift for you," he said, handing me the velvet box.

I caught my breath when I opened it. The seal necklace.

"How could you possibly know that I loved this most of all?"

"I just hoped that you might love something that was associated with the huge island I love so much." He fastened the carved silver seals around my neck, and again, I shivered for joy.

VI

My parents came hastily to Copenhagen to say good-bye, and *Mor* acted as if it would be forever. Her eyes were red-rimmed, and she clasped and unclasped her hands distractedly.

They met Stig in *Frue* Steinsen's parlor, and I thought he was charming beyond belief, but *Far* was openly hostile to him. He refused to shake hands. *Mor* looked at Stig accusingly, as if he had slung her daughter over his shoulder and carried her away against her will.

Only Frederik was totally thrilled with Stig. He asked him about polar bears and whales and sled dogs and how cold it got in Greenland.

Discerning the effect that extremes would have on my parents, Stig evaded them.

"Ah, polar bears!" he said. "They're clever beasts. If you can imagine a creature weighing nearly a ton creeping up on anything, picture the bear advancing on a seal. He puts his paw over his black nose to remain invisible in the white landscape."

"Have you killed one?" Frederik asked eagerly.

"Many times. I got the last one with a rifle shot to the spine. He was nine feet from nose to tail."

Frederik persisted while my parents and I fidgeted with impatience. They had things to say to me, and I needed to finish packing. *Frue* Steinsen, fussing about with coffee and cakes, was fascinated, however.

"What did it look like?" she asked, holding out her Royal Copenhagen platter of cakes like an offering to a conqueror.

"A young bear's hair is ivory or pearl, but it grows more golden with age," Stig said. "The last one I killed was the shade of wheat. They have pale violet mouths and gray tongues."

"A lovely combination," *Frue* Steinsen said uncertainly.

Frederik was at it again, asking, "How do you find a bear to kill?"

"If you see a raven or two, it's a sign of bear, or you can look for seal breathing holes. When you discover the bear's tracks, you can predict the condition of your prey. The toes of a thin bear turn inward, and a fat bear's toes turn out."

"Alexandra," *Mor* said, "I'd like a word with you in the kitchen."

We slipped away as Stig was saying, "The polar bear flattens himself like a toboggan and slides toward his prey."

I pulled out a chair for *Mor* at *Frue* Steinsen's small kitchen table and sat down opposite her, feeling much as I had when I'd broken one of her favorite dishes in my childhood. The cheerful red and blue stencils above the wainscoting were at odds with my emotions as I looked at her worried face and felt the first true measure of our parting. My destination seemed to be north of the heart.

I was almost afraid to ask, but I said, "Do you like him?"

"He seems to be a decent man, but you can't know everything about a person in a few days, Alexandra. He's enough older that I should think he would realize that--for himself as well as you."

"I love him, and we'll be married by the ship's captain."

"I had hoped that you would be married in church," she said with a catch in her voice. "It seems that each generation gives up a little more of the faith."

"*Mor*, I would gladly do that, and I'm sure Stig would, too, but the banns and the preparations take too long. Stig says he must be back to make arrangements for a film crew coming in June. There's no time to waste!"

"If you love each other, it will wait," *Mor* said.

I fingered the silver seals around my neck and said, "I *can't* wait, *Mor!* I can't bear to be separated from him, even for a few hours."

She sighed deeply. "Well, I suppose I'd better tell you the things a woman needs to know about married love."

"I know those things, *Mor*."

40

"Dear God!"

"Oh, don't be alarmed. I have married friends, that's all."

Looking visibly relieved, she reached across the table and took my hands. "I have something for you."

The packet she handed to me was puzzling. What were Acme Suppositories? *Mor* blushed under my questioning eyes and whispered, "You put one you-know-where to keep from getting in the family way. I couldn't bear to think of a little baby being born into all that ice and snow!"

I hadn't thought about that at all, and I said, "Eskimo babies are born there all the time."

"That's different!"

"How did you get these, *Mor*?"

"At my age, it was quite embarrassing, I assure you!"

Touched, I blinked back tears and thanked her.

She sighed deeply and said, "What can I say?"

"Just wish us happiness."

"I do--with all my heart!"

I stood so quickly that my chair fell over backwards and rushed to her arms. She seemed to have shrunk. Through the years I had burrowed into ever-higher portions of her anatomy until I overshot her height. Now, looking down at the severely straight part in her salt-and-pepper hair brought tears to my eyes.

"God bless you!" she said, disengaging my arms and moving to join the others.

As she left the kitchen, *Far* came in. He gave that funny, false cough he always employed to avoid surprising anyone.

Thrusting the suppositories behind my back, I blinked away my tears and faced him, waiting for him to speak first.

"So, Alexandra," he said. "have you gone completely crazy? How can you give yourself to a stranger?"

"We're not strangers, *Far*. If something is meant to be, you know it right away. And I know I'm going to love his daughter, Nauja."

"I read about that daughter," he said. "She's half-Eskimo."

41

"And half-Danish. My understanding should reach at least halfway to her heart."

"But you're no more than a baby yourself!"

"Then it's time I grew up!"

"Don't sail out farther than you can row back, Alexandra. Can't you give this a little more time and be absolutely certain it's right for you? I wouldn't lend money to a man I'd known for such a short time--"

"Whoever was business-like about love?"

"I absolutely forbid this marriage!" His voice rose and his face reddened.

"Please don't say that, *Far*." I dropped the parcel on a chair to grasp his upper arms and look into his face, hoping to see it soften, but instead, his expression grew stonier. "Must you make me miserable at the happiest time of my life?"

"You'll find out what misery is if you go through with this."

"Then so be it!" I turned my back on him, too angry to cry.

He sighed deeply and left the room with a heavy tread. I wanted his blessing so desperately, but I wouldn't beg for it. The tears started to flow. I sniffled like a small child and squeezed my eyes shut.

"Alexandra!"

Mor was back, wiping my cheeks with a handkerchief perfumed with her familiar 4711.

"So you two are at it again," she said. "He only wants the best for you--surely you know that!"

"You know very well that he wouldn't let me marry Saint Peter himself!"

"But this is so drastic, Alex! if you don't like it in Greenland, you can't run home to Aalborg very handily."

"I know, *Mor*."

"And you hate the cold."

"I have considered that, and if I must endure it to be with Stig, that's what I'll do. You should see the anorak he bought me! The hood is trimmed with the most beautiful fox fur! Wait here, and I'll

42

get it."

I rushed to my room and put it on, returning to the kitchen to model it with the exaggerated poses of a Paris mannequin.

Mor blinked and gathered me into her arms. Her voice was husky as she said, "You looked just like that when we pulled you up Skovbakken hill on your little sled."

I went into the parlor to model the anorak, hoping to touch *Far's* heart with the little-girl image that had moved *Mor*, but he wouldn't look at me. He was standing near the door with his hat on ready to leave. Stig could see how things were and helped me out of the anorak which was much too warm for Copenhagen in May.

The family soon left to catch a train, taking with them the clothes I could not possibly use in Greenland, including a georgette gown of lapis lazuli blue and the pumps with the highest heels. *Mor* kissed me and put a fold of paper in my hand. Frederik punched my arm in farewell, and *Far* maintained an icy silence.

After they were gone, I looked at the folded paper. It was a check made out to me in the amount of five thousand *kroner*. I never had possessed that much in a lump sum, and I started to calculate how long I would have to work in the silver shop to earn it. No, I thought, I wouldn't do that. My career as a sales person had ended almost as soon as it started. How had *Mor* dared to write a check for such a sum without consulting *Far*?

I handed the check to Stig, saying, "Our first wedding present."

His brows lifted at the sum, and he said, "Your father is a generous man."

"No, my mother is a generous woman. Can it be cashed in Greenland?"

"If there's no time to deal with it here--and I'd rather not travel with that much cash--we can find a bank in Julianehaab. Go to bed, now, Alexandra. We sail tomorrow, and you must be rested for the journey."

I came into his arms, and we kissed for a long time, causing *Frue* Steinsen to forget about the coffee cups and plates for the time being.

43

"If only we were married right now!" I said. "How soon can the captain perform the ceremony?"

"As soon as we're underway, I believe. That's why I took the liberty of booking just one cabin. Come along, now. Up you go!" He pointed me toward the stairs and gave me a pat on the rear as if I were a five-year-old.

If he wanted me to be a little girl at this stage of the game, I would go along, I thought. But soon he would have to realize that he was marrying a New Woman, equal to him in more ways than he realized. Not that I could open a tin can with my teeth, and I certainly had no intention of going to a dance hours after giving birth, but I had a strong sense of myself that would never endure a patronizing husband.

I flashed him a sideways glance and a smile. "Good night, my love!"

Turning away to avoid watching him out of sight, I hurried to my room to read the directions for Acme Suppositories. All I really knew about such matters was that Claudine had been fitted for a pessary that effectively prevented what she called "the harvest of love." I was amazed that my mother knew about such things. Maybe she didn't. I decided to rush to the neighborhood chemist's shop as soon as it opened and make my own inquiries.

I thought we had seen the last of Leif, but I was mistaken. He had collected some of the writers, readers and just plain hangers-on who came to the literary evenings and was standing beside the gangway of the Hekla when we arrived.

"Hail the happy couple!" he shouted, brandishing a bottle of champagne.

Babette and Claudine were there, and so was Holger Petersen. Holger waved a sheaf of pages and called to Stig, "I got it copied for you, *Hr.* Brand!"

Stig thanked him and tucked the unwieldy manuscript into a pocket, taking my elbow to guide me up the gangway. Leif and the others fell in behind us, and when they were stopped by a uniformed official, Leif wheedled, "We just want to offer our friends a farewell

44

toast, officer. We'll be off in a flash!"

"This is not the Mauretania!" the sour fellow said.

The Hekla was a small steamer--so small, in fact, that I wondered how she dared to brave the Atlantic. She had no amenities to speak of, either, and we crowded into a stretch of the second deck for our farewells. No glasses were to be had, it seemed, so each drank from the bottle and passed it on.

"To the happiness of our good friends, Alexandra and Stig!" Leif proposed, looking deeply into the eyes of Claudine as he passed her the champagne. She drank with a *"Skoal!"* and passed it to Hjalmar. When one bottle was finished, another miraculously appeared. The laughter grew louder, and the handful of other passengers stared at us disapprovingly as they passed by in the process of getting themselves situated.

In all the confusion, Leif cornered me and spoke into my ear, "You'll be back, you know."

"I expect that I will."

"This is what the Americans call a flash in the pan. It won't last."

"Why not?" I asked angrily.

"Because you're too civilized to live in a place like that. Why bury yourself in ice? Stay here where the action is!"

I laughed shortly. "Action? Have you harpooned a polar bear lately, Leif?"

"No, but if that's what it takes to get you to sit up and take notice, I will!"

"Oh, Leif, we'll be friends forever if you want it that way, but that's all."

"I wish to hell I'd never taken you to that press conference!"

"It wouldn't have changed anything. This way, you just know how things are sooner."

"What a cruel wench you are!"

"Not cruel, just honest. Take my hand and wish me well."

He took it and kissed it, saying, "I know you'll come back to me."

I laughed, shaking my head, and then the whistle blew and the "All ashore!" call went up. Holger Petersen bowed to Stig and said, "A very great honor, sir! I can't tell you how much it means to me to know you'll be reading my poem--in the very place that inspired it."

"Perhaps you'll come to visit us there one day, Petersen."

I nudged Stig fiercely, thinking Holger would be the house guest I wanted least.

Claudine had to be supported down the gangway, having drunk too much champagne. Finally the whole party assembled on the dock and waved to us as we leaned on the rail high above them. They left before the ship did, as no Dane likes to watch a friend move out of sight. It's considered to be unlucky. It was a sheer accident that my eyes followed Leif until he disappeared. I really was looking at all the harbor landmarks, memorizing them to remember if I could not come back for years, and Leif was centered in the picture.

The first motion of the ship was so slight that I thought I imagined it, but then the people and the buildings ashore began to slide in dreamlike slow motion. We were leaving! I had never been outside of Denmark, and a week ago, I wouldn't have dreamed of such a thing, but I was leaving my homeland and family behind. I was sailing into my future with a stranger. I shivered, and Stig put his arm around me and drew me close.

"Cold?"

"No, just terribly excited. You do love me, don't you?"

"Not a bit," he said dryly. "I just have this penchant for collecting a lovely girl every time I return to Denmark."

"And marrying her aboard the ship?"

"Lord, no! Eskimos can practice bigamy if they have the wherewithal, but Danes had better not try it--not even in Greenland."

"Good! I wouldn't want to share you."

We embraced, and by the time the Hekla cleared the harbor and sailed into the Oresund, I almost believed I had found that magic meeting place of sea and sky.

VII

Captain Nielsen was in no hurry to perform our marriage. First, he had to check cargo lists. Then he had to inspect the hold. The ship moved through the night slowly, it seemed to me, and the lights of Copenhagen could be seen for hours.

I had dressed for my wedding in a gown of rose silk and stood at the rail shivering slightly. Stig pulled me close.

"I'll go and speak to him again," he said. "If he's not ready this time, why don't you go to bed? I'll find somewhere else to bunk."

"Oh, no!"

"It's not my favorite idea, either, but I know you're tired. We have the rest of our lives to be together."

"Are you sure this is legal?"

"Good enough for Greenland. I married Naika by carrying her to my bunk."

"But will Denmark recognize our marriage?"

"Does that worry you?"

I looked down at the white foam that formed a line where the ship cut the water and considered. "No, I guess it doesn't."

He kissed me long and hard, then said, "You needn't worry. The King's administrator in the Julianehaab district is on board, and I'll ask him to be a witness."

Stig held me tight for a moment, then went to search for the captain again. I stood at the rail marveling at how my life had changed in a matter of days. Last week at this time, who could have guessed that I would be sailing into the unknown with a man I'd just met in defiance of my father's wishes?

Furthermore, if our unorthodox wedding plans were thwarted, I was quite willing to be married Greenland style. The thought of Stig carrying me to his bunk was quite appealing, actually. The moment that thought occurred to me, the New Woman in me was appalled, but I suppressed her. Life would be much more basic in

Greenland, and the New Woman might not thrive there.

At length, Stig returned to lead me to the tiny dining galley. "Everything's all set," he said. "The captain is putting on his coat, and *Hr.* Thielemann is coming down with another witness, *Hr.* Bech.

Captain Nielsen had put on his coat with gold braid over a seaman's shirt, and *Hr.* Thielemann wore a dark suit like those of the managers of the Stroget shops. *Hr.* Bech, the representative of a herring canning company, carried a small bottle of aquavit. Aalborg, my home city, was the aquavit capital of the country, and I knew my brands. *Hr.* Bech had excellent taste.

"Well, now, *Frøken* Lund," the captain said, "have you no lady to attend you?"

I shook my head, momentarily regretting the absence of my best friend, Karen. We had talked about our weddings since we were little girls--what we would wear, who would sing Grieg's *Jeg Elskidag,* how the champagne bottle would be pulled from the *kransekage.* But none of that mattered. Only Stig mattered, and his faded blue eyes were warm with love.

He introduced the witnesses to me and took his place at my side.

"Let us proceed, then," said the captain. "Dearly beloved, we are gathered here in the sight of God and man to unite this couple in holy matrimony. If anyone objects to this union, let him speak now or forever hold his peace."

No word was spoken, but the ship hit a swell, nearly causing me to lose my balance. Was the sea objecting?

"Stig Andrew Brand, do you take this woman, Alexandra--" he broke off and asked me, "Do you have a middle name, *Frøken* Lund?"

"Yes, it's Marie."

"Very well--do you take this woman, Alexandra Marie Lund, to be your lawfully wedded wife?"

"I do," Stig said in a deep, steady voice.

"And do you, Alexandra Marie Lund, take this man, Stig

Andrew Brand, to be your lawfully wedded husband?"

My eyes welled with tears, and I could only suppose that I was weeping for joy as I made my answer firm, "I do."

"Then, by the power invested in me by the parliament and in the name of his majesty, King Christian X, I pronounce you man and wife."

It was over so quickly. Stig kissed me while the witnesses signed the necessary document.

"You'll have to excuse me," the captain said. "I have to see to a broken gaff.

As he hurried out, a sailor came from the galley with a *kransekage* carried high on a platter. Stig pulled out his pocketknife and cut through the towering rounds of almond paste to uncover a bottle of champagne.

"How did you ever manage that?" I asked. Forming, baking and constructing the *kransekage* was a major undertaking that took time.

"I ordered it the night we met in Nyhavn."

"So soon?"

"The inevitable pays no attention to time."

I was dizzy with love as we sat down with *Hr.* Thielemann and *Hr.* Bech to drink the champagne, demolish the almond rounds and toast the occasion in aquavit.

Hr. Thielemann patted his lips delicately with his handkerchief and sighed. "Now that I've thawed out properly, it's back to eternal winter."

Hr. Bech, who was making his first trip to Greenland, looked apprehensive. "One gets used to it, I suppose," he said.

"Some do," *Hr.* Thielemann nodded. "Some do."

"Where are you headed?" Stig asked.

"To Holsteinsborg. My company may be interested in investing in a halibut cannery there."

"Ah, yes," Stig said. "There's a tall mountain peak near Holsteinsborg called Womanhood. You'll know why when you see it." He caught my hand and pulled me to my feet. "Now if you gentlemen will excuse us--"

51

I looked back at the shattered wedding cake, remembering how beautiful it had been when it was whole. *Mor* would be pleased to know that our wedding had one thing traditional, at least. I'd write to her about it. And, I suddenly realized, she wouldn't get my letter for a year. But maybe the time lag wouldn't seem so terrible--no worse than starlight that has been on its way to the human eye for thousands of years.

We went to our cabin, which was so compact we couldn't move without bumping into each other--just right for newlyweds. I made quick and surreptitious use of *Mor's* parting gift. Then, colliding and embracing, we undressed each other eagerly and fell on the lower bunk. The ultimate embrace was not long in coming, and Stig took me with such passion that my imaginings of the act were overwhelmed and forgotten. Only this driving, shouting Viking could give me what I must have from now on.

When the urgency was stilled for a time, he stroked my cheek, my breast, my belly and whispered, "You're so beautiful."

I touched his body, fingering a broad, keloid scar on his thigh. "What's this?"

"I harpooned myself."

"How could you ever do that?"

"I was sliding down a harpoon line to the bottom of a crevasse to look for a place where the dogs and sleds could come down, and I impaled myself on the harpoon tip on the spliced line. I couldn't go either way until I pulled the tip out. It hurt like the devil, and I bled like hell, but they found me in time. I was out of it for days."

I kissed the scar and said, "Promise me you'll be more careful from now on. You belong to me, and I want to keep you."

The ship rolled, throwing us together and then apart, and I caught a glimpse of his face. That far-away look in his eyes frightened me as I remembered him saying, "Those who love Greenland are lost."

Then, without another word, Stig was asleep. I sat up beside him on the narrow bunk and inspected the rest of his body, particularly his scarred and battered feet. This man, my husband, often went barefoot on the ice, he had told me. It was the best way to keep one's footing. I swore that I'd keep him from taking such awful risks in the future.

I lay down, molding my body against his, and pulled the coarse sheet over us. Stig smiled in his sleep, and I put out the light.

He had more faith in my ability to cope with his frozen world than I did, and I wondered how he had decided that I would work out? Leif once had called me "a spoiled banker's daughter." It was when I went with him on an assignment to cover the maiden voyage of a tourist barge on the canal, and I said, "If this is supposed to be a pleasure, I'd hate to experience what these people call misery! I'm freezing to death!"

The tourists were British and layered with tweed, which probably accounted for their stoicism.

The tiny cabin still contained the heat of our loving encounter, and Stig exuded warmth like a tile stove. As long as I had him, I wouldn't have to worry about being cold. He turned to the wall, and I molded my body to his back, clutching him to keep from falling out of the narrow berth.

He awoke with a start, and then he turned and held me, whispering, "Shall I go topside and give you some room?"

"No, please stay!"

We settled into a snug embrace, but not to sleep. Our hearts pounded and the ship's engine thumped.

"Do you hear what it says?" Stig asked.

"Love me, love me, love me!"

"Hmm," he said, "perhaps it does. But I hear Greenland, Greenland, Greenland!"

We awoke quite late the next day, and Stig had to invade the galley to find breakfast for us. I was feeling light-headed, almost dizzy, and the strong coffee was just what I needed.

"How are you today, *Frue* Brand?" he asked.

"I think I've been loved to death!" I whispered, not wanting to share that information with the strange men who were lingering over their coffee in the dining area. "Am I the only woman on board?"

"One of two," he said. "When I took my turn on the deck before you woke up, I met an Eskimo woman named Kullabak. I'll introduce you."

"What was she doing in Denmark?"

"Visiting relatives."

I had a momentary resistance to the idea of Danes being related to an Eskimo, and it shamed me. After all, I was on my way to becoming the mother of a small Eskimo girl named Nauja. The thought reminded me that Stig had loved her mother before he loved me, and that distressed me, too. I would take care not to think of it again.

"Where are we?" I asked.

"On the Kattegat. We passed Helsingor in the night."

"Oh, I wish I had been awake to see it!"

I loved Hamlet's castle, Kronborg, built by Eric of Pomerania, and I hadn't seen it since Leif had tried to "modernize" my view of it.

"Shakespeare never saw it and Hamlet never saw it," he said. "Don't tell me you really believe the ghost looks out through the parapets of the Knights' Hall!"

"What I really believe and what I want to believe may be two different things," I told him with a haughty look.

"Has *Frue* Brand gone off somewhere?" Stig asked, holding a morsel of pastry to my lips.

"I'm here. When the ship pulled away from the dock in Copenhagen, I felt that we were leaving, but we haven't gotten far from home, have we?"

"Not really. You can still jump ship fairly easily if you decide you've made a mistake. I understand we'll be putting in at Fredrikshavn to replace the gaff that delayed our nuptials."

"That's not far from our summer beach house. Oh, I wish I could show it to you! We had so many happy times there--"

Most of my memories of *Far* were in that setting, and I was reminded that my new happiness was an act of disobedience to him.

"There's a cloud crossing your lovely face," Stig said.

54

I forced a smile, and he added, "The eyes are still behind the cloud. What is it, Alexandra?"

I didn't want to create a breach on both sides by telling him what *Far* thought of our marriage, and I said, "I've never been outside of Denmark. I suppose I'm a bit frightened."

He took my hand and looked into my eyes."I will take care of you, and actually, you won't be far from home when we land in Greenland. Almost everyone speaks your language."

Kullabak did speak Danish, but she expressed herself with such indirection that I frequently thought she was talking about a third person--one who was invisible.

After Stig introduced us, he left us on the deck and went to talk to the sailors. Kullabak regarded me with the narrow slits that were her eyes and said, "A woman once knew Naika."

"Yes?" I said with a look of encouragement.

"Somebody is thinking *Hr.* Stig's kamiks will be supplied with grass again."

I hadn't the faintest notion what she was talking about, so I just smiled and sat back, watching the sun glint on the waves as the Hekla sailed toward Fredrikshavn.

Kullabak seemed to be about *Mor's* age, and her skin resembled tanned leather, but her glossy hair was still coal-black. We sat together in comfortable silence until Stig came for me.

How many times daily would we dress and undress in those days at sea? As often as any healthy honeymooners, I supposed.

Now, as we lay together in blissful lassitude, I asked Stig about Kullabak's mode of speech.

"She refers to herself as `a woman' or `somebody.' A Polar Eskimo will never mention himself or herself by name. A jealous spirit might be listening and cause trouble."

"Do you believe that, Stig?"

"That depends on where I am," he said with a laugh.

"She also said something about grass being supplied, but I can't remember the other word."

"Ah, she must have been talking about *kamiks*, sealskin boots.

55

It's the duty of a wife to put a new layer of dried grass between the two pairs of soles in the boots every day."

"I suppose I can do that--"

Stig laughed and gave me a hug. "A person is glad to hear that," he said.

As the Hekla approached Frederikshavn, I felt a sense of loss. Among so many red-roofed beach houses along the distant shore, I could not identify our own with any certainty. All my life, I had believed it to be unique.

Stig tried to comfort me, and the fact that he was charmed with my childishness accomplished that comfort.

We stood together at the rail and watched the drama of colliding seas near Skagen, where the Kattegat and the Skagerrak clashed with high, white foam. It was the grandest thing I'd ever seen, but he said, "Wait until you see ice floes collide in the light of the Aurora Borealis."

The Hekla entered the North Sea for a calm passage of time when we spoke only to each other, keeping to ourselves and needing nothing more.

When the ship took on coal at Methil, a small port on the Firth of Forth in Scotland, we disembarked and walked along the dock. My legs still thought they were at sea, and I took Stig's arm to steady myself.

"This is so foreign," I said, referring to the sailors and dock workers speaking a thick, incomprehensible language; the high houses with many chimney pots; the mounds of bright fishing nets; and the blue flag with the white X.

"We're the foreigners here," he said.

We followed that foreign coast for a long time, passing between the mainland and the northern islands. When the Hekla nosed into the Atlantic, a ground swell moved the vessel massively, and I feared that I would be seasick, but the moment passed.

We went to bed and were rolled so wildly in our berth that our love-making was seriously affected.

"One just has to catch the tide," Stig said, and when we did, we seemed to be in tune with the universe.

"Love me, love me, love me!" the engine thumped. But I knew that my husband heard, "Greenland, Greenland, Greenland!" His spirits had risen with each nautical mile in a northerly direction.

VIII

We sailed the North Atlantic forever, it seemed, and I was content with the routine that evolved. The harmony of our bodies in the night became the harmony of our companionship in the daytime. Stig would rise early, out of long habit, and walk the deck until I awoke. Then he would bring breakfast to our crowded cabin and put the tray between us on the lower bunk.

"The first time I came out, I slept in a hammock," he said. He tilted my chin for a kiss and added, "I like this better."

I sipped my coffee and ran my fingers through my tangled hair, still slightly embarrassed at being studied so minutely by a man while in such a state of undress. With no time to assemble a trousseau, I wore a school-girlish nightgown that made me feel less than alluring.

"We should catch sight of Cape Farewell before sunset," he said. "Ships usually stay too far away from the coast to see it, but the captain tells me the ice isn't as far out as usual. I'd say the Cape wants to welcome the bride."

"Just one more day in the open sea?"

He nodded, eyes bright with anticipation. What I felt was more like trepidation. After being loved and listened to and spoiled for this timeless interval, I was about to confront reality. I would be judged by Stig's friends and acquaintances. I would be measured and possibly rejected by Nauja, a child who would forever remind her father of his first love.

Stig picked up the tray and brushed the crumbs from the sheets, saying he would leave me to get dressed.

I caught his hand and pouted.

He laughed and put the tray down. Going down on one knee beside the bed, he placed my foot on his thigh and kissed its arch. The beard tickled, and I laughed, too. Then, instead of getting dressed, I helped him undress.

I needed to know the origin of his passion for the far north, and God knew if he'd ever have time to explain it once we landed, so I struggled out of the melting lassitude that followed love-making and asked.

"One of my ancestors was with Bering," he said. "His name was Peter Brand, and I found his battered sea chest in our attic."

"What was in it?"

"A compass, a dented metal cup, *kamiks* worn to shreds--the usual northern gear. I was just a boy when I found it, and I ignored the thing that came to mean the most--his diary. Eventually, I pieced the crumbling paper together and read what he had to say on that last voyage with Bering. He expected to die, and somehow that didn't frighten him. He wrote, `The secrets of the universe are in this cold vastness, and soon I shall know them.' That statement seized my imagination."

"Did he die on the voyage?"

"No, he died in his own cozy Danish house under a feather *dyne* with his wife and six children at his side."

"You'd better plan to do the same!" I said with mock ferocity.

Kullabak was at the ship's rail when we finally emerged from our cabin. Her narrow eyes grew even narrower as she stared across the slate-gray waves toward her invisible homeland. She wore a leather jacket with a hood over leather pants rather than the dresses she had appeared in at the beginning of the voyage.

"It won't be long now, Kullabak," Stig said.

"A person is not unhappy," she said, smiling broadly at us before returning her eyes to the sea.

The administrator approached and greeted us. Stig squeezed my shoulder in farewell and strolled on with him, leaving me with Kullabak.

In companionable silence we watched seabirds whirling low above the water and riding the waves.

Finally I said, "Did you have a happy time in Denmark?"

"Somebody smelled smoke. Heard big noise all the time. Many people."

I nodded, realizing that I scarcely noticed the industrial annoyances of Aalborg or the crowds of Copenhagen. I wondered

60

if I could get used to pure air that was too cold to breathe and sparse habitation. I shivered and told Kullabak that I must go to my cabin for another sweater.

"A person thinks *Frue* Stig should eat more fat," she said.

While I was digging for the sweater in my case, I found the parcel of costume jewelry I had bought to gain goodwill among the Polar Eskimos in Stig's remote outpost. I decided to give a *faux* amber pendant to Kullabak.

She hadn't moved an inch while I was gone, and I touched her arm to gain her attention, offering the necklace in a twist of tissue paper.

She smiled broadly, showing incredibly short teeth. Stig had told me that Eskimo women chewed hides so constantly that frequently they outlived their teeth by many years.

"For what reason does *Frue* Stig give presents to a person?"

"Because a person likes somebody," I said, in the gleeful belief that I was learning to speak in the Eskimo manner.

"Then somebody must look among worthless possessions to find a gift that will answer."

"Oh no, Kullabak! That isn't at all necessary."

She unwrapped the pendant and looked at it thoughtfully. "The sun is caught in this," she said, wrapping the chain around her work-thickened fingers and holding the tear-drop pendant in her palm.

"Shall I help you put it around your neck?"

She shook her head. "A person wants to hold it."

Stig reclaimed me in time for the midday meal, and when I told him Kullabak recommended a change in my diet, he said, "Wait until I introduce you to my favorite delicacy, rotten mattak."

"That sounds disgusting! What is it?"

"It's huge flakes of narwhale skin kept in a cache for several years until it ferments and tastes like walnuts. The blubber turns green, and it has a sharp flavor--like roquefort cheese."

"Stig, you're making me sick!"

He laughed and said, "It's not on the menu for *middagsmad*."

I heaped my plate with pickled herring, hoping that my new

61

husband had a good supply of tinned goods in his house at Thule. I was almost afraid to ask.

I told him about giving the necklace to Kullabak and how she refused to put it around her neck.

"She wants to hold it and possess it," he explained.

"She told me the sun was caught in it."

"It's an amulet to her--a symbol of warmth and wealth. You chose well for her, Alex."

"Better than I knew! I just thought it was pretty."

After the meal, *Hr.* Thielemann wound the small Victrola he was taking back to Greenland and played some American jazz. *Hr.* Bech called it cacophony, and the counsel cheerfully lifted the needle and substituted another record, something called "The Pineapple Rag."

The jazz reminded me of the bohemian gatherings at Claudine's apartment--of everything modern that I was leaving behind to return to the nineteenth century, if not to an earlier time. Looking at Stig, who smiled faintly and tapped his toe to the music, I knew I would go anywhere--into any time--to be with him.

Kullabak was the first to spot the faint outlines of Cape Farewell. She shouted excitedly in her own tongue, and everyone rushed to the ship's rail.

The coast was gray in a silver mist with shafts of sunlight streaming down to illuminate the forbidding granite mountains. This somber blue barrier was crowned with snow, and the sea ran high on the rocks, foaming and crashing with awesome force.

I backed into Stig's arms, and he held me close. "Isn't that a sight?" he said. "I've never seen the Cape so clearly."

I fingered my seal necklace, needing an amulet for the confrontation with this evil beauty. Warmed by my neck, the silver comforted me, but I doubted that I was equal to this adversary.

"In the days of the sailing ships, it would have taken us anywhere from 34 to 44 days to get here," he said.

I would have liked that, I thought.

A southeaster blew up suddenly, blowing sheets of water

around the ship like smoke. The Hekla was carried seaward, and the fearsome Cape was hidden from view. Stig said it was just as well. If we came any closer, we might hit ice floes and pack ice.

"What's a floe and what's pack ice?" I asked.

"In the summer, ice along the shore partly melts and partly breaks. A floe is a free-floating chunk of ice, and a pile-up of floes is a pack. One floe riding on another is a raft, and pack ice breaks into growlers and brash--"

"Complicated, isn't it?" I said.

"More complicated than you know," he said. "The Eskimos have more than a hundred words for the various forms of ice, but the real experts on the subject are the dogs. They can sense unsafe ice, and they spread out and move slowly. When it's really thin, all a human can do is lie down and wriggle like a snake."

I looked at him with horror, and he laughed.

The Hekla put in at Julianehaab just after dinner, and we said our good-byes to *Hr.* Thielemann.

"I wish you every happiness," he said. "The next time you come to Julianehaab, do call on me. *Frue* Thielemann will be happy to meet you.

The town seemed to have a good many Danish-looking houses with steep roofs to shed the weight of heavy snow, and the language we heard from the dock was Danish, even if the accent was not Copenhagen. The portion of the cargo destined for Julianehaab would be unloaded quickly, Stig said, and he thought we should stay on board. I had to content myself with sight-seeing from the deck.

"The place looks quite civilized," I said.

"This is the gentler Greenland," he told me. "They have a sheep station here, they grow potatoes, and the only savages are the mosquitoes."

As we pulled out of the harbor, he directed my gaze to a hillside where I saw nothing but a blurry movement at first. Then I made out the forms of humans--Greenlanders waving to the ship. Their clothes were the browns and dull greens of nature, and they seemed to be part of the landscape.

"No matter what time a ships puts in, somebody waves from the hill. There's always someone awake in the colony, and they find it amusing to wave at the summermen," Stig said.

"Summermen?"

"Tourists. They hold them in great contempt."

"Then why do they wave?"

"The Eskimo always says what he thinks you want to hear, and he sees no dishonesty in that."

"Well, I think it's indecent! My grandmother always says, `An open enemy is better than a false friend,' and I believe it!"

"*My* grandmother used to say, `Follow the customs or leave the country.' Give that a little thought, my love." He hugged me as he spoke, and I concentrated more on the embrace than on the words.

Later, as we passed the distant lights of Gothaab, Stig told me about the big celebration there earlier in the year. "The king came to mark the 200th anniversary of the arrival of Hans Egede, the apostle of Greenland."

"I read something about that in the papers at home."

"It was quite an affair. People came from all the remote settlements, and we had a procession from the high school to the church. The pastors were all dressed up, and I marched right along in my red anorak--not quite the thing for the occasion.

"They gave the king a kayak, but he wouldn't try it out, and that was a big disappointment. The next day, they had a big banquet on the king's ship. He was handing out knighthoods right and left, but what I got was the branch of a beech tree in a bottle!"

"Why that?"

"His majesty thought I would appreciate a green touch of home in these frozen climes.

"And did you?"

Stig rolled his eyes and laughed.

We steamed up the Davis Strait to Holsteinsborg, the last port before the Hekla headed home. This was our temporary destination and the place where *Hr.* Bech would stay. He was visibly

64

apprehensive about conducting business in this outlandish place, and as we stood watching the gangway being lowered, he said, "I don't know why I'm fretting, *Frue* Brand. My commitment is nothing compared to yours."

"That may be, but I suspect you don't love fish canning as much as I love my husband!"

Just then, Stig came up to us and pointed out the peak called Womanhood. It actually did look like a breast. Then we walked around to the far deck to watch some whales at play. They were white, and as their bulbous heads broke the water, they seemed to smile widely.

We brought as much of our luggage as we could manage to the gangway and left it for the porters while we went ashore and walked along the dock. Although it was past midnight, the light resembled early twilight in Denmark.

We saw many Eskimos, and Stig told me Holsteinsborg was the stopping point for Eskimos travelling down the coast in one season and up the coast in another.

Someone called his name, and we turned to see three elderly Eskimo women grinning broadly and hurrying toward us. Stig spoke to them in their own language, then told me, "This is Arnaluk, Manik and Iva, old friends of mine." I heard my own name in a rush of words I didn't understand and knew he was completing the introduction. I smiled and went on nodding and smiling until he ended the conversation and started to walk away.

"How did you meet them?" I asked him.

"When I first came out, they were unmarried young girls. I danced with them at trading post parties."

"But that was only fifteen years ago! They're ancient!"

"Not in years," he said. "Life is hard on Eskimo women."

Stig needed to make arrangements about some goods being unloaded from the cargo hold, and I stood aside to wait. Kullabak came toward me, struggling with Danish suitcases in both hands and skin-wrapped parcels clamped between arms and body. Her eyes searched the busy crowd on the dock patiently and apparently fruitlessly. Then she saw me and smiled as she put her burdens down.

She pulled the *faux* amber pendant from the neck of her jacket and pressed it to her lips. "Remember to eat much fat," she said. Reaching inside her jacket, she brought out a gift for me. It was a small soapstone figure of a woman with generous breasts. "Somebody wishes you much love."

"Thank you, Kullabak." My eyes moistened as I prepared to give up the only woman I knew in what was clearly a man's world.

She was already gone from me as she heard a man's shout. He was too young to be her husband--a son, perhaps--and her face was radiant as she picked up her burdens and hurried toward him.

I realized I had appropriated Kullabak as a substitute for the mother I had left in Denmark, but she probably wasn't old enough for that. If the three women I had just met were any indication, Kullabak could be my older sister or a very young aunt. I fingered the amulet she had given me reflectively. Standing on the dock in trousers and anorak, I needed all the help I could get to remember I was a woman.

Stig had found some Eskimo boys to carry our personal luggage, and they walked behind us to the house where he had taken a room for us for the next two months--until the pack ice receded enough to allow a boat to land at Thule.

He had made inquiries and learned we had beaten the film crew to Holsteinsborg, which pleased him mightily. He whistled a few bars of jazz as we approached a house painted brilliant blue and rapped on the door.

The woman who answered was *Frue* Rasmussen, the wife of the Lutheran pastor. She welcomed us with coffee and showed us our room very soon. It was, after all, more than an hour past midnight, and she was tired. So were we, but it was not too late for love.

IX

The morning sun came through lace curtains much like *Mor's*, and for a moment, I forgot where I was. Then I remembered. I was finally planted on Greenland soil, what little of it there seemed to be. The impress of Stig's head was in the pillow next to mine, and he was nowhere to be seen. I sat up and stretched luxuriously, watching the door open a crack.

"Awake?" he asked softly.

"Ummhmm."

"Here's coffee and kringle." He turned and backed into the room, swinging the tray around like a magician producing something amazing from his hat.

We sat side by side on the bed to enjoy our breakfast, and it was much easier here than on the ship. I commented on the piercing brightness of the light that flooded the room.

"We'll have to get you some bone goggles with narrow slits to protect your eyes," he said.

"*Frue* Rasmussen seemed surprised to see me last night."

"Small wonder. When I booked the room, I was a disconsolate widower."

"And now?"

He took the cup from my hand, removed the tray, and kissed me into a reclining position. "And now the blissful bridegroom," he said.

I had been about to ask what we were going to do on our first day in Holsteinsborg, but that could wait. Today, Stig made love with the intense restraint of a starving man offered a huge meal and trying to spare his body the ravages of too much too soon. This resulted in exquisite pleasure for me, but I also wanted to break down that control, invade the place where he retreated--even from me, wallow in excess, live in the spirit of summer.

Something was different about our coming together here. As we

67

lay in each other's arms, I pushed back a delicious lassitude to think what it was. Stig shifted his body, pulling the covers from my shoulders and bosom, and I knew. The calendar might say it was summer, but the air still held the chilly burn of the menthol salve *Mor* rubbed on my chest when I had a childhood cough. The North was putting me on notice that things were different here.

At home, my parents and Frederick would be at the beach house, and my brother would be diving into the breaking waves. Here, submerging one's body among the bobbing ice floes probably would be fatal. I pulled the covers over me and clung to Stig, shivering.

"What's this?" he said. "You can't be cold, we're still in south Greenland."

"How much worse does it get?"

He laughed and said, "I'm not sure you want to know. Get dressed, and I'll show you the town."

I put on a wool skirt and sweater, heavy stockings and walking shoes, an outfit I'd worn for autumn walks on the moors near Aalborg. As soon as we walked out the door, I walked right back in to fetch my anorak, but Stig seemed impervious to the chill in the air.

"Stig, I just remembered the check *Mor* gave us. Do they have a bank here?"

"What passes for one, but I doubt their entire assets would be as much as that. Just keep it in a safe place. We won't be needing it."

I wondered if *Mor* had told *Far* about that check. If not, she wouldn't have to face the consequences for a long time. She was such an innocent in matters of finance, it seemed to me, and I had resolved to be better informed.

The sun was painfully bright, bringing out the blazing purple of the saxifrages blooming between the houses and the white heather that looked like a sifting of snow. Bumblebees maneuvered their big, clumsy bodies into the blooms, and the whine of mosquitoes was in the air.

We walked past the school, a bleak, wooden structure unused in the summer, and when I commented on the terrible condition of the roofs on several houses, Stig laughed.

"The Eskimos knock them down on purpose. It's their version of spring cleaning. What a day this is! If we were in Thule, I'd take you to the bird cliffs, but there'll be plenty of time for that."

We soon came to Pastor Rasmussen's church with its soaring cross, and I asked, "Can we go in?"

Stig tried the door and found it open, but it took awhile for our eyes to adjust to the gloom inside. At last we could see the sailing ship suspended in the nave, the symbol of the storm-tossed human condition, and the figure of Thorvaldsen's "Kristus" at the altar.

"I feel right at home," I said.

"I told you that's how it would be."

I held out my hand and said, "Kneel with me?"

"Weren't the Captain's words enough?"

"Yes, but--"

He clasped my hand, and we knelt in a beam of amber light coming from the narrow window above the altar.

"I, Stig, take thee, Alexandra," he said. "To be my wedded wife as long as we both shall live."

"I--" My throat filled with tears, and I swallowed hard. "I, Alexandra, take thee, Stig, to be my wedded husband as long as we both shall live."

We kissed with a prolonged and tender pressure of our lips, and I thought, *Live. The question is, where?* I had enough New Woman attributes to question the traditional "Whither thou goest" female response, but so far, I was following that tradition without a murmur.

We returned to the painful brilliance of the sun, and Stig said, "You've seen two-thirds of the main features of the settlement. Let's finish the job."

The store was a long, low building with goods laid out on planks resting on sawhorses. Again, it took some time for our eyes to adjust to the dim light inside. Stig found some bone glasses with slits for me and told me to look around for anything else I fancied.

What I liked was a pair of white beaded kamiks, but he said, "Sorry, those are for young girls."

"Am I so old?" I asked indignantly.

"Forgive me, *Frue* Brand. I should have said `unmarried girls.' Married women wear red kamiks."

"The red are prettier, anyhow!" I said with a sniff, and he laughed. So did an Eskimo going through a pile of coats.

"Better get some leather trousers, too," Stig said. "When the film crew gets here, we'll be heading for the ice cap. Most women make their own, but I won't ask you to chew leather on your honeymoon."

I whirled to give him an indignant look, which only intensified his amusement. It wasn't funny to me, as I supposed his first wife had chewed leather without complaint.

The next day was Sunday, and while I'd skipped services often after moving to Copenhagen, I half-expected Stig to take me to church--especially since we were living in the home of the pastor. He slept late, however, and when we heard the Rasmussens leave the house, we made love without restraint. This was the first time we hadn't worried about being heard.

"We're not going to church, I gather," I said.

"I could take you to an *angakok*, I suppose."

"What's that?"

"An Eskimo holy man. He goes into trances and then interprets the visions that come to him. Once I told Pastor Rasmussen that he ought to try it, and he was scandalized."

Even as I looked at him, loving the way his eyebrows arched, feeling the warmth of the big hand that capped my shoulder as we lay back against high-piled pillows, I realized how little we knew of each other. How much of himself had he revealed to Naika? How much did she demand to know? How much did I need to know?

"How does one go into a trance, Stig?"

He laughed. "If your ambition is to become an *angakok*, forget it! They're always men."

"You didn't answer my question," I pouted.

He kissed the pout away and said, "Sometimes they stop eating and drinking until the mind begins to hallucinate. Other times they go to a lonely place and rub a stone in a circle on a rock for for hours or days--as long as it takes. The state of unconsciousness is important to the Eskimos. Even the children can make it happen by tightening the cords of their hoods until they turn purple."

"That's terrible!"

"They think it's wonderful--until there's an accident and someone dies. The Eskimos have no benevolent deity, only protective spells and the help of *angakoks* to keep the evil spirits in nature from overwhelming them. It's the *angagkok's* job to find out how the people have offended the spirits and tell them what to do about it."

"And what might that be?"

"They usually lay some taboo on the women--like forbidding them to eat the meat of the female walrus for a certain length of time."

"That doesn't seem fair."

"Perhaps not, but women are considered to be unclean."

"Do you believe that?" I asked in a menacing tone.

"I believe only what I can see--and I see you, Alexandra. At this moment, I see only you."

We made love again to take advantage of our solitude, then rose to wash, dress and pour ourselves cups of coffee from the pot on the back of the stove. *Fru* Rasmussen had left us a plate of pastries covered with a linen napkin.

I sipped the strong brew contentedly, repeating to myself the words of Emile Coue, "Day by day in every way, I am getting better and better." On such a gorgeous summer Sunday I had no need for his other auto-suggestion, "It'll soon be over."

We went for a walk, and when I squinted painfully in the bright sunlight, Stig reached into his pocket for the bone "glasses" he had bought for me.

"Welcome to the North, Madame!" he said, putting them on my

71

face.

"That feels much better, but it cuts down on the view."

"You can't have everything, much as I'd like to give it to you."

We walked down to the water, where some Eskimo boys were playing tag in their kayaks.

"They're getting in practice for the August seal hunt," Stig said. "They paddle far out to sea and harpoon the seals."

As one boy was about to tag another with his paddle, the pursued flipped his kayak until it looked like a Turkish slipper floating in the water.

"Stig, he'll drown!" I cried.

"Keep watching," Stig said with a grin.

I did and saw the boy right his craft and paddle swiftly away, water streaming from his hair. I knelt to feel the temperature of the water and found it even colder than I expected.

"That poor boy must be wet to the skin," I said. "He's sure to catch pneumonia."

"I wouldn't worry about it," Stig said. "He turned himself over because he was feeling kayak dizziness. The sun on the water hypnotizes them until they can't move their arms, and they feel they're sinking. That's when they take the cold water treatment."

We went on, approaching a low, rambling structure that reeked with a strong, fishy odor. Black flies swarmed everywhere, getting into our eyes, nose and ears. I started to run away from the place, and Stig followed.

"That's the halibut cannery," he said. "I thought we might run into *Hr.* Bech."

"On Sunday?"

"Oh, I suppose not."

So much for my judgment. The voice calling Stig's name obviously belonged to *Hr.* Bech, who had emerged from the cannery and was walking quickly toward us. He had exchanged his formal businessman's attire for the expensive casualness of a country squire, but his facial expression was as anxious as ever.

"How's it going?" Stig said, extending his hand.

72

"I wish I'd never left Copenhagen!"

"Why do you say that?" I asked. "Aren't you finding this to be an adventure?"

"Ah, *Frue* Brand, young lovers find adventure in everything, but to me, the exotic just means one difficulty after another."

"What seems to be the problem?" Stig said.

"These people promise you everything and give you nothing!"

"They simply say what they believe you want to hear, *Hr.* Bech. They want everything to be peaceful and pleasant, and they live one day at a time."

"That's impossible! Progress is what we're after, and you don't accomplish that by being peaceful and pleasant. Furthermore, planning is the key to success in any undertaking, and living one day at a time amounts to letting the future walk all over you!"

"You can't change them, I'm afraid," Stig said, "and you can learn a lot from them--if you will."

Hr. Bech thrust his hands deep into his pockets with a short, angry exhalation. "So *I'm* the one who has to change, is that it? For one thing, I'll have to find out how to use my leisure. I can't seem to read here--can't concentrate--keep reading the same sentence over and over."

"That's what endless daylight does to a person," Stig says. "You feel a certain kind of confusion from over-stimulation, I suppose."

"What do you people do for amusement?" he asked.

Stig looked at me and grinned, and *Hr.* Bech reddened. He said, "I've found a decent place to live, at least--with a Danish widow, *Frue* Kjaer. If you'll tell me when you can come, I'll ask her to make a dinner for us."

"Would tomorrow be too soon?" Stig asked.

"I shouldn't think so. Let's say six o'clock. They do everything earlier here, I've discovered."

"Tell *Frue* Kjaer that we'll bring the dessert," Stig said, and I almost gasped. My cooking skills were minimal, and I was scarcely ready to create a dessert for a dinner party.

73

After we parted from *Hr.* Bech, I said, "Just what do you expect me to make for this affair?"

"Nothing. I'll arrange it."

About an hour before we were to leave for *Frue* Kjaer's house the next day, Stig went out while I was dressing. It was the first time he had left me alone, even for a few minutes, and I wasn't sure how I felt about that.

He returned with a glass bowl containing some golden berries in a kind of golden fluff.

"What is it?" I asked.

"Eskimo ice cream. I asked an old friend to make it."

I asked no more questions then, not about the dessert or about the person who made it. *Hr.* Bech asked *Frue* Kjaer to dine with us, and I noticed that she did not serve herself from the glass bowl.

The meal and conversation were pleasant, and we visited for a time in the bright gloaming before Stig yawned elaborately and said it was time to turn in.

"Oh, yes," *Hr.* Bech said, reddening again, "of course."

We strolled back to the parsonage, the sides of our bodies just touching in an intimacy that the casual observer would not notice.

"That dessert was quite good," I said. "What was in it?"

"Cloudberries in a mixture of seal oil and chewed caribou tallow beaten like whipped cream."

I felt slightly sick, but I took myself in hand firmly. "I have a lot to learn about Greenland cuisine," I said.

And about everything else in the place, I thought.

X

The arrival of the American film crew created a sensation in Holsteinsborg, and the way they talked and dressed was as strange to me as it was to the Eskimos. Stig and I stood on the shore as their ship anchored waving our greeting, and it seemed that the whole town had turned out to do the same.

We watched them struggle onto the barge that would bring them quayside.

"The first thing we'll have to do is get them outfitted," Stig said.

Jimmy Manzoni, the director, wore plus-fours and a baggy cap with a bill. A half-smoked cigar jutted from the corner of his mouth. As soon as the barge bumped the quay, he leaped from it, hand outstretched.

"You gotta be Brand," he said.

I understood some English but never tried to speak it. Stig's English seemed to be quite good, and when it was clear that I was being introduced, I smiled and offered my hand.

"Hello, Sweetheart!" Manzoni said, removing his cigar long enough to plant a smacking kiss on my cheek.

Eskimos and other townspeople lined the quay, offering helping hands to the people trying to debark, and Manzoni turned and shouted, "Hey, Ziggy! What's that guy doing with the camera? Tell him to keep his hands off!"

"Take it easy," Stig said. "Everybody helps unload any ship that docks here. It's the custom."

"If he busts that baby, we're in the soup!" Manzoni said.

The man called Ziggy wore an aviator's helmet with the goggles pushed up, giving him an authority that regained custody of the camera.

When the entire party was ashore, we met the rest of the group. Ziggy Handelman was the camera man, Vernon Banks did wardrobe and makeup, and Mel Torreli, Jimmy's nephew, was the general flunky.

"We're a stripped-down outfit," Jimmy said, "but we'll get the goods. You sure about the ice and snow? After all, it's summer."

Stig laughed. "I'm sure. The ice and snow is 10,000 feet deep in the mountain valleys, and you'll see plenty of action on the ice cap."

"Have you got the Eskimos lined up?"

Stig nodded. "They think it's pretty silly to build an igloo just to take its picture, but they're game."

Manzoni re-lit his cigar to discourage the midges swarming about our faces and asked about hiring a guide.

"You can," Stig said, "but it's expensive. He gets a crown for every 24 miles plus a daily salary for as long as he's away from his family. Besides, anyone who gives advice can claim to be a guide and collect the wages of one for the entire trip."

Manzoni laughed. "Sounds like they got all the angles figured, but we might have to go for it. I sure as hell don't want to get lost out there and freeze to death!"

"Me neither!" said Mel, sniffing, "I already got a cold."

"I can guide you," Stig said, "and if I think this journey is safe enough for my bride, why should you worry?"

The rest of their goods came off the barge and was piled on the dock: a generator, a record player, the camera with its huge tripod, and their personal cases.

"Where's the hotel?" Manzoni asked.

Stig called to some Eskimo boys and told them to take the luggage to Mrs. Sorensen's house. Then he told the crew to think of their accommodation as a boarding house.

"Jeez," said Vernon, "this is like the Wild West! They got a dance hall here?"

"No, but there will be a dance tonight--a chance for you to meet some of your stars before we set out for the ice cap."

"Oh, you kid!" said Mel, doing a little dance on the dock.

We got them settled and then took them to the store to be

outfitted with anoraks, hide trousers and kamiks. They postured and posed in their new gear, laughing at each other like children.

When we left them, I asked Stig how he had managed to arrange this expedition. He'd scarcely been away from me for a minute, and yet everything seemed to be well planned.

"I did most of it before I came away," he said. "If I hadn't, it wouldn't have been done--not with the lovely distraction I brought back with me."

We retired to our bedroom in the middle of the afternoon, and I caught Mrs. Rasmussen rolling her eyes as I closed the door. Was she disapproving or jealous? I didn't much care as I went into Stig's arms.

After we made love, we piled the bolsters behind our shoulders and lay back to talk, arms around each other. He taught me to say "*Assavakit*," which means "I love you," and "*Ab*," which means "Yes."

After the kissing involved in that lesson, I asked, "How did you get involved with these film people?"

He laughed and said, "Manzoni sent a wire to 'the guy in charge' at Godhavn, and when I came here to meet the mail boat last April, someone handed it to me. He said he wanted to do a documentary on Eskimo life and asked 'the guy in charge' to arrange it, so I did. If it hadn't been for that wire, you probably wouldn't be *Fru* Brand."

"Why not? We would have met in the same way and fallen in love."

"But you would have wanted more time, and I would have given it to you. We'd still be in Denmark, and I doubt that we'd be married."

So these brash Americans were responsible for the dramatic turn my life had taken. They deserved thanks from me thus far, but I wasn't sure how long this would be the case.

The dance began quite late by European standards, but when it's light all night, what difference does it make? Held in the school, it was unlike any dance I'd ever attended.

The music was strictly rhythm, a monotonous beat made by hitting skin stretched over a circle of bone with a short, thick stick. Stig told me that early missionaries tried to discourage drum dancing, which they considered to be a heathen practice, but they failed.

Manzoni listened for awhile, and then said, "Hey, Mel! Go back and get the phonograph. We'll show 'em what dancing is all about."

Vernon was busy inspecting the beadwork on the kamiks of the girls, and I strained my English to tell him they were unmarried because their kamiks were white. I was inordinately proud of my small nugget of knowledge.

"Nice beadwork!" he said, and then he spoke out of the corner of his mouth, making his words harder to understand than before. "See that dolly over there?"

I followed his gaze to an Eskimo girl whose damp hair was caught up like a horse's tail. "She's lovely," I said.

"Yeah, well I'm going to ask her to dance when Mel gets back with the phono. I'll show her what dancing's all about!"

It seemed to me that she already knew. Her feet came down with the beat of the drum, and her partner did the mirror image of her steps.

The light in the room was like deep twilight, but Stig said no lamps would be lit. No one in the Arctic wasted oil just to make a room brighter. Ziggy muttered about the light as if he were behind a camera, which he wasn't.

Stig took my hand and said, "Let's dance."

Instead of holding me European style, he faced me and began to move three steps back and three steps forward with an almost sexual thrust. I made a timid attempt at the same movement, and he said, "That's it--just let yourself go."

Just as I was getting the hang of it, Mel returned with the phonograph, and everything stopped. The dancers gathered around to watch him wind the machine and set the needle, and the first notes of a fox trot brought startled laughter.

Stig swung me into the dance, and the tightly-packed crowd

78

moved in on us for a better look until we had no room to continue.

Vernon asked the girl with the swinging tail of dark hair to dance, and she covered her mouth and laughed, but when he continued to gesture and reach for her, she went into his arms. They worked against each other at first, but then she caught the rhythm and really danced with him. Vernon, however, looked distressed. He finally broke from her and came over to us.

"Do these people piss in the corner or what?" he said, "Whew!"

Stig laughed and said, "Some of the young ladies dress their hair with urine. That's one of their beauty secrets."

"Oh, Stig, you can't be serious!" I said.

"I only mentioned it because I thought you might like to try it," he teased. "It might deepen the amber of your hair."

The record came to an end, and the drumming began again. The room grew closer and hotter, and some of the guests were removing their garments. Vernon's young beauty pulled off her shirt, and her breasts shone with perspiration, golden almond in the dim light.

"Jeez!" said Vernon, "I'd like to get next to that, but I don't know if my nose can take it!"

"We ought to have the camera rolling on this," Manzoni said, clamping the unlit cigar tighter in his teeth.

Mel stood on the sidelines patting the outside of his thighs to the rhythm of the drums until a young girl pulled him onto the crowded floor and motioned for him to copy her movements. Her white kamiks flashed in the gloom, matching the white flannel trousers he wore, and they were a strange couple but somehow well-met.

Stig whispered to me, "This is all very entertaining, but I can think of something I'd rather do. Shall we go?"

The insistent drumming had given me other ideas too, and I nodded, but I said, "Is it safe to leave those four here without you?"

"Hmm. That's a good question. They just might commit some cultural *faux pas* that would affect the filming. I'll tell them we'd better get to bed so we can start early tomorrow."

He went over to Manzoni and spoke with him earnestly while

79

I waited at the door. When Mel picked up the phonograph, there were cries of protest, but the drumming soon resumed, and the six of us walked into the eternal daylight of the arctic night.

"Boy, could I have got some shots if I'd had my camera!" Ziggy said.

"You're shooting what I tell you," Manzoni said, "no more and no less."

"Yowsah, Boss!"

Holsteinsborg, which had seemed so primitive to me when we arrived, became much more civilized in comparison with the ice cap. Ten dogs hitched in a fan shape pulled the sled I rode on, and other teams drew sleds carrying the film crew and the equipment. Stig strode along with the contingent of Eskimos that walked beside us, and he said more of them would meet us. It was freezing cold, and a high wind blew the snow into drifts.

I sat low on the sled with a bar against upright poles to support my neck if I leaned back. The dogs' claws made a scrabbling noise on the hard snow, and their breath rose in clouds of steam.

The pure white of the icebergs shaded to palest blue with a hint of violet, and sometimes they looked pink. I was glad for my bone "glasses" in the glare of the sun. Riding into the wind, I held my mittened hand to my face for warmth and wondered where in this vast wasteland we were headed and how long it would take us to get there.

Manzoni shouted his request to stop so frequently that Stig finally told him, "We really should move on and set up camp. What you're seeing will be repeated for hundreds of miles."

"When the light's right, you do it," the filmmaker said.

"In the Arctic, man is not the boss," Stig told him.

He planned a shorter run than usual on the first day, deferring to me and the Americans, but still, it was eight hours, and I was tired and frozen stiff when the sleds came to a halt in the middle of nowhere.

"Why here?" I asked him, "Not that I mind stopping."

His answer was to pull a gun from his pack and fire into the air.

A shout was heard, and Eskimos poured over a snowy ridge, waving as they came. They greeted the people who had come with us, and soon all of them were busy making a cooking fire and starting to cut blocks for the igloo Manzoni wanted to film.

I took my share of the food eagerly. The boiled seal meat was strong and sweet--not too bad. I wasn't too sure about the dried eggs, but after Stig told me how they were prepared, I knew I'd never try them again.

"They drink the whites from the shell, then take the yolks into their mouths and spit them into a long, dried seal intestine and hang the whole thing to dry in a dark place."

I groaned and said, "I'm not asking any more questions. A few more answers like that, and I'll starve to death."

Mel, who had heard that little interchange, got up quickly and hurried away.

Ziggy snorted and said, "'Every man to his own taste' said the old geezer as he kissed the cow!"

I didn't quite understand that, but as I've said, my English was not the best. Another thing I didn't understand was how Stig knew when to stop--where the others would be. Every milestone on the ice cap looked the same to me.

The dogs were released from their traces, which were put on a high platform made with slender poles and a piece of hide. I watched them milling around, regarding us with the hard, yellow eyes of wolves, and felt a trace of fear. I asked Stig if someone would feed them to dispel their ravenous look.

"We don't feed our dogs the way you feed pets," he said, "especially not in the summer. They dine about twice a week, and yes, they will eat people."

I looked at them with horror as he told me of burying an empty coffin for such a victim and shooting the killers.

"Ziggy," Manzoni said, "You're going to have to take that camera to bed with you to keep it from freezing up. God, can you believe it's July?"

I certainly couldn't, listening to the creaks and groans of the moving glacier. Feeling a physical urgency, I looked around for a place to relieve myself where the all-male company couldn't see me. Beyond the ridge, I decided. It wasn't far.

But it was farther than I expected. With no landmarks, distances were hard to measure, and I walked for some time before I could claim that visual barrier. Using a bucket just inside the doorway in the settlement had been bad enough, but this was worse. I lowered my hide trousers and made as quick a job of it as possible, but the cold was pervasive and painful. Men had it much easier. I removed a mitten and scooped up a handful of snow to clean myself. That was painful, too.

Then I was surrounded by dogs fighting over the excrement, and I ran from them in terror.

XI

We slept that night in Stig's sleeping bag, a large hide pouch with the fur inside. He quickly stripped before climbing into it, but I refused, pleading both modesty and comfort. His body gave off heat like a tile stove, and he finally convinced me I could take better advantage of it unclad. Between the two of us, my clothes were removed, and the Eskimos, who seemed never to sleep, were making remarks that I was just as glad I couldn't understand.

The Americans were tossing and turning in their bags, too chilled to go to sleep, and when Stig suggested they join forces as we had, they were indignant.

"Whatdya' think we are, a bunch of queers?" Manzoni said.

At that remark, Vernon rolled over to turn his back to the director, and Ziggy laughed. "Don't worry, Vern, old boy," he said, "You ain't his type."

One of the Eskimos, Awala by name, called to Stig, and I watched my husband's face as he listened with amusement and answered, "*Namik.*"

"What did he say and what did you say?" I asked.

"He asked me if I had offered my wife to my guests, and I said no."

"*Namik* means no?"

"*Ab,*" he said, kissing the tip of my nose, "and that means yes. I didn't teach you *namik* because I don't want to hear it from you."

"Do they really do share their wives in Greenland?"

"They really do."

"And have you accepted such offers?"

"On occasion. It would be rude to refuse."

"Oh Stig," I wailed, "I hate hearing that!"

He kissed me thoroughly and would have done more, but I whispered, "No, not with all these people around!"

"Good night, then," he said. "*Assavakit!*"

Stig had the ability to fall asleep instantly, I had noticed, and he did it now, leaving me wide awake. I stared at the bright sky, let my eyes sweep across the sleeping bags ringing the dying fire, saw the dogs curled in hairy circles. The yellow eyes opened from time to time, catching the faint light from the fire, and I wondered what was to prevent them from devouring us in our beds.

I felt totally weary and almost light-headed, but I could not sleep--had not slept well since arriving in this land where the sun never set. Resolutely I closed my eyes.

I must have slept, for when I woke, the igloo had taken its basic shape, and the Eskimos were carrying hides to the mouth of the long, low passage, passing them to somebody inside.

Stig brought me coffee and a chunk of something frozen. "Eat it," he said, "you need your fat quotient to stay warm."

"What is it?"

"Seal blubber."

I wrinkled my nose, but a took a bite and chewed it vigorously. At least it wasn't nasty. It tasted like candlewax.

"Come and see the igloo."

First, I had to dress, and I wondered how Stig had managed to do that without waking me. I concluded that he had exposed his entire body to the frigid air for my sake, and I couldn't bear the thought. Every time I moved, I seemed to let more icy air into the sleeping bag, and my teeth chattered as my bare arms moved out of the bag into the sleeves of my anorak. If I had to live like this for the rest of my life, I couldn't bear it, I thought, but surely Stig's house at Thule would offer some kind of comfort.

I crawled along the low passage after Stig, and when I stood up under the main dome, I was amazed at the spaciousness of the snow house. The inner walls had been hung with hides to serve the insulating purpose of the tapestries in old castles, and a moss wick burned in a shallow stone tray filled with some kind of oil.

Some of the Eskimos were sitting on platforms around the chamber, laughing and talking as they waited for Ziggy to set up his camera. The enclosure seemed warm to them, and some had taken

84

off their anoraks. Their tea-colored torsos gleamed in the flickering light from the oil lamp.

"Mel!" Ziggy yelled, "Take the hide down from behind those two guys. It's eating up the light."

Sniffling miserably, Mel did as he was told, then took off his mittens to blow his nose.

"Damn it all!" Stig said to me. "That cold of his will be all over Greenland in nothing flat! These people never have a cold unless somebody brings it in, and they have no resistance to germs of any kind."

Remembering that Naika had died from a disease brought from the outside world, I said nothing. I just nodded to show I had heard.

I had to leave the igloo to make room for cast and crew, and I amused myself by making big patterns in the snow with my kamiks. All that trampling kept me reasonably warm.

I had told Stig about my fear of the dogs, and he gave me a stout stick to carry at all times. I used it now to form the more delicate details on the huge flower I had made in the snow.

Suddenly the dogs set up a terrific chorus of barking. I looked around and saw two sleds, tiny in the distance, with their teams fanned out and going full speed.

Stig emerged from the igloo, shaded his eyes, and then waved at the approaching sleds with both arms high above his head.

"It's the women," he said. "Right on schedule."

"What women?"

"The future film stars. They're bringing caribou meat to cook and some hides to chew for the camera."

Their approach seemed to take forever, but at last the women shouted "*Ayey-ayeh!*" to bring the panting dogs to a halt. They greeted Stig like an old friend.

Not until one of them addressed me in Danish did I realize that I knew her. It was Kullabak.

"One is glad to see you again," she said, smiling broadly.

I threw my arms around her and almost wept for joy.

She introduced the other women, Naterk, Kasaluk, and Ivalu,

and they put up a hide platform on poles to keep their belongings from the dogs before carrying their gear into the igloo.

As they bent to enter the low passage, I could see the strip of bare skin between trousers and anorak. It was dark brown and as weathered as old leather. Why on earth didn't they make their jackets longer? They must be completely oblivious to physical misery.

"Stig, did you know that Kullabak was coming? If so, why didn't you tell me?"

"I didn't know. I sent a message to Ivalu, telling her to find three friends for this project, and I had no idea that she'd recruit Kullabak."

"Do the others speak Danish?"

"Very little. You'll have to communicate through women's intuition."

They were in the igloo for what seemed like hours before Manzoni emerged and declared himself satisfied with the shoot.

"I can't believe they really chew hides like that," he said.

Stig laughed and said, "That's a wife's chief duty in these parts."

Manzoni laughed too and pinched my cheek. "Not in your book, eh, Sweetheart?"

"You're quite right about that," I said.

I could, at least, keep the fire going--once Stig got it started. It was ready for the caribou meat.

The women's lead dogs and our lead dogs were jockeying for supremacy, and we could scarcely hear what anyone was saying above the savage yelps and snarls. Stig strode among them with a stout stick and laid about him until they subsided to a whimper.

"A lead dog is the world's most arrogant male," Stig said. "He bosses all the others around and is the only one allowed to mate with the bitches."

"Around here, a dog's life isn't so bad," I observed, and my English was good enough that the Californians understood it and laughed.

Now we couldn't hear above a booming sound that frightened me until Stig explained it was the forming of crevasses as the glacier moved over uneven surface.

Kullabak added, "The noise is kind to one. Seals do not fear guns because they hear this always. If a person misses a shot, the seal will not run away from the gun, and one has another chance to bring home food."

They had brought a supply of *imiak* (Greenland beer) with them from their village, and Kullabak was proud of offering it as one would in Denmark--in bottles. The beer, however, had frozen stiff, and she was forced to break away the glass and offer the icy forms for us to suck. It tasted a bit like sour dry cider, and the necessary mode of consumption surely would reduce the likelihood of getting drunk on the stuff.

Mel was doing his best, however, taking huge bites of beer and reducing it to slush in his mouth. None of us noticed his departure, and even if we had, we would have assumed he had gone to relieve himself and thought nothing of it.

"Mel!" Manzoni yelled, "Get the generator and the processor going. I want to show these good folks some rushes."

Hearing no response, Manzoni looked around and said, "Where the hell is he?"

Vernon glanced at the women and tried to be delicate. "Answering the call of nature, maybe?"

Ziggy laughed and said, "That call don't come so quick when you have to bust open your beer."

"I'll find him," Stig said, and one of the Eskimo men joined him. As they slogged toward the south, they looked like brown bears walking upright.

"How does he know where to look?" I asked Kullabak.

"He does not know. He will walk out, plant a stake and begin to circle."

Manzoni chewed his unlit cigar fiercely. "Why in hell did the kid have to wander off like that? I want to get this shoot over and get back to someplace where I can thaw out."

A gloomy Ziggy wrapped his camera in a blanket and marched in place to keep his feet warm. His aviator helmet was fastened under his chin now, not flapping jauntily as it had when he landed.

Vernon was busy powdering the faces of the younger women, and they giggled under his ministrations. My own face felt chapped and sore, and I longed for the lotion I hadn't brought.

Kullabak invited me to join her in the igloo, and when we were seated on a hide-covered platform, she pulled the amber pendant I had given her from the neck of her anorak and caressed it. I wished I had brought her gift, the soapstone woman, to show her how much I valued it, but it was safe at *Frue* Rasmussen's house.

"Is there to be a baby?" she asked.

I blushed and shook my head. "I don't think so--not yet."

In that moment the full weight of her question staggered me. Stig had told me how Eskimo women gave birth and rose to prepare a meal or even go to a dance. At home, the doctor came to deliver the child and the mother was kept in bed for at least ten days. She was as carefully protected from drafts as her infant was.

Stig had told me I had too many adjustments to make to consider motherhood very soon. He offered to practice coitus interuptus, which I smilingly rejected. I had the preparation *Mor* had given me with such embarrassment, but I also had found time before our sailing to buy a case of the contraceptive jelly manufactured in Friedrichshafen, Germany. Claudine swore by it, although she said the best stuff came from Holland. Now I worried that it might freeze, break down and become ineffective. Like the frozen beer, it might not have the expected effect.

Then Kullabak told me the amulet she had given me brought many children, healthy children, and I tried to look pleased at the thought. My real pleasure was in leaving the thing in Holsteinsborg, too far away to work its magic.

She took up a seal skin and began to chew it, which effectively limited our conversation. I wondered how she could bear the taste of hide with bits of clinging flesh.

Manzoni came into the igloo, beating his hands together

impatiently. "Might as well get some footage while we wait," he said, directing Ziggy where to position the camera.

"I'll get out of the way," I said.

"Nah, stay there. Put your hood up, and you'll pass as long as Ziggy don't shoot you head-on."

I picked up a skin and pretended to be looking for a spot to chew. Leif would be impressed by my debut as a film star, I thought. Until now, I hadn't given Leif a thought, but now I remembered my unlucky accident of watching him until he was out of sight.

"Cut!" said Manzoni.

I put the skin down, but Kullabak went on chewing, and when the men left the igloo, the younger women came in. Naterk pulled off her anorak and searched it for lice. Kasaluk and Ivalu followed suit, and as they killed the vermin with their teeth and ate them with relish, I felt my skin crawl.

The hours passed slowly as we waited for the return of Stig and his companion, Imenak. Vernon complained that it was too cold to play solitaire, his favorite diversion during the long delays of film-making. Manzoni paced and reduced his unlit cigar to shreds. Ziggy repaired to the igloo to take a nap.

Kullabak broke several bottles of beer and melted their frozen contents over the fire. We drank and waited. I limited my intake, thinking of the inevitable result of consuming liquid.

At last we saw one dark figure on what seemed to be the western horizon. Was it Stig or Imenak? Whoever it was seemed to be motioning for us to come. I started off at a run, and my feet slid out from under me immediately.

Kullabak helped me up and said, "Walk like the bear." She demonstrated the sliding shuffle with spread legs. It worked, but it was slow, and I was desperately anxious about my husband.

Naterk and Kasaluk stayed behind to tend the fire and control the dogs, and the only evidence of our forward progress was the diminishing size of their bodies. The igloo seemed to melt into the ice cap and become invisible.

By the time we were close enough to recognize Imenak, my breathing was painful and rasping, but I managed to gasp a question to Kullabak. "Where is Stig? What has happened?"

She shouted to Imenak and listened to his brief reply, then translated it for me. "He who sneezes fell in crevasse. Your man waits to be lowered and bring him out."

I imagined the crevasse, bottomless and shining cruelly, self-satisfied with swallowing Mel and anticipating a more challenging mouthful. I tried to speed my bear gait, get there and beg Stig not to be a hero, but I was the last to reach the scene. Stig was nowhere to be seen.

The Eskimos had tied harpoon lines together to lower him into the crevasse, and I was afraid to look.

"More!" he yelled from the depths.

Sending up a prayer without words, I watched them add to the lifeline.

"Why can't they just throw the rope down to Mel?" I asked.

Kullabak asked the men and was told that Mel hit his head when he fell. He was unconscious on a small ledge and in great danger of falling deeper.

Manzoni alternately swore and prayed. "What the hell am I going to tell my sister? I promised I'd take care of the kid!"

I crept close to the edge on my hands and knees, then flattened myself to look down. I could see the top of Stig's hood, the loop of the line around his thigh, his mitten sliding down the glistening wall of ice. His body obscured a view of Mel.

"Almost there," he shouted, and the sound seemed to come from inside a drum.

"Oh God, let him be OK!" Manzoni said. "Ziggy, you ready to shoot?"

I couldn't believe it, but Ziggy had brought a small, hand-held camera to the scene of this disaster, and he made ready to use it.

What if the lines broke? What if the walls of the crevasse collapsed? Why had I ever left the civilized safety of the Stroget?

"Got him! You can pull now."

90

The ascent seemed to go on forever. When my husband's head appeared, I could breathe again. He held Mel against his chest with one arm, and the rope was wound around the other. Over the edge they came, and the Eskimos shouted with excitement.

Mel was still unconscious, and his hood had fallen away, allowing his ears to turn the curious dead shade of frostbite. He was just a boy--a boy with a bad cold--and thanks to Stig, he'd probably live to be a man.

Izzy cranked his camera furiously, and Manzoni said, "We'll wrap it up with that. I couldn't have planned it better!"

Imenak and one of the other men carried Mel back to the camp, where Manzoni passed out *kroner* to the Eskimos and told them it was all over.

Kullabak looked around the igloo with regret as she collected the hide wall hangings. "Not much life for this one," she said.

The men were shouting at the end of the entrance passage, and she motioned for me to leave with her. I soon learned why.

Stig said, "When you leave an igloo, the last thing you do is relieve yourself in it. Then the dogs are let in to clean it up."

"Will Mel be all right?"

"I hope so. I'm afraid he has more than a cold now, and I'll feel better when we get him closer to a doctor."

"I was so worried about you! Why didn't you let Imenak go down for him?"

"I didn't even think of it."

"Or of me?"

"He didn't answer. He just pulled me close and held me. The boom of another crevasse opening made me bury my face in his chest.

XII

I walked some of the way back, as Mel had to lie down on the sled. He had regained consciousness after his fall, but all he said was, "I slipped."

"Did you ever!" Manzoni said, punching his shoulder with rough affection.

We hadn't gone far when Mel went into a delirium. He tried to strip off his clothes, insisting he was burning up, and the only way to stop him was to tie him to the sled. I walked beside him pressing snow on his feverish forehead.

Stig told Manzoni he was sorry the expedition had been cut short, but the filmmaker waved the apology away.

"That's OK by me! If this is summer, I'd hate to see winter around here!"

"There's not much difference between the two on the ice cap."

"Don't worry, Brand, I got the picture, if you know what I mean. This Flaherty guy goes off and lives with people for months before he shoots a frame, but I got you."

Mel was in bad shape by the time we reached Holsteinsborg, and the doctor was up the coast at Egedesminde. Stig prevailed on *Fru* Rasmussen to nurse the boy.

"We may have to leave before we know he's all right," Stig said. "Our ship will be in sooner than I expected it."

"I'll do my best for him, *Hr.* Brand," *Frue* Rasmussen said.

Manzoni was beside himself. "You gotta get him fit to move!" he said, "The last thing I want to do is miss the boat in a place like this, beggin' your pardon, Ma'am!"

I offered to help, and I spent a great deal of time sponging Mel with cold, wet towels and trying to get him to eat. I tried to talk to him, too, but my English wasn't good enough to carry it off. I could understand much more than I could say.

He was restless and raving, talking about a girl named Sheila, calling for his mother, and apologizing over and over again to

"Uncle Jimmy."

Why didn't the doctor return? Why wasn't there more than one in this God-forsaken town?

Hr. Bech heard we were back and came to call. When he saw the seriousness of Mel's condition, he hurried back to *Frue* Kjaer's house to raid the elaborate selection of medicines he had brought from home. The bottles and containers he returned with held nostrums for everything from headaches to tuberculosis, and nobody in the house knew what to prescribe.

"It's pneumonia," *Frue* Rasmussen said darkly. "There's nothing for it but to wait until God expresses His will."

The Californians took up a vigil in the Rasmussen kitchen. Vern played solitaire, Ziggy drank *imiak* from a coffee cup, and Manzoni shredded one cigar after another.

Stig said the Rasmussens were anything but puritanical, having seen the dregs of human behavior in their parish. As far as they were concerned, Jimmy Manzoni could have lit his cigars, but he was too polite.

Frue Rasmussen said she would recognize the signs of the crisis, and she did, but there was little she could do. Mel DeVito died in the brightness of midnight a week after his fall into the crevasse.

I wept for him, and there was little time for even that because Stig insisted we be packed and ready for the departure of the M/S Frederica which had entered the harbor during the death vigil.

As we were leaving for the quay, Jimmy Manzoni came running after us, highly agitated.

"Brand! Wait! You gotta help me!"

"What do you need?" Stig said.

"I gotta take that boy home to his folks, and they say they ain't got no embalmers here. What do I do?"

Stig stopped and set down the cases he was carrying. He rubbed his beard while he pondered. Such a question was beyond me, and I had no hope of Stig being able to solve the problem either, but much to my amazement, I heard him try.

"In the old days, they shipped corpses in hogsheads of wine. It preserved them quite well, I remember reading."

"They got that much wine in this place?"

"Perhaps not, but *imiak* should have the same effect. *Hr.* Bech may have a receptacle at the halibut cannery, and I'm sure there's enough malt extract, brewers' yeast, sugar and hops to make the brew."

"But who would do that for me? And won't it take a long time?"

"*Frue* Kjaer will help you, I'm sure. The process takes five hours."

Manzoni pumped Stig's hand. "Thanks, Buddy, I'll never forget what you've done for me! But why the hell can't it be Vern? He'd think he'd died and gone to heaven--floatin' in all that beer."

As we went on, I shook my head and said, "I really can't believe what I just heard. It's horrible to think of poor Mel sloshing around in a barrel!"

"Poor Mel won't care, and at least he won't rot in transit."

The barge was waiting for us and our gear, and when we left it to board the Frederica, I looked back at the rooftop sheltering the brewing operation that would start Mel on his long journey home. When Vern heard about it, would he ever touch *imiak* again? I wasn't sure I would.

We were subdued at dinner that night out of respect to Mel, and as we ate our *sagosuppe* flavored with rum, I said, "I'd like to get off at Egedesminde and find that doctor who might have saved him. I'd stamp on his foot and call him a murderer!"

Reasonable as always, Stig said, "Perhaps he went there to save another life. He had no way of knowing Mel would throw himself down a crevasse and catch pneumonia."

"Oh, you're so tolerant that you make me sick!"

"There's something about the Arctic that forces one to be that way. Everything superfluous is eliminated, and you really get down to the basics of human existence--or non-existence, I guess. You feel a touch of eternity."

I declined Stig's invitation to walk the deck that night, preferring the relative warmth of our cramped cabin. I seized the opportunity to take a piece-meal bath, washing, drying and clothing my body one part at a time. Clean and ready for love, I waited for him, and he was a long time coming.

I pondered the chain of events that had brought me to this moment--my determination to define myself in Copenhagen, meeting Leif by chance, going to a press conference under false colors, and being pressed to a decision by the necessities of Jimmy Manzoni. The time in Holsteinsborg had been a kind of southern vacation, Stig had given me to understand. Now we were sailing north to reality--and the child, Nauja. Somehow I would have to prepare myself to share Stig with his daughter, and the prospect recalled my much-younger self. When other children came to visit, I clutched my dolls tightly and shouted, "Mine!" When Stig finally came to me, I clutched him just as tightly. The same shout was silent, but I thought it. Oh, how I thought it.

Perhaps it was Mel's death that gave me such a sense of dread. Somewhere on these cold seas he was sloshing about in his barrel, deprived of a future by the pitiless North. The lovemaking that put Stig to sleep so quickly left me wanting more--enough to keep me from thinking. I burrowed into Stig's arms, then broke free to toss and turn. When I did sleep, I dreamed that a huge polar bear was inching toward me like a glacier, a paw over the black coal of its nose.

"It's no use," I screamed at the beast. "I know you're there. Let's get it over with!"

I awoke struggling in Stig's arms.

"What is it, Alex?"

I shuddered deeply. "A bear. He tried to hide his black nose, but I knew. He may get me, but he'll never fool me."

Stig rocked me in his arms, singing a lullaby that he probably sang to Nauja. The tune was strange, but the words were Danish: "Sleep, *lille pige.*" I would have bristled if anyone else called me "little girl."

The next day the Frederica threaded her way among icebergs the size of apartment houses. Some resembled castles and cathedrals. They looked like frosted volcanic isles in the pale green water, and the bright sun glinting on them colored them intense blue with mauve and pink shadows. I wondered what Hans Christian Andersen would have made of this incredible beauty.

The scene was not without frightening undertones. The pack ice near the shore had broken into small chunks called growlers and and a mixture of chunks and finely-ground ice called brash, Stig told me. Those ice forms did seem to growl as they threw themselves against the hull of the ship.

At mid-morning we saw a flotilla of kayaks, motionless on the water until sleek shapes broke the surface and harpoons tied to inflated bladders flew through the air. The seal hunters were out in force.

"I hope the seals get away," I said.

"They're not pets, Alex. They're the difference between life and death for these people. Food, clothing and light all come from the seal."

I bore the lecture I supposed I deserved with as much grace as possible.

Farther up the coast whale hunters had dragged their catch up on the rocky shore, tail in the air and head in the water. Stig borrowed binoculars for me, and I watched the Eskimos at their flensing with sharp spears. They carried blood away in buckets and cut the blubber into squares. The whole thing made me feel queasy, but I supposed I might feel the same if I visited an abbatoir at home. I wouldn't do such a thing at home. I'd simply ignore all that and enjoy my beefsteak well cooked. Here, whole layers of civilization were removed, and it was back to the basics.

Stig had told me how the sun on the water hypnotized the Eskimos in their kayaks until they couldn't move their arms and felt they were sinking. I felt something like that now, but if I sank, I would have experienced a great love, at least.

The captain intended to stop at Upernavik, but he received word of a suspected smallpox epidemic and was sufficiently well-provisioned to sail on.

"Who the hell could have brought smallpox in?" Stig said, scowling at the curls of smoke from the dwellings on the shore."

He brooded about it until we came to some bird cliffs with baby gulls filling the air like a snowstorm.

"Next year we'll be home at the best time, and I'll take you to our bird cliffs," he said. "We'll catch some little auks with nets on long poles and make ourselves a *giviak*."

"What's that?" I asked with a doubtful look.

"A sealskin bag lined with blubber is filled with the birds and buried under the rocks. The sun mustn't shine on it, but it's warm enough to let the blubber seep into the birds and cure their meat. It's delicious."

"Do you clean the birds?"

"No, just take them out of the net and kill them by pressing your thumb under the breastbone to stop the heart. Then the wings are braided together, and into the bag they go."

"I don't think I could kill a bird that way. Poor, little auk!"

"Your sensibility does you credit, but I doubt that you've ever been hungry."

"I most certainly have! I was lost on the moor once for a whole day, and I was ready to eat a live sheep."

He smiled at me with a kind of indulgence that made me furious, and we talked about something else.

That night I saw the Aurora Borealis for the first time and felt the impersonal power of the universe so strongly that I had absolutely nothing to say.

First it was wisps of pale greenish light in an irregular band that changed shape like whirling smoke. Almost imperceptibly, the color changed from green to rose and lavendar. A sudden brighter light to the north unfurled like a brilliant pennant, billowing and turning and throwing out streams of light. The green band separated into dancing forms that pulsed and paled, and another swath of light made a zig-zag across the sky. Below the curtain of light was a shining strip, vividly rosy, and then the whole spectacle was gone.

"Oh, Stig," I breathed.

"The Eskimos say it's the dance of the spirits--men who died in the hunt and women who died in childbirth. Others say it's stillborn children dancing and playing football with their umbilical cords."

"Maybe it's Mel."

Stig sighed deeply. "Poor lad. He was a pleasant kid, but I'm not sure he'd be capable of anything that grand. The Aurora never fails to move me. The day it does, I'll know I'm ready for the grave."

The Arctic in its mildest season had something more to show me before we reached home. A storm blew up as we sailed into Melville Bay, bringing a rain that made a sheet of fresh water ice on the surface. The Frederica cracked and groaned, and the motion of the ship threw me to the floor in our cabin.

Stig lifted me quickly, struggling to keep his own balance. "Are you hurt?"

"No, but I might be sick." I caught a glimpse of the dipping porthole as it seemed to fill with sea behind its frozen, isinglass face.

"Then come on deck. Fresh air always helps."

I clenched my teeth and nodded. No matter how bad it got, I refused to give in to the elements in this god-forsaken place. I was almost as afflicted as I had been when Dorte insisted that we become blood sisters by joining our cut wrists. The sight of blood made me feel faint, but I wouldn't admit it, and I decided I'd rather see my own than hers. I made the first cut, and *she* fainted.

Before putting on my anorak, I rummaged in my suitcase for the seal necklace. The smooth silver on my throat had become my amulet.

"Getting ready for a party?" Stig asked teasingly.

I couldn't speak. My fingers trembled on the clasp until he did the fastening for me.

The most sheltered spot on the deck still afforded little relief from the curtains of sleet that swept the ship, and we were forced to go below. I couldn't afford to let my anorak get drenched. Stig, on the other hand, paid little attention to whether he was wet or dry. Somehow he had learned to ignore his personal comfort level, and I wondered if I could ever manage that.

Clutching the seals at my throat, I tried to tell myself that I was out for a summer sail on the Kattegat and everything was fine. It almost worked, but when I finally had to give in to the urge I could no longer fight, Stig held my head, wiped my face and whispered endearments.

"I love you so," I said hoarsely.

"And I you."

"Even when I'm like this?"

He nodded and held me close.

XIII

At last the Frederica came to North Star Bay and turned into Thule Fjord. The water with its bobbing icebergs was surrounded by mountains with the icecap beyond, and Sauders Island with its huge bird cliff was covered with a lace of whirring wings. Three glaciers spewed icebergs into the water. I was so quelled by the scenery that it took me some time to notice the human dwellings on the rocky south shore of the fjord.

"There's our home," Stig said, pointing out a small, dun-colored building. "It's a patent house we put up as an experiment, and the kids had a great time throwing stones at it when the mortar was soft."

I strained my eyes to see my new home until I was distracted by a welcoming flotilla of Eskimos in kayaks. The waves swamped one of them, and he allowed himself to be turned completely upside-down before righting his craft with an artful body twist.

"Oh, Stig! How will he ever get dry?"

"He can't be very wet. His suit is watertight sealskin, and the manhole of the boat is covered with skin that closes around his waist with a wooden ring. His hood and sleeves are tight, too. Believe me, he's quite dry."

Just looking at the fellow made me shiver, but he grinned and paddled on with the rest of the welcomers.

Stig laughed and said, "We'll have to teach you to paddle the *umiak*. That's a round skin boat that looks like a deep soup bowl, and it's rowed only by women. It's the Greenland trolley."

I returned my attention to the shore with its sprinkling of turf huts, a long wooden building, and the rock-studded mortar house that would be my home.

Stig was exhilarated, more so than I had ever seen him, which gave me a sense of being abandoned. As soon as the Frederica's anchor dropped, he did leave me, rushing off to see to our goods.

Clouds of mosquitoes met us at the shaky, little dock. I slapped at them frantically, dodging the Eskimos who had abandoned their kayaks to help with the unloading. I couldn't even see Stig until he suddenly appeared beside me.

"Everything is accounted for. Now I'll take you to our castle."

The house did not improve with a closer view, but I kept that opinion to myself as Stig carried me over the threshold and proudly pointed out the features of the three rooms: double window glass, well-insulated wooden walls inside, boards nailed to the top and bottom of the doors to cut the draft, and an outer hall to perform the function of the long, low entrance to an igloo.

The place smelled like stale, cold grease, and I couldn't wait to make it more habitable. When Stig kissed me, I decided I *could* wait. Making love in our own home for the first time was of prime importance. Naked except for the silver seals around my neck, I claimed the promise of Kullabak's soapstone Venus--but not all of it, I hoped. Having a baby here was a terrifying prospect.

Stig held my hand as we walked to the trading post along a rutted icy path. We were going to fetch Nauja, and I was almost holding my breath in anxiety. I was ready to love her, but was she ready to love me? Stepmothers were in bad odor in my country. My grandmother with her inexhaustible supply of proverbs always said, "The hand of the stepmother is hard."

We passed a few sod huts with wooden doors and shaggy walls. Fur garments and other belongings were piled on the roofs, and Stig told me that was to keep the goods from the sled dogs staked out at intervals that prevented them from interfering with each other. The dogs were fed infrequently in the summer when they didn't have to work, and they would eat their leather traces and anything else they could get their teeth into.

Stig had left his ten dogs and his daughter in the care of Harald Kaarup and his wife, Semigaq. As we approached, a big, blue-eyed dog with a white ruff pulled at his tether and barked joyously.

"That's Minik," Stig said, "he's the king of the string. I almost

102

named him 'Pastor' because of the white neckpiece."

Minik didn't so much as glance at me, but he moved his head in ecstasy as Stig scratched behind his ears. The other dogs took up the barking, but Stig didn't approach them.

"Why does he get all the attention?" I asked, "It doesn't seem fair."

"They're used to it. Minik gets everything, and he bosses the rest of them."

We entered the long, low trading building, and *Hr.* Kaarup came from behind the counter with an outstretched hand, saying, "Welcome home!"

"May I present my wife, Alexandra?"

"I did not know that you anticipated such happiness," *Hr.* Kaarup said.

Stig laughed and said, "Neither did we, but fate was kind."

Hr. Kaarup bowed and called toward a rear door covered with a hide, "Semigaq, bring Nauja."

I scarcely saw the woman who appeared, only the child she pulled by the hand. Apparently the little girl had just wakened from sleep. Her glossy black hair was tousled, and her expression was querulous until she saw Stig. Then the eyes, which were rounder than the Eskimo eyes I had seen so far, widened and brightened.

"Papa!" she cried, running to hug his knees.

He picked her up and held her high at arm's length to look at her. "Well, Nauja, you've grown a foot since I went away! Have you been a good girl?"

Semigaq said, "She has cried for you. She was afraid a polar bear had eaten you."

Stig hugged and kissed the child. "Never, never, never! Your papa is much smarter than any old polar bear. Come now, Nauja, hold out your hand to your new mama."

I held out my hand hopefully, but the child's expression darkened, and she hid her face in her father's shoulder. I was crushed, but I tried to speak lightly. "Give her time, Stig. She had no warning of a new mama."

We were invited into the Kaarups' quarters in the rear, and Stig presented a packet of coffee to Semigaq.

"Oh," she said reverently, "one is happy beyond measure." She pushed the kettle onto a burner of the small iron stove, and I expected coffee to be served, but when the hot liquid was poured, it was weak tea.

The men were talking business. Stig offered a list of the goods he had brought back from Denmark, and Harald nodded with approval.

"Did you get a good price for that white fox fur you were so proud of?" Harald asked.

"The best," he said, glancing at me.

Now I knew where the fur trim for my anorak had come from. It was the cream of the trading goods. When had Stig found time to purchase knives, saws, axes, guns, kettles, sewing boxes, needles, scissors, pipes, tobacco, coffee, sugar and packets of matches? It would take me forever to choose all those things, but he was decisive beyond belief.

I tried to coax Nauja into my lap, but she hid behind Semigaq and refused to look at me.

"Alex," Stig said, "we must get some kamiks for you. Danish shoes will not do in Thule."

Harald told Semigaq to let me try on one of hers, and I took it from her reluctantly. The thigh-high leather boot was worn and stained with spills, and when I put my foot into it, the woman's body heat obscurely offended a fastidiousness I knew could not last long in Thule. The comfort of the kamik was remarkable, however. That dried grass padding was soft and springy to give the sensation of walking on air.

Semigaq wore short pants which didn't quite meet the top of the boots, and the skin of that exposed strip was dry as leather and dark as mahogany. Although it was high summer, it was colder than Copenhagen winter, and I was suffering, even in my layered sweaters. An anorak trimmed with rare white fox was a start, but something would have to be done about my wardrobe before the next frigid season came on. I'd have to see to Nauja's wardrobe, as well. Her little coat seemed tight on her.

The visit ended with Stig picking up a bundle of the child's belongings and a chunk of caribou meat for our next meal. Nauja trudged along at his side, as far from me as she could get.

"I wish she liked me better," I said.

"She'll get used to you."

"That's not good enough!"

He shrugged. "We take what we can get until we can get more."

"If she can't call me `Mama,' what about `Alex'?"

"Suit yourselves," he said.

We had not locked the door when we left, and suddenly I remembered that we had not unlocked it when we arrived. The house had been open the whole time Stig was away. I told him I was surprised that everything hadn't been stolen in his absence.

He laughed and said, "We might have found someone else living in it when we returned, but we got lucky. Everyone takes what he needs when he needs it here. There's no such thing as theft."

"And no such thing as private property?"

"That's about it. Eskimos even share their wives."

I looked at him in horror. "You wouldn't share me, would you?"

He gave me a long look and said, "I would find it difficult. However, unless you prove to be very good at thawing and scraping hides, I won't feel obliged to lend you to a hunter going after musk-ox." He spoke with utter seriousness before the tiny twinkle in his eyes erupted into full laughter.

"Oh, you are so bad!" I scolded, trying to hide my relief. I wasn't used to Stig's kind of teasing, but I vowed I would learn to recognize it sooner.

As we turned to enter our house, I looked back at North Star Bay with its crush of ice, the cruel-looking mountains surrounding the fjord and the distant icecap. The hour was late, but the night was bright as day, showing off a desolate beauty.

"Nauja should be in bed," I said.

"We'll eat first," Stig told me. "Good little Danish children may go to bed at eight o'clock, but we don't worry about things like that up here."

Once inside, Nauja started to take off all her clothes, and I asked Stig if she had pajamas. The rooms were downright cold, and I was afraid she would take a chill.

He shook his head and then nodded toward her, indicating that I should watch what she was doing. She turned her coat inside out, and the little fingers probed the seams, pinched at something and brought it to her lips.

Stig could see that I didn't know what was going on, and he said, "We'll leave her to that while I show you your new galley."

He put his arm around me and guided me behind a partition created by a hanging blanket. The tiny area held a small iron stove and a rough table with a metal basin. Stig took a big iron skillet from a nail pounded into the wall and handed it to me.

The stove was filled with heather and twigs that ignited readily at the first match he struck, and he told me what a joy that was.

"Once we lost our matches down a crevasse and had to rub sticks together. It took hours! You have to move fast, and you can't afford to slack off when your arms get tired. The shortest pause cools the friction, and you have to start all over again."

I looked at the chunk of caribou meat I was to prepare and felt repelled. It seemed to be covered with bits of dirt and had the brownish color of dried blood. "Is that edible?" I asked.

"Eminently." He rummaged on a high shelf and brought down a container of something even more evil-looking, a greasy, dark amber lump. "Blubber to fry it in."

Kullabak had told me to eat more fat, but I hadn't thought of it in these terms. Having consumed nothing but weak tea since getting off the boat, I was ravenous, but I wasn't sure I was hungry enough to eat this.

Waiting for the stove burner to heat, I asked Stig if he had any canned goods.

"Not much," he said. "During the last trading season the Eskimos decided to have a party at my house. I wasn't home when it started, and when I got here, I found they had opened most of the cans and dumped everything into the kettle for a giant stew. Ever eat stew with canned peaches?"

"It sounds better than that awful stuff that turns green!"

"Ah," he said with a light in his eyes I would have been proud to inspire, "what I wouldn't give for some rotten mattak right now!"

I shuddered and then remembered to ask him what Nauja was plucking from her garments.

"Lice," he said. "The Eskimos have an old saying, 'We'd rather be a little chilly and be the only ones in our clothes.' By the way, lice are considered a treat."

Furious at myself for being so suggestible, I itched all over.

Eventually, the stove grew hot enough to draw oil from the blubber, and the caribou meat began to brown--even smell good. Stig brought a kettle of snow inside to melt for drinking water. When the meat was ready, Stig called Nauja to the table, which I had set with the blue and white Danish ware so common at home. Stig had ordered it for Naika, I supposed.

The small, tea-colored girl was still naked and did not seem uncomfortable, but I couldn't stand to see her like that. I begged Stig to ask her to dress in something for my sake.

He shook his head indulgently, saying he'd been on the verge of joining her in total undress. "When that stove heats up, it gets very warm in here."

"I hadn't noticed," I said.

He spoke to Nauja in the Eskimo language, and she slid off her chair to humor the strange woman her father had brought home.

The caribou wasn't bad, but it was tough and required a lot of chewing. At least our stomachs were full, and I felt I had made some kind of a start in the outlandish domesticity of this place.

"The settlement will be expecting a coffee party soon," Stig said. "It will be a celebration of our marriage."

"How many people will come?"

"All eighteen who live here and anyone else who hears about it and can get here."

"What shall I serve?"

"Don't worry about that. I have the coffee, and that's the main thing. I suppose you noticed how thrilled Semigaq was with the coffee we gave her?"

"Yes, and I expected to have a cup, but she put it away."

"Coffee is more precious than gold around here."

"Do you have enough for that many people?"

"It doesn't take much. They boil it over and over again, and the last batch tastes about like rain water, but they don't seem to notice. It's the idea of it--as long as they see grounds, they believe they're drinking coffee."

Nauja, her round cheeks greasy with blubber, was sliding in and out of sleep. I rose to gather her in my arms and put her to bed, but she woke instantly and stiffened with resistance. Tears welled in my eyes as I released her.

"I guess you'll have to put her to bed."

Stig lifted the child, and she relaxed instantly, burying her face in his shoulder. I was glad to see him carry her to a corner of the room where we sat and pull off her clothes, settling her in a sleeping bag of hide with a lining of fur. I couldn't have borne it if she shared our bedroom.

It occurred to me that Nauja should brush her teeth before going to sleep, but I said nothing. The way I thought things ought to be obviously was not the norm in Thule.

I heated the rest of the melted snow and looked for soap to wash the dishes. I could find nothing that remotely resembled soap, and finally I had to ask Stig.

"There isn't any," he said. "Use that bit of hare skin on the shelf."

I did as I was told, revolted by the dull patina of grease that remained on the plates, and propped everything on the table to dry. If my parents could see me now, *Mor* would be appalled, and *Far* would think it was no better than I deserved. Frederik would think

108

it was all a lark.

While we were at the Kaarups, somebody had brought our luggage to the front of the house, and I stepped outside to retrieve the case I would need immediately. It contained a bar of soap. Pouring the remainder of the melted snow into the all-purpose basin, I started to take a sponge bath. Stig watched me scrubbing and shivering and finally said, "That's enough of that! Come to bed, amber lady!"

"I want to wash the lice away!"

He laughed. "I doubt that you have any--yet. Besides, they don't mind water a bit. One time I soaked a shirt that was filled with lice overnight, and when it dried, the little devils were active as ever. You can't freeze them to death, either."

I ran to his arms with a cry, and he carried me to bed. Naked against fur, I wondered momentarily if Naika's body had warmed to Stig in these coverings, but he soon gave me something else to think about.

XIV

I worked hard at wooing both Nauja and Minik, and sometimes I wasn't sure which of them was more difficult. Stig had brought the dogs home, and every time I stepped outside the house, they barked and strained at their traces. Minik's beguiling blue eyes were cold, and the others gave me a harsh, yellow stare as they bared their teeth at me.

"Why do you hate me, Minik?" I asked, keeping a respectful distance from him. "Is it because you want all of Stig for yourself?"

Stig was coming up the path after spending the day putting mud on sledge runners--his and several others. Soon it would be too cold to get the job done.

Minik went wild at the sight of his master. I watched Stig hug the dog and sighed. Finally it was my turn to be greeted, and I lifted my face for a kiss.

"You look so unhappy," he said. "Has Nauja misbehaved?"

"No," I said, realizing my answer wasn't strictly true. "I just can't seem to make friends with the dogs. I never had that trouble at home."

"Don't worry about it. They aren't meant to be pets, after all."

I wanted to tell him that one needed all the friends one could get in this desolate country, but he wouldn't understand. To him, it wasn't desolate in the least. In fact, he laughed at me when I shivered and frowned, saying I hadn't even experienced the long darkness yet.

It was coming, though. September had arrived. Each day the sun was lower in the southern sky, and the endless daylight was giving way to the darkness that Semigaq said she welcomed.

"People get so tired from all that light that they get crazy," she said.

I nodded, thinking that I was feeling a bit crazy myself. I was never totally warm and never totally clean, and Nauja would have none of me.

Why hadn't I brought her a storybook from Denmark? The tales of Hans Christian Andersen beautifully illustrated, for instance?

Since I hadn't, I took out my stationery that morning and tried to draw some pictures for her--the princess on the pea, the ugly duckling, the little mermaid. I balked at the little match girl, who always made me cry. They weren't bad, I thought, but they certainly lacked color. I touched them up with a bit of rouge and tried to lure Nauja to the table to look at them.

I knew that she understood some Danish, though I'd never heard her speak it, and I spoke to her slowly and warmly. "Come, Nauja, look at the pretty pictures. Wouldn't you like to see?"

She shrank back onto her pallet, clutching a doll made of bone. Its features were incised and darkened like scrimshaw, and it wore a dress made from a hare pelt. Naika had made that doll for her.

"Maybe your dolly would like to see the pictures, Nauja."

She looked at the doll and spoke to it earnestly. Then she shook her head and rolled up in a ball, pretending to be asleep.

I looked at my drawings through a film of tears and was tempted to tear them up and throw them in the stove. However, I stacked them carefully and put them away. There was always another day.

"Let's go to the store and visit Semigaq," I said, and Nauja came to life eagerly.

Semigaq was the only woman I knew in the settlement, and probably the only one willing to make friends with the sole European woman in Thule.

Nauja ran to greet Semigaq, who picked her up and hugged her, wiping the child's nose with her own hair. The sight made me swallow hard, and I could not imagine the love and acceptance that would engender such an act.

"Someone is glad to see you," Semigaq said. "Come near the stove."

We could scarcely carry on a conversation because Nauja wanted Semigaq's attention. She chattered away in the Eskimo tongue, pulling at Semigaq's sleeve whenever the woman turned from her to look at me.

Nauja needed better manners, it was clear, but I also realized that Eskimo women were extremely indulgent with their children.

"She wants a story," Semigaq said. "I told her it must be in Danish so her papa's wife can hear it too."

"I'd love to hear it."

Nauja was scowling, but she didn't protest aloud, and Semigaq pulled the child into her lap and began.

"In the beginning there was nothing but water. Then one day stones and rocks began to fall from the sky, and there was land. But it was dark all the time, and in the darkness words were born.

"The fox met the snow hare in the darkness. `Dark, dark, dark,' said the fox. He wanted it dark so he could steal meat from the caches people made among the cliffs. `Light, light, light,' said the hare. He wanted it light so he could see to find his food on the ground. The moment the hare said the new word, `light,' it was light. And it stayed that way until the fox's turn and the darkness came. And so it went, the fox and the hare taking turns, and that's why we have night and day."

I said, "As long as I've been here, the hare has had the lion's share."

"The fox's night is coming fast," Semigaq said. "Then all of us can get some rest. Nauja, look in the lower drawer. There's some marzipan your papa brought from Denmark, and you may have a piece."

The child's smile was beautiful to see--like the sudden burst of dawn--and I wondered if it would ever beam on me. I was not above any kind of bribery to make it happen.

I talked with Semigaq about our coffee party, and she advised having it soon. If we waited, she said, the fully-formed ice would bring traders from everywhere, and our house might not be big enough. It occurred to me that she might be trying to avert coffee watered down until it was no pleasure to drink--my concern as the hostess, surely, but hers, too, in a place where the edges of ownership were blurred completely.

I had decided to bake something Danish for the occasion, but I knew I didn't have skill or patience to create decent kringle. Folding the pastry in thirty-six layers was a chore that daunted even *Mor*, and she'd never undertake it with something like fifty people to be served. I'd do a simple pastry puff.

Talking to Stig about it, I asked how we'd ever have enough coffee cups for that many, and he told me they would bring their own.

Semigaq went into the back room and returned with the kamiks she had made for me. The sealskin boots were so tall that I joked about climbing on the table and jumping into them, but that wasn't necessary. I sat on a chair to pull them on and luxuriated in the softness of the hare skin stockings inside. Semigaq gave me a muslin bag of dried grass, correctly assuming I had no supply at home for daily layering between the two soles.

Not wanting to fly in the face of custom, I didn't tell her I thought I could use the same layer of grass for several days.

"They are so beautiful, Semigaq. What is the fur at the top?"

She fingered the long hairs, white with just a tinge of gold, and said, "It's the mane of the male bear. Unhappily, one's brother did not shoot a bear with the longest, most beautiful mane. You will need a fox fur coat for the cold time coming."

"Can I buy that in your store?"

"We will set traps."

"Semigaq, I will never be able to chew skins to make a coat, never! Can I pay someone to do that for me?"

She smiled and said, "If you were a man, you could not."

As Nauja and I walked home, I smiled and nodded at the women sitting outside their huts making stockings of hare pelts. Stig probably needed a new pair or two, and I now realized what a problem this would be. Eskimo etiquette did not allow a woman to make clothing for any man but her husband, and I certainly was not prepared to chew and sew hides. I hoped he had properly outfitted himself while he was a widower and thus exempt from the ban. My

114

legs were toasty in the new kamiks, and Nauja was touching the tip of her tongue to a marzipan pig, trying to make it last as long as possible.

Now, I poured coffee for Stig and me and cooled a small cup of it for Nauja with melted snow. I still worried that the child never drank milk, but Stig laughed at me and said, "Look at her teeth. Did you ever see any that were stronger and whiter?" I had to admit I had not.

I asked Stig if he had spent the whole day on the sledge runners, and he said, "Almost. We did put in some windowpanes for Inuiyak. Wanted to get that done before the walrus hunt."

I looked through the double glass of our own front window and thought that I must wash the outside of the panes before it got any colder. Stig followed the direction of my gaze and said, "Inuiyak's windows aren't glass, fortunately. I've never learned the glazier's art."

"What are they, then?"

"The dried intestines of the big bearded seal."

"Nothing is ever wasted here," I said, remembering how Nauja had rushed to save the grounds I was preparing to throw out when we finished the first pot of coffee I made in my new home. I had dumped them onto a newspaper and was just folding the edges when she clambered onto a chair and brought down a dish. She tugged at the paper until I let go and stood back; then her tiny hands scooped the grounds into the dish. She put it on the shelf and said something I couldn't understand. I remembered the words, however, and asked Stig what they meant.

"For the next time," he told me.

"Oh, Stig, I can't bear watered-down coffee!"

He gave me a quizzical look and said, "When in Rome--"

That's how I came to the furtive practice of pouring fresh coffee on old grounds. When the increased bulk became noticeable, I spooned some of the grounds into the stove. There was no place to dispose of refuse, actually. The ground was too hard to dig a pit of any kind. This didn't seem to matter to anyone else. I was the only

115

one who ever had anything left over. Everyone else in the settlement used whatever they had until it was totally consumed or disintegrated.

The seal meat boiling on the stove for our supper would disappear completely. Stig and Nauja ate every bit of what I served them, but I would push the hard-to-chew bites to the edge of my plate and give them to Minik, bribing him to love me. So far, it hadn't helped. The taste of the seal was strong, and it was sweet as sugar. The liver was a special delicacy, tasting like preserved cranberries.

Our coffee party was set for September 23, when day and night would be divided equally. The day before, Stig went through the settlement knocking on doors to say, "Come visit my house!"

"Isn't that rather short notice?" I asked.

He laughed and said, "It isn't news to anyone. The word has been around for weeks."

I had scrubbed the floors with melted snow, and now I was struggling with my pastry puff. The eggs called for by the recipe were out of the question, and so was the butter. I couldn't expect the puff to rise, and I had to hope that sugar and almond flavoring would overcome the taste of blubber.

I gave Nauja a wooden spoon and a small bowl, and she was mixing ingredients with rapt concentration. The smooth ovals of the lids over her downcast eyes made her a miniature of her father; made me want to catch her up in my arms and kiss her. But I didn't dare.

I tripled the puff recipe, but I could bake just one at a time. The first was flat and anything but delicate in flavor, but at least it had a nice, golden color. I trickled sugar water frosting over the top while it was hot and took it outside to the meat rack to cool. Stig had gone to one of his caches for provisions, and it was hard to find a flat spot on the rack.

Nauja's tiny puff was baked along with my second pan, and I had to watch closely to see that it didn't burn. She watched, too, so interested in the fate of her creation that she forgot to shrink away

116

from me when our bodies touched.

When I started toward the meat rack with the second puff, I caught the movement of Minik's great plume of a tail atop the rack, saw the convulsive gulps, and knew that the first puff was consumed. I rushed back to the house with the second puff and found the stick Stig kept next to the door of the entry room.

"*Ayeh-ayeh*!" I yelled, so righteously angry that I forgot to be afraid. I'd picked up the words from the sled drivers on the ice cap, and I knew they meant "Stop!"

Minik turned his cold, blue gaze on me, licking chops rimmed with sugar-water frosting. He had chewed through his traces, eaten the most obvious offering on the rack, and intended to start the main course as soon as he got rid of me.

I'd heard tales of killer dogs and how an empty coffin was buried to commemorate their completely devoured victim, but I still wasn't afraid. I was furious that Minik had eaten the puff I'd worked so hard to make--that my reputation as a hostess would be ruined.

"Nauja!" I yelled, "Find Papa."

The door opened, and I saw her take one look at the dog on the meat rack, pull up her hood and run toward Inuiyak's house.

Every time Minik took his eyes off me and started to nose the meat, I hit the ground with the stick and shouted, "*Ayeh-ayeh*!"

The rest of the dogs bayed and barked as if they were fairytale creatures about to be changed into human form. It seemed like hours until I heard Stig call to his lead dog from a distance. Minik's head shot up, and he ran to his master.

I watched them, father, daughter and dog, and felt excluded. Stig actually wired Minik to a steel post behind the house, quieted the other dogs, and rounded the house with Nauja on his hip.

"Brava!" he said, bending to brush my lips with his, "You've saved the family honor."

"Thank you, Nauja," I said. I extended my hand, and to my joyous surprise, she took it.

117

XV

I scarcely slept the night before our coffee party. Stig promised he would take care of things and do what was expected. All I would have to do would be to smile, look pleasant, and keep the coffee coming. Even so, I was worried that things would not go well and our guests would feel sorry for him because he had married such an unworthy wife.

I was dashing about in the house touching things--moving chairs a fraction of an inch--wishing for vases of flowers, of all things--when Semigaq arrived. She had promised to be my interpreter, and I was glad that she came early. I didn't want to miss a thing.

Much against Nauja's will, I had brushed her hair with my hairbrush and tried to push it into waves, but it was straight as a stick, and it hung in wisps over her eyes. I found a red ribbon to tie it back, but she pulled it off and put it on our dresser. Just when I had hoped we were becoming friends, she was being difficult again.

Stig had shaved and put on a new flannel shirt to greet our guests. He called Nauja to him and whispered to her. As a result, she fetched the ribbon and brought it to me.

"Someone thinks Nauja is beautiful," Semigaq said.

Just then, a voice called from the entry hall. I couldn't understand what it said or what Stig answered, so Semigaq began her translation.

"'Hereby somebody comes visiting,' they say, and your man says, 'The bad hunter welcomes you, though you could have chosen a worthier home.'"

I was indignant that Stig would speak of our home in such terms, but Semigaq whispered, "Someday you will understand. It is not what you think."

The couple came in, and I recognized Inuiyak and one of the women I had seen making hare skin stockings. Her name was Atakutaluk. They sat down and loosened their anoraks. Stig and

119

Inuiyak talked--about the weather (it was snowing outside) and about dogs, Semigaq told me before she got too busy making conversation with the wife.

Others arrived singly and by twos and fours, always announcing their presence in the third person. One young mother had a baby on her back inside her anorak, and when the child answered the call of nature, she stripped her upper body and wiped her back--and the baby--with her hair.

The coffee was at a boil, I had cut the surviving puffs into tiny squares, and I was wondering when to serve my refreshments when Stig said something in the Eskimo language that obviously was particularly meaningful.

Semigaq made her way to me through the crowd, and it wasn't easy. All the chairs were occupied, and everyone else sat or reclined on the floor, leaving no room to walk about.

"He says, `Do you happen to want something to eat?'"

I turned toward the kitchen, thinking it was time to serve, but Semigaq touched my arm and translated Inuiyak's words: "Someone would never expect anything to eat, but if you want to give us food, there is no place in the world where we would find better refreshment than in this house."

Thinking of my poor puff, I swallowed hard, but I supposed I would have to produce it. "Shall I bring the puff, Stig?" I asked.

"Later," he told me. "There's a scene to be played first."

I watched him strike his chest and stride toward the door, saying what Semigaq translated as, "Bad luck for you! I am a terrible hunter, and I have nothing to give you as a treat. However, if you will lower yourself to taste the poor offering I have, I will fetch it."

We all watched as he disappeared into the entry hall and went out the front door. Our guests had a better idea of what was coming next than I did. Even Nauja seemed to know.

He returned and threw a large bag on the floor, taking an ax to it until he chopped loose a bit of something all pink ice and feathers.

Semigaq went on translating as he grimaced and said, "Alas, I have to take this back out to the rack. It has an awful taste! The dogs have soiled it, I fear."

My hand flew to my mouth. Surely Minik hadn't!

Stig went on, "I simply can't serve this to my excellent guests," and as he stooped to pick up the bag, the guests fell upon it, crunching and chewing with their mouths rimmed with feathers.

"What a treat!" Semigaq said. "This giviak is two years old and has a wonderful flavor."

"What *is* it?" I asked, repulsed.

"Dovekies--little auks. You skin a seal through the mouth, and after you drag the body out, you braid the wings of the birds and fill the skin with seven or eight hundred of them. Then you tie the opening shut and cover the bag with stones. It has to be kept out of the sun until winter. The seal blubber cures the meat. Try one."

Now I remembered. Stig had told me about this delicacy, and now Semigaq demonstrated how it should be eaten, holding a bird by the legs with her teeth and stroking it with both hands to brush off the loose feathers. Then she bit the skin loose around the beak, turned it inside out and pulled it free of the bird, sucking it into her mouth to get all the fat before swallowing it in one piece.

Other guests were chewing the frozen birds in a less orderly manner, spitting out the feathers and bones, and Stig offered me one, which I took reluctantly.

"If you happen to get a fully developed egg inside a bird, it tastes like heaven," he said. "And if you get the clot of blood that gathers where they displace the heart with the thumb, that tastes best of all."

I looked at the poor, dead bird in my hand so doubtfully that Stig took pity on me and told me to bite down on one side of the breast bone of the bird he was eating. Somehow I got the liver, and it tasted like green cheese.

Having done my duty, I started to pour coffee, a difficult task in such crowded quarters. I was pleased to see the expressions of approval as they tasted the coffee and enjoyed its robust flavor. As a joke, I went about pouring and murmuring, "My coffee is really disgustingly weak. I must have forgotten to grind fresh beans for at least a year!" Semigaq didn't hear me, but Stig did, and he reached into one of my tall kamiks and gave me a playful pinch. I grinned at him and said, "When in Rome--"

The rooms grew hotter and hotter, and I was just beginning to be comfortable when the guests started taking off their clothes. Some of the children searched their garments for lice and slaughtered them between their front teeth.

The eating went on apace, and the giviak was still at least half full. Even so, I brought on the Danish puff, and it was better received than it deserved to be.

The first belches and farts startled me, but Stig was quick to tell me they were the hallmark of the polite guest.

A man named Oosugtaq was speaking, and this time Stig translated for me. "He says, `Is Spring coming in September? It sounds as if the auks on the cliffs are squawking. Are there really birds in here, or is it women?'"

"Doesn't he think women should talk?"

"They will, whether he thinks so or not," Stig said.

And sure enough, after a slight let-up everyone laughed and the noise quickly built to its previous level.

The giviak diminished more, and some of the guests pillowed their heads on an arm and went to sleep. I smiled at the women and tried to look interested in their incomprehensible words, and I moved about with the sugar bowl, expecting them to put it in their coffee. Instead, they scooped it into their mouths and replaced the damp spoon in the bowl. I had to edge my way into the kitchen several times to replenish it.

As I moved among the men, my kamiks touched their bodies. With such a crowd, it could hardly be otherwise, and I hoped I wasn't violating Eskimo etiquette in some way. They looked at me appraisingly, I thought, grinning and speaking to each other and to Stig in words that Semigaq did not translate.

When I asked her what they were saying, she said, "Someone does not find their words to be of any importance."

Stig, however, heard my query and said, "They like your looks,

Alex. We are discussing a trade."

He said all this to me with a completely straight face, laughing only when my expression told him I was embarrassed and horrified.

The party went on for hours, and I found myself wishing for the hostess's nightmare--the food or the coffee running out. Obviously, this was the only thing that would put an end to the occasion. I found myself dividing eight hundred by fifty and determining that each guest would have to consume sixteen little auks before the giviak was empty. As for the coffee, Stig had told me to use a whole year's supply if necessary. He would lose face if anyone held up a cup that could not be filled.

Nauja was playing with some other children on her own bed, and I was gratified to see her showing off the drawings she had scorned when I made them for her. She seemed closest to a brother and sister, a girl of about ten and a boy I judged to be five or six.

"Who are those children?" I asked Semigaq.

"Patlok is their father. Their mother died last winter."

Motherless children, just like Nauja. I would invite them to our house again, I decided.

Now I was ready to lie down and sleep, but that would be too rude. I stifled a yawn and picked my way among the guests to the entry hall. It was time to collect another kettle of snow to melt for coffee.

I thought of a crowded apartment in Copenhagen with everyone sitting on the floor like this and wished Leif could see me now. We could laugh together about the difference between the two occasions--one an arrogant pretension of intellectual superiority and the other an escape from isolation and the everlasting cold.

Stig's sealskin coat was handy, so I put it on and went outside. As soon as the door closed, the Arctic silence was ascendant. I felt totally insignificant as I scooped snow into my kettle.

I prayed that this would be the last pot of coffee. My grandmother often quoted the proverb, "After three days, both fish and guests stink," and while our guests hadn't been with us that long, it certainly seemed as if they had. If I could have joined in the conversation, it would have helped.

Harald Kaarup made his way into the kitchen to talk with me, and I was almost startled to hear words that I could understand.

"Well, *Frue Brand,* I'd say you've done your husband proud."

"I'm happy to hear it. I don't know what I would have done without Semigaq to speak for me."

"She's pleased to help you feel at home, which is more than she was made to feel when we were in Gothab last year. The Danes there invited me to the dining room but told her to eat in the kitchen."

"How rude! How did you respond to that?"

He laughed without amusement and said, "I told them we'd both eat in the kitchen."

"I was just remembering some literary gatherings in Copenhagen that were as crowded as this. We drank wine at those parties, and sometimes things got out of hand. I'm glad we're serving nothing stronger than coffee tonight."

Kaarup grinned and shook his head. "These people can get drunk on nothing. On poems, for instance, or drum dances."

I clapped my hands. "An Eskimo literary gathering! I can hardly wait. Of course, I'd better wait until I learn the language or it will be lost on me."

"Some of the poems are quite beautiful," he said. "Sometimes they're funny, too. Let me see if I can remember the old man's song--'I have grown old, I have lived much, Many things I understand, but four riddles I cannot solve. The sun's origin, the moon's nature, the minds of women, and why people have so many lice.'"

Hearing Kaarup's words, one of the men started to sing, "Ha-ya-ya-ya!" and others took it up. The storekeeper put a tune to Eskimo words, and the whole house rocked with the refrain. Even I was singing "Ha-ya-ya-ya!" For the first time, I half-way believed that I might come to feel at home in this place.

At long last the giviak was a limp sealskin bag and the coffee was down to the grounds.

"Come, Semigaq," Kaarup said, "we must go home."

A sharp knife of cold entered the house as they departed, reminding someone else to follow their example.

Patlok woke his children, who were sleeping in a tangle of childish arms and legs on Nauja's bed, to take them home. They whimpered a bit as they woke, but as soon as they were fully conscious, they obeyed their father instantly. They would have a good effect on Nauja, I decided.

At length, everyone had put on their clothes and gone home, and we were left with a houseful of auk fathers and a mountain of coffee grounds.

Stig folded me in his arms and said, "Well done!"

"Are you sure everything was all right?"

"Everything was wonderful, and they can't stop staring at your beauty. Your hair is like sunrise, they say."

I had taken to letting my hair fan over my shoulders for warmth rather than pinning it into a classic knot, something I never would have done at home. If my new friends and neighbors considered it beautiful, so much the better.

I struggled in Stig's arms, saying I wanted to get the broom and clean up, but he said, "Drudgery will always keep. I had something more interesting in mind."

On the way to our own bed, we paused to cover Nauja and watch a dream leave its brief mark on her little face.

Auk feathers floated from our covers when we made love.

Stig often fell asleep immediately afterwards, but this time he didn't, and somehow I didn't dare ask what he was thinking about. Had there been a coffee party when he married Naika? Something to remember and compare?

I said, " I like Patlok's children. What are their names?"

"The boy is Mala and the girl is Naterk," he said sleepily.

"How did Patlok's wife die?"

"In childbirth."

Feeling a cold clutch of fear, I burrowed deeper into my husband's arms.

125

XVI

I was thrilled by the beauty of the October sky in Thule--all reds, blues and yellows--but I soon discovered this was one of the few good things about the early part of the month. Too much ice had formed to hunt with kayaks, too much water remained to use the sledges, most of the birds had departed (the loons were the last to go), and all the dogs needed new harnesses.

At least we were catching up on our sleep, now that we had dark nights, and in fact, I was now regretting my complaints about long daylight hours. I'd been warned that I'd catch my last glimpse of the sun for four months on October 26.

"This place can do nothing in moderation," I complained to Stig.

"You make it sound as if the Arctic does these things to you on purpose. Actually, the Arctic is cold, dark and indifferent. It simply doesn't care how you feel."

"I wish I had brought more books," I said. "After all, how many times a day can you make love?"

"Oftener than I had supposed," Stig said with a leer. He put down his coffee cup and pushed away from the table.

The men of the settlement were going seal hunting on the newly-formed sea ice. I had asked to go along, but he told me women were not welcome. Instead, he said, I could climb to a promontory above North Star Bay and watch the action through binoculars for as long as I could stand the cold.

"What shall I do about Nauja? I'm sure she'll get bored waiting around for something to happen."

"Take her to Patlok's house. She can play with Mala and Naterk for awhile." He stroked my cheek with one finger. "I suspect it won't be for long."

I kissed him good-bye, waited until he had time to join the others and move onto the ice, and then bundled up to take Nauja to

Patlok's and find my vantage point. I carried the binoculars inside my anorak to keep them warm, and when I took them out and brought them to my eyes, they steamed up.

I wiped the glasses on my sleeve, and then I had to blink away tears brought on by the cold before I could pick Stig out among the Eskimos. He was a head taller than any of the men. They pushed white screens mounted on skis onto the ice, and I wondered how they knew where to go until I focused the glasses on the dark speck that was a breathing hole.

The seals breathed five to eight times per hour, Stig told me, and always at the same hole. The men would lie flat on the ice and pretend to be seals, even to the point of rolling over and flexing their legs as if scratching fleas with hind flippers. When the seals had breathed and submerged, the hunters would creep forward behind their white screens.

Seals were sensitive to some noises, Stig said, but they couldn't hear while exhaling, and that was the time to move toward them. Shooting one as it surfaced to breathe would not warn the others, he said, as the shots sounded much like the banging of ice pans or icebergs breaking up.

I watched for what seemed like a whole hour, seeing nothing. My eyes teared behind the binoculars and my arms grew intensely weary. Just when I thought I couldn't stand it for another moment, a glistening dark head popped up from the hole. In a single instant, I was on the seal's side, warning it to duck, and then I remembered that my husband's dearest wish was to kill that glossy creature. What a terrible conflict.

The shot rang out and reverberated. Immediately, a harpoon with a rope struck the dark body and the men emerged from behind their screens to pull the seal onto firm ice. They dragged it out of range and disappeared behind their screens once more.

The next head to emerge seemed larger than the first, and it disappeared before a shot could be fired.

Already women were moving across the ice toward the fallen seal to attend to it. Stig hadn't told me it was my place to join them,

128

and I was thankful for that. I wouldn't know where to begin, anymore than I would know how to go about butchering a hog, a skill my mother had brought to her marriage and never used.

The skinning was unusual, it seemed to me. They were cutting spirals around the animal's body, and I couldn't figure it out until it occurred to me it was like peeling an apple. The unbroken corkscrew of skin would make ropes or traces for the sled dogs. Ingenious. That accomplished, the blubber was hacked off and cut into squares.

A long time passed before another seal surfaced to breathe, and I wondered at the patience of Arctic hunters. They got this one, too. I had no way of telling who fired the killing shot or who threw the first harpoon. These hunters would get the best parts, according to Stig's explanation, but everyone would get a share. Since I didn't know good parts from bad, I decided not to worry about it.

What did worry me was the numbness of my feet and hands. I had been out quite long enough. What I really wanted to do before picking Nauja up was visit Semigaq and not have to share my friend with the child. That was out, I supposed, as Semigaq would be with the women down there on the ice. I stamped my feet, beat my hands together, and set off for Patlok's house, a poorly-kept turf hut beyond the store.

I knocked at the door and waited, marching in place to restore the circulation in my feet. Again I knocked, and there was no response.

"Naterk!" I shouted, "It's Mrs. Brand. Let me in!"

Nothing. I lifted the latch and pushed. All doors in this frigid wasteland opened inward to keep wind and snow from imprisoning people in their own homes. The shaft of daylight admitted by the open door was a dramatic contrast to the soft gloom inside. Seal intestine windows were better than none, but I wouldn't want to read long by the light they let in, I thought.

I heard harsh breathing and the small grunts of children exerting great effort before I saw them, Nauja and Mala, trying to lift or hold up Naterk. I rushed forward and grabbed the older girl, and as the children let go, I felt the dead weight of her body and saw the leather noose tightened around her throat. The other end was fastened to a stout peg high on the wall.

"What have you done?" I struggled to loosen the noose with one hand, and Mala's small fingers tried to help but only got in the way. Nauja had backed up to the wall and was whimpering softly.

"Get a knife, Mala," I said, but he refused to understand Danish.

"Nauja? Can you find a knife for me?"

She spoke to Mala in Greenlandish, and he scrambled to a leather bag in a corner of the room. The tool he brought me was dull, but it was better than nothing. Exhausted by Naterk's weight in my left arm, I sawed away with my right hand. It was such slow work that I was sure I could chew through the leather faster, and the two children wept loudly as I struggled to sever it.

Naterk's limp form nearly threw me off balance when the leather finally broke. I knelt to lay her down on a walrus skin pallet and caught my breath in horror. Her face was dark, engorged with blood. Her mouth was open in a silent cry, and her eyes were wide and unseeing. I laid my ear on her chest and heard nothing. Somewhere I'd read about holding a mirror to the nose and mouth to see if life remained, and I grabbed my binoculars to use for that purpose. When I held the lenses close to Naterk's nose and mouth, they did not cloud. The child was dead.

Why would one so young take her own life? I held out my arms to the younger children, and they came to me. Holding each other, we all wept.

The horrible part of it all was the warmth of Naterk's body. If I had come sooner, I could have saved her. Kissing the tops of two small, dark heads, I got up to do what I could for the girl who would never grow up. She would never fall in love, never marry, never have a child. Why? Why had she done it?

I forced her eyelids down, and they sprang open again. When I pushed her chin to close her mouth, it gaped as soon as I removed my hand. I took a deep breath and exhaled shakily, then covered the girl's face with a portion of the hide she lay upon.

"We must go home, Nauja," I said. "Tell Mala to come with us."

She spoke to the boy, and he pulled on his anorak and hood. The string to tighten the hood was missing, and the head covering gaped and slipped off. When I saw that Nauja had the same problem, I demanded an explanation.

The children refused to look at me, and when I grabbed Nauja's shoulders to make her face me, I saw the leather noose around her neck. Mala was wearing his hood string the same way.

"My God!" I said, "What is this?" My fingers trembled as I untied the slip knots and re-threaded the leather into the hoods.

Holding the hands of both children, I dragged them through the deserted village. When the hunters and the women came home with the fruits of their success, there was to be celebration. Now the seal meat would be bitter in Patlok's mouth, and the others would mourn with him.

Our house seemed cold, and I filled the stove with dried heather, trying to fight the chill of death. It was no use. Even while I held my hands over the flames shooting from an open burner, my teeth chattered.

The thought of Patlok coming home to the corpse of his daughter without warning was intolerable, and yet I was afraid to leave the two children who had put their heads into nooses. They would have to come with me, and with their short legs, the journey to the ice would take forever.

The children lay on Nauja's pallet, each of them rolled into a tight ball of misery. I didn't know what to say to them, so I said nothing.

I paced, still trying to decide whether to hurry to the butchering site or wait at home for Stig. Finally, the image of Patlok's homecoming was too much for me. Nauja had a small sled, and I could pull both children on it.

Minik barked at me as I lifted the sled down and the other dogs took up the cry. The light was waning. I checked Mala and Nauja to see that their hoods were tied and their mittens pulled on securely, then sat them down on the sled wordlessly and started off.

They were so little, and yet they seemed to weigh so much! The sled hung up on the bare spots, and I hurried to an expanse of unbroken snow packed hard by many feet. Voices carried a long distance in the cold air. I could hear Stig's booming laughter but couldn't make out his words among the others.

It started to snow. The wind blew the small, pellet-like flakes into my eyes, so I bent my head and trudged along in utter misery. I hadn't been home long enough to warm up before going outside again. I could feel the children staring holes in my back as I pulled the sled. The voices sounded closer, and when I raised my head, I could see the fire somebody had started on the bank of the frozen bay.

"Stig!" I cried as loudly as I could.

The wind blew the sound back to me, and my hope of shortening the trek faded. Clearly, I'd have to find him and pluck at his sleeve to get his attention. This situation was a severe test of my romantic notion that we were bound so closely together that we shared every thought.

A figure was coming toward me, however, and I felt a great sense of relief when I recognized Semigaq.

"One is pleased to say that your husband has claimed some choice portions of the seals," she said.

"Oh, Semigaq, she's dead! Naterk is dead!" I dropped the sled's leather pull and ran to her. "Where is Stig?"

She turned and pointed, then asked, "How did Naterk die?"

"She hanged herself!"

Semigaq sighed deeply and shook her head. "It is not what you think. Somebody will let your husband explain." She turned, pointing, and I saw Stig, ruddy in the firelight.

I shouted his name, and he started toward me at a normal walking pace. When he was close enough to see my face, he broke into a run.

And when I could see his face, I was appalled at his blood-rimmed mouth. "Stig, how did you hurt yourself?"

He looked puzzled; then comprehension dawned, and he said, "The blood, you mean?"

I ran to his arms with a cry. "Yes, for the love of God! The blood!"

"Alex, I've just had a drink of warm seal's blood. It's nothing."

By this time, I had forgotten the children on the sled, and when Nauja's small hand tugged at the leg of her father's sealskin trousers, I was startled. I was also ashamed. I had rushed to Stig for my own comfort, not thinking how much his daughter needed him.

He scooped her up in one arm and held both of us while I told him what I had discovered in Patlok's house.

"She didn't mean to kill herself, Alex. That's just a game the children play. They get a pleasant, almost sexual sensation from cutting off their air, and they usually stop in time."

"When I came in, the little ones were trying to hold her up, but they weren't strong enough."

Nauja broke in, telling her father what happened in the language I couldn't understand. Mala joined in, and when they had told their story, both cried bitterly.

Stig told me what they said. That Naterk had strung them up briefly by their hood cords, and when it was her turn, she stepped off a stool, accidentally kicking it over. Instead of putting the stool within her reach, the children tried to hold her up and couldn't do it. Apparently they had been trying for a long time when I arrived.

"Wait here," he said. "I'll go to Patlok and tell him."

Semigaq apparently had passed the word to the women. The laughing and chattering among them diminished and died out altogether.

I sat on the sled and invited both children to come to my arms. Who was protecting whom from what was a good question.

When Stig and Patlok approached, Mala went to his father wordlessly and the two trudged toward home. The thought of them uncovering Naterk's dead face made me sick.

Stig cleaned his mouth with a handful of snow and kissed me.

He kissed Nauja's forehead. Then he loaded the sled with seal meat, blubber and a liver and we started for home. At first, I carried Nauja and he pulled the sled. When she cried piteously, I suggested that we switch.

"You're spoiling her," he told me.

"After what she has seen today, I would deny her nothing."

XVII

Naterk's burial in the small cemetery beyond the settlement took place quickly--before the ground could become flintier than it was--and a cairn of stones protected her primitive coffin from marauders of any kind.

Patlok was not a Christian, but he followed a prescribed ritual for the disposition of the dead. The men who placed Naterk in her coffin and carried her to her burial site took off their mittens and put them under the stones. Those mittens had touched a corpse and could be used no longer. They stepped in their own footprints returning from the cemetery, and the last man in the party erased the tracks with his knife so death couldn't find them and follow the men home. Naterk's name was not to be mentioned until it was reborn in an infant, and Stig said that might be a long time. No family was eager to name a baby for a loser of the "breathless" game. Names combined the qualities and talents of all the persons who had been called by them, and the Eskimos wanted the best.

I felt the need for some evidence of mourning, but Stig told me it wouldn't happen. He said, "They're not afraid of death. In fact, they're quite indifferent to it. They concentrate on life."

As soon as Naterk was out of sight and unmentionable, she was out of mind as well, and the settlement busied itself with preparations for the trading season.

Harald Kaarup unpacked some of the goods Stig had brought back from Denmark: knives, red cloth, sturdy boxes of sulphur matches, saws, tea, sugar, and strong sewing needles. None of the dainty cross-stitch needles for these folk. They required strong steel shafts with huge eyes to accommodate thin strips of hide.

By October 20, the ice had firmed, and sledges were arriving from all directions, coming out of the dark with a shout of greeting. The villagers came from their houses to greet the visitors, and someone would take them home.

Our guests were a man named Orfik, his wife Aneenak and their boys, who were twelve and ten. Their sledge was piled high with something under a covering of skins, and Stig told me not to speak of it. Fox skins were never mentioned until the second day.

Orfik staked his dogs far enough away from ours for safety, although barked challenges were exchanged. The boys helped him hoist his bundles on top of the meat racks.

I had been boiling seal meat all afternoon, and I offered it to Aneenak. She declined until Stig went through the song and dance about how rotten it was and that his worthless wife hadn't the faintest idea how to cook it. Then, after saying she wasn't at all hungry, she accepted a large chunk.

Knowing she couldn't understand me, I told Stig, "You're taking a big risk--translating the way you insult me. I might find an interesting way to get even."

"I don't mean a word of it--and they know it and you know it."

"Then why waste time saying it?"

"Life is difficult up here. We need some kind of diversion."

Orfik came into the house with the boys, and this time I offered the seal meat with a disclaimer, even if they couldn't understand a word of it.

I said, "This meat came from a sickly seal that my cross-eyed husband shot by accident, and I was too stupid to skin it before I put it in the pot, so if you get some hairs between your teeth--"

Stig chuckled and said, "Woman, I'm warning you!"

Our visitors found our house much too warm. They stripped down as far as modesty would allow, but they were still too hot. One by one, they left the table and stepped outside to cool off.

After we ate, the men began to talk about everything but the central issue--trading fox skins. They discussed the weather, the dogs, their luck at summer hunting, the scandal of the man who left the door of someone else's house ajar and allowed the dogs to eat everything inside that wasn't metal.

Finally Stig put the question casually, "Were you able to catch any foxes this year?"

136

Orfik laughed. "Foxes? One is the worst hunter in the world, but even worse than that when it comes to foxes."

"What a shame," Stig said. "I was hoping to send some skins back to Denmark on the summer ship, and I knew you would have some that were first-class."

"Oh no," said Orfik, "you don't know how bad one is at catching foxes, and if one happens to fall into the trap by accident, it is a poor specimen. Besides, if I did have some skins, how would I get them tanned? My lazy, dirty wife knows nothing of such matters."

I looked at Aneenak to see how she was taking all this, and her face remained expressionless. In my own case, every thought and emotion showed on my face. This could be inconvenient, and I resolved to practice Aneenak's polar impassivity.

Stig said, "What a pity. I was hoping those bags out on the meat racks contained some fox skins."

Orfik studied his kamiks and said, "Well, there may be a couple of skins in those bags, but they're filthy. We used them to wipe the grease from our hands, and they're nothing for you to bother with."

"Oh?" Stig said, "Even so, let me take a look tomorrow."

He gave me a look that told me it was time to serve tea, which I did. Our visitors' sons were fascinated by the Danish cups, tracing the gulls on the china with one finger.

Nauja, who had been quiet and withdrawn since Naterk's death, was just beginning to respond to the boys, and the children grew noisier by the moment.

Orfik and Aneenak didn't seem to notice this annoyance, and when I tried to catch Stig's eye and signal for him to do something about it, he wouldn't look at me. He was intent on Orfik's continuing disclaimer.

"When you finally see my skins, you and everyone else will laugh so hard that I can never come back here again," he said.

Eventually we all settled down for the night, and with relative strangers on pallets of skins a few feet from our bed, Stig and I forwent lovemaking.

Orfik and Aneenak had no such scruples, but they were relatively discreet. Coupling close to one's sleeping children encourages discretion, Stig whispered, and then he planted a series of silent kisses from the top of my throat to my breasts. Restriction had its own excitement, I decided.

The serious bargaining the next day took place at the store, where Stig had access to the goods he had brought from Denmark. I visited with Semigaq while it went on, and Nauja and the boys played with the children of other traders.

Stig opened with, "Will you please bring in those greasy fox skins you told me about last night?"

Orfik groaned. "What? You want to see those filthy things? Am I to be disgraced so early in the morning?"

"You did bring the bags with you, didn't you?"

Orfik turned toward the door, Aneenak following him, then stopped in his tracks and turned. His wife bumped into him and gave a small cry. "Oh, Mr. Stig, this is so hard on one!"

"Do me the favor, Orfik."

The two went out and returned with two heavy sacks. About fifty blue fox skins tumbled out of each, and Stig said, "You wiped blue grease with these, I see. Orfik, these skins are the best of the season. I'm sick about missing out on them."

Orfik said, "Are they too disgusting for you to accept?"

"Not at all! It's just that I have nothing to pay you with. The trading goods this year are of such bad quality that they couldn't possible buy these fine skins."

"Buy?" Orfik yelled, "Do you think I would stoop so low as to take pay for these poor skins? One will be happy if you will accept them as a gift."

Stig considered, knitting his brow. "Well, if I can't pay for the skins, I might take them and show my gratitude with some gifts. Poor gifts though they are, what might you want if I should take the skins?"

Orfik shrugged. "Am I a man with wishes? One doesn't know what one wants."

138

Semigaq spoke to me in a low voice, explaining, "Now Mr. Stig must tell him what he wants."

"Don't you want a gun?" Stig asked.

"I have dreamed of a gun, but why should I have one? A terrible hunter like me?"

"I will give you a gun. And a knife, too. You'll need some tools, and what else?"

"One could look," said Orfik, and when Stig nodded, he motioned to Aneenak, and they started to go through the merchandise.

Orfik took down all the guns and looked them over carefully. Aneenak hefted every kettle, tested all the knives. Orfik went through a pipe rack, sucking on every stem. Aneenak checked out all the needles, scissors and dry goods.

After what seemed like hours, Orfik gave a passionate speech on the merchandise, praising the axes and the knives, the guns, the kettles. He never said he wanted any of them.

"Just wait," said Semigaq.

Then Aneenak broke into his spiel, apologizing for the brashness of her husband, a man who has nothing of value to trade.

"Ah, no!" said Stig, "Those skins are marvelous, the best I've seen." Then he spoke to Aneenak, "What about you? Don't you want something?"

Annenak colored and stepped behind a flour barrel as if to hide. "What should I want? Haven't I been a guest in your wonderful house? Haven't I tanned the fox skins miserably?"

Stig ignored her protestations and asked, "But isn't there something you'd like to have?"

"Why should a worthless person like me have anything?"

"Please, I want you to have something to remember us by."

"Well, maybe a few needles. Not that one can sew, but it's nice to have such things because others do."

She moved along the aisles of the store, touching the scissors and thread, which she wanted, and a mirror "even though one would never look in it," and a cup and a pot.

Orfik felt the necessity to interrupt. "Let me take this shameless woman outside and beat her! To ask for so much! Where is my whip?"

Stig shook his head, and Aneenak caressed a sewing box, saying, "Of course I don't want it!"

"We're coming close," said Semagaq.

Stig consulted some figures he'd written on the back of an envelope and said, "I will write down what you may have."

He handed the list to Orfik, and he, in turn presented it to Harald Kaarup, who began to collect the items allowed.

"It's time for us to go home," Stig told me, "It saves time and money for me to be someplace else during this part of the process." He also told me to start getting lunch ready, because food was the only way to stop the dealing.

I began to see what he meant when Orfik came back to the house the first time.

"I forgot to ask for tobacco when you were kind enough to ask what I wanted. That's what I want--some tobacco."

"Fine," said Stig, and off he went.

Aneenak came back next, saying, "I didn't see the red cloth when I was walking down the aisle. I'd rather have that than some of the things you wrote down, but I hate to give those things back, too."

"Keep them and get the red cloth," Stig said.

"Stig, are they getting the best of you?" I asked.

"I allowed for this," he said.

Then Orfik was back, offering to trade the hatchet he'd asked for for a saw, yet bemoaning the loss of the hatchet. Stig let him have both and told him that lunch was ready.

Semagaq had helped me with the menu: whaleskin, bear meat, and frozen duck eggs plus tea with sugar. Our guests were so busy chewing that they couldn't bargain anymore.

When it was time for them to load their sledge, we all went outside to help.

"Oh," said Orfik, "I forgot matches--"

140

"Alexandra will bring you a box from our kitchen," Stig said, and I hurried to do so. He also had told me they would expect a packet of tea and sugar when it was time to go, so I brought that with me too, hiding it for the moment inside my anorak.

Orfik now remembered that he needed a file and a small axe as well as the large one he had chosen.

Stig looked hesitant long enough to trigger the next act. Orfik whipped out four more fox skins that had been held back for just such a moment.

"Done!" said Stig, and his tone told me it was time to pull out the packet of sugar and tea.

Aneenak and the boys climbed on top of the sledge, Orfik got the dogs to their feet, and I offered the parting gift.

With a crack of the whip they were off, and we still heard their voices after they disappeared from our sight in the darkness of the afternoon.

"They'll be back in the spring," Stig said. "Well, what did you think of our first house guests?"

"They seem decent enough, but I simply can't understand why they can't be straightforward about things. Why couldn't the two of you just say so many fox skins for so many tools?"

Stig laughed and said, "If we did that, how would we spend the rest of the day? We're amusing ourselves, Alex."

I thought of the Georg Jensen silver shop on the Stroget and wondered how that kind of amusement would work there? *Hr.* Hertz would have apoplexy, I decided. Just thinking about the shop made me yearn for a Danish autumn with the leaves of the beech trees yellowing just a bit by this time in October and the sun still warm on the tables and chairs of the outdoor cafes on bright days.

XVIII

After several trading parties had come and gone, our meat supply was low. Stig proposed a bear hunt, and I was terrified by the prospect.

"Can't you buy meat from some of the others?"

He laughed and said, "In this part of the world, a man kills his own meat. We have no Arctic butcher shop."

"But you could be hurt--or even killed."

"That's the chance one takes. The Eskimo definition of happiness is coming across fresh bear tracks ahead of all the other sledges and meeting the bear with one's whole life."

"Part of your life, at least, belongs to me now," I reminded him.

He took my face between his hands and kissed me lightly on the lips. "Then you must lend me that part temporarily. Would you like to watch from the sledge, or would you rather stay at home?"

"I'll go. Whatever I see can't be as bad as what I would imagine. I'll ask Semigaq to take care of Nauja."

The child had been watching as we spoke. She understood much more Danish than she had before I came, I was sure. When she was alone with her father, he spoke to her in Greenlandic. I was not progessing with her language nearly as well, but I did know what to call a bear--*pisugtooq*--the Great Wanderer.

I told Nauja that perhaps we would have nice, white fur to make her a new pair of pants, and she shook her head violently.

"Why do you shake your head, Nauja? Wouldn't you like a beautiful pair of pants?"

"*Pisugtooq* looks in window. Bites off Nauja's head if she is bad."

"Who in the world told you that?"

She didn't answer; simply shook her head again.

"Stig?" I appealed.

He spoke to his daughter in Greenlandic and reported, "She

can't say the name of the dead. Naterk told her that."

I put my arms around her, which she allowed, much to my surprise. "Nauja, we will protect you from the bear. *Pisugtooq* will not come to our house."

I held her close, enjoying the warmth of her small body. She ate enough fat to radiate heat like a small furnace, and I still was working on my intake. I was always cold, a hellish condition for any Dane.

Both of us were afraid of *Pisugtooq*, but for different reasons. Despite my respect for Stig's knowledge of the Arctic and my belief that he could take care of himself and of me, I sensed the profound indifference of the North. Courage and foolishness seemed to merit the same reward.

We were in the grip of winter now, and the late November sun shone no more than four hours a day. Stig said it was too late to go out until the next day.

I gave Nauja a quick kiss and put her down to attend to our next meal. The seal meat on the rack outside would be frozen stiff, and it would take time.

As I reached for my anorak in the entry hall, I glanced at the small mirror beside the door and momentarily thought I was looking at someone else--someone like a plain woman from the country just arrived in Copenhagen. The hair was pulled back severely and tied with a ribbon--oily from lack of washing and about the color of the khaki uniform I'd seen on an American doughboy during the war. I'd been Stig's amber lady once, but how could he love the drab creature I'd become?

Standing on tiptoe to find the meat in the gloom, I felt the soft snow slide into my kamiks. I kept a watchful eye on Minik, who was standing and eyeing me banefully. The other dogs were curled in balls in the snow, tails across their noses. At least Minik had stopped barking at me savagely every time I came out of the house. But now he was doing something new--whining.

"What's wrong, Minik?"

He whined again and lay down in the snow, panting. How on

144

earth could the beast be hot in this climate?

With Nauja safely in the hands of Semigaq, whom I rewarded with several pieces of costume jewelry brought from Denmark, we started out at first light. Although we did not plan to be out long, Stig told me to pack some seal meat in case our return was delayed.

"We might find a cache somewhere," he said, "but you can't count on it."

He had told me that anyone who needed food took it from whatever cache they could find. They replaced what they took if possible, but it wasn't always possible.

"So if you put something away for your own use, you can't count on it being there when you come back?"

"That's right. It's the only way to even the odds between humanity and the North."

The dogs fanned out and began to run. The wind cut my face so severely that I had to turn and look at where we had been rather than where we were going. As we approached the fjord, the sledge slowed. I had heard no command from Stig, and yet the dogs were inching along.

He explained, "They know they're coming to sea ice, and the salt will hurt their feet."

"Is it safe for us to go on the ice?"

"If it isn't, they'll know."

"What do you do next?"

"Park you, unhitch Minik, and hike upwind to find a seal's breathing hole."

"Stig, how cold is the water under that ice?"

"Minus ten, maybe. Don't worry about it."

I huddled in a seal robe, watching him unfasten Minik from the traces. The big dog was eager to be off, straining and barking, inciting the others to a barking chorus. If a bear were in the vicinity, he surely would lay low, I thought. It would be "he," as only male bears hunted in the winter.

Stig came past the sledge and kissed me good-bye, then walked north across the ice, following the rapidly vanishing Minik. Soon I couldn't see Stig, as he was wearing a white anorak to hide him from his quarry. His rifle was wrapped with white cloth for the same reason.

Minik had stopped barking, and when I heard him again, the sound was greatly diminished. He must have sniffed out a breathing hole. The other dogs set up a hue and cry, and I tried to quiet them. It was hopeless.

I turned slowly to take in the forbidding mountains that surrounded the fjord, let my eyes rest on Saunders Island which many of the birds had abandoned until a gentler season, and finally focused on a speck that turned out to be Minik with his camouflaged master. Stig was bringing the dog back before beginning his bear watch.

I stamped my feet to keep the circulation going and clutched the seal robe tighter. This whole episode was just beginning, and already I felt close to the end of my endurance, but I would never admit it.

When Stig was close enough to speak in a low voice, he said, "The hole is just beyond that pressure ice, and I saw a raven, which means a bear is somewhere in the neighborhood."

I tried to follow his gaze, but when it came to terms for ice, I was hopeless. The Eskimos had more than a hundred words for its various forms, and I didn't know one from the other in any language. I did remember Stig saying paleocrystic ice was several years old and looked like rolling prairie. Not knowing what rolling prairie looked like left me pretty much in the dark. I knew that pack ice was a large thick field of the stuff in constant motion and that dogs on unsafe ice spread out and moved slowly.

"Point it out to me again," I said, and I followed the line of his mittened hand. If only there were some way to mark it. I did see ice broken and piled into ridges--pressure ice, no doubt.

Stig left me again, and the long wait began. I fixed my eyes on the spot, wondering how on earth I'd ever see a white bear and a white-clothed man in that landscape. I sang songs in my head--"It's a Long Way to Tipperary," Grieg's "I Love Thee," some of

146

Grundtvig's nature-loving hymns. Would Grundtvig have loved nature so much if he had seen her Arctic face?

Soon I tired of being so far from the action. Wrapping the seal robe around me, I started to walk, following Stig's deep footprints in the snow. The dogs barked, as if to tattle on me.

On I trudged until I had to stop to catch my breath. I could see the dark head of a seal bobbing up in the breathing hole, and then just the faint outline of what looked like a pale tobogganer. It was the bear. He had flattened himself to move toward his prey. But where was Stig?

A shot shattered the stillness. The bear roared and rose up on his hind legs. Then he dropped and began to run at an astonishing speed. The gun went off again, and I saw Stig raising it for a third shot as the bear raced toward him.

"Dear God!" I shrieked, "don't let it--"

That third shot brought the huge animal down, and he wasn't more than a few meters from Stig, who seemed to be kneeling with his gun.

I started to run, and the seal robe was so heavy that I shrugged it off, thinking I would pick it up on the way back. I didn't know I was in trouble until I felt a wave of cold that nearly stopped my heart. Running across young ice hidden by the snow, I had gone in to my waist.

Stig heard my screams and came running to pull me out. He sat me down in the deep snow and told me to roll.

"It blots the water," he said.

"I've got to get back to change!" I gasped. Water sloshed in my kamiks, which he pulled from my feet and emptied, replacing them quickly.

"The best way to dry your clothes is on your body," he said. "Just keep moving--sit, stand, and kneel. Might as well come over and have a look at what I bagged."

My teeth chattered uncontrollably as I said, "I s-s-s-aw h-h-him run at you."

I walked in the circle of his arm to where the giant bear lay, his

147

blood staining the snow. Bullet wounds in the shoulder and high in the neck were still pumping crimson, and the third and fatal shot to the heart was hidden by the way he fell. His pelt was the color of pale sunlight, and his last snarl was frozen on his muzzle forever.

Stig looked so proud, and he was completely oblivious to my misery. "Congratulations," I said. "Now may I go home and change?"

"Oh!" he said, as if he'd forgotten my misfortune. He scooped me up and carried me, stopping to retrieve the seal robe where I dropped it. "I'll have to have help dealing with that carcass, anyhow. I'll bet there's a quarter-ton of meat there. Hope you like bear meat."

"I've never tried it," I said, convinced that I wouldn't survive to taste it. I looked back and saw two dark specks moving on the dead bear.

Stig saw them too and said, "Ravens. I owe them a few pecks for marking the territory."

He took me home and built up the fire in the stove, then went to fetch Nauja while I removed my sodden clothing and rubbed my body hard with a towel. I had other clothing, but the kamiks were my only pair. I would not be able to leave the house until they dried.

I was waiting for a sneeze, a cough, some sign of the fatal pneumonia that was sure to carry me off after this terrifying experience, but all I felt was a glow. I even fancied myself some sort of Norse goddess--invincible. I made myself some tea, and when Stig returned with Nauja, I was ready to invent a story for her about *Pisugtooq*.

Along the way Stig had recruited helpers to skin, flense and cut up the bear meat. As the victorious hunter, he had first choice of the meat, but he said there was plenty for everyone.

"What do we get, heart and liver?" I asked.

"The heart is fine, but never the liver. Polar bear liver gives you a headache and makes you vomit for days."

Nauja and I saw him off and then settled down for our story in another seal robe that had stayed warm in the house.

148

"Once upon a time a big polar bear named *Pisugtooq* came to North Star Bay to spy on little children," I began.

"He looked at somebody," she said.

"But he passed by the Brand house. The little child in that house was so good that he never could catch her doing anything wrong."

Nauja giggled, and I rejoiced in the happy sound that was heard from her so seldom.

"But *Pisugtooq* scared some of the other children, and they didn't know what to do. Well, actually, they did know. They could have been good, and that would have been the end of it, but that was too hard for them."

Nauja looked thoughtful.

"Finally, one boy said, `Let's make friends with the ravens and ask them what to do.' And they did. They put out food for the birds, and the birds began to talk to them.

`Why are you so nice to us?' the ravens asked. `What do you want?'

"One little girl said, `We just like you. You are very nice birds.'

"The ravens puffed their breasts in pride and said, `You are very nice children, as anyone can see. You have been so kind to us that we would like to return the favor. What can we do for you?'

`We are afraid of *Pisugtooq*. Can you get him to leave us alone?'

`We just might be able to do that,' said the ravens, and off they flew.

"They flew all over the ice on the fjord until they found the seals' breathing holes. That was where polar bears could be found. And that was where hunters came. When a hunter saw ravens, he knew bears were near."

Nauja finished the story, "The ravens told Papa, and Papa shot *Pisugtooq*, and he won't look in windows anymore."

"That's right," I said, "and everyone will live happily ever after."

Not quite. When Stig came home hours later, filthy with blood and grease, he told me that Patlok had nearly bled to death when his flensing knife slipped and cut an artery in his inner thigh. The wound was deep, and one of the women had closed it with an ordinary needle and thread.

XIX

The day after Stig shot the bear, Minik obviously was seriously ill. He lay stretched out, panting, making no attempt to curl his body against the cold or cover his nose with the brush of his tail.

The dog had not been my friend, but I was sorry to see him suffer and even sorrier to feel Stig's desolation.

"Can't we cover him with some hides?" I asked.

"He'll just shake them off. He's burning up with fever."

"What could it be?"

"Something brought in by the traders, I suppose. We had a thing like this a few years ago. Some of the Eskimos tied crosses around their dogs' necks to protect them from it, but it didn't seem to help, so they went back to their old amulets."

"What will you do if you lose him?"

"Mequsaq doesn't have as much heart, but he'll do, I suppose. The problem will be convincing him that the king is dead."

Mequsaq was ordinary, the type of dog you could see staked out beside any dwelling, but he worked well in the traces. I went into the house for melted snow and tried to pour some into the side of Minik's mouth with a spoon, but it simply ran out and froze on his fur.

"Greenland needs some veterinarians," I said, frustrated to the point of tears. "Should we try to bring him inside?"

Stig shook his head. "He'd be terrified and much too hot."

The other dogs paced and whimpered, dragging circles in the snow around their stakes.

A few hours later Minik was dead, his blue star fixed forever. Stig released Mequsaq from his stake and pulled him toward the body. Mequsaq struggled, afraid to approach the lead dog even now, but when he passed some invisible line without harm, he started to advance cautiously, sniffing and whining.

"You'd better go inside now," Stig said.

"Why?"

"I don't think you'll enjoy watching an act of cannibalism."

I turned but not quickly enough. Mequsaq went for the throat, and I vomited on the snow. I'd never been given to queasiness, and I was shocked by my physical reaction to this stark situation. Shaking, I went inside to make myself some tea.

From the fierce barks and snarls I could hear, I gathered that Stig had freed the other dogs to join the baneful feast.

Nauja, who was playing with a doll made from a bone and some fox fur, spoke to her "baby" rather than to me, but she must have wanted me to hear. She said in Danish, "Minik go dance in the sky."

I nodded, sipping my tea. It seemed fitting that such a magnificent animal should race forever in the Aurora Borealis.

When Stig finally came inside, he accepted the tea I offered wordlessly. After one huge swallow, he set his cup down and buried his face in his hands.

"I'm so sorry," I said.

"I saved his life when he was a pup--just a round ball of fur."

"Tell me."

"I was up at Etah visiting a man named Sorqaq who had a litter of pups, and another old fellow named Tatterat showed up, too. Tatterat loved puppy meat, and he had quite a way of getting it. He'd pick up a pup, always the fattest, and just by accident drop it and kill it. Then he'd do the owner the favor of disposing of the corpse."

"You knew this about him?"

"Of course. Everyone did."

"Then why didn't the dog owners prevent him from picking up their puppies?"

"It has something to do with an elaborate code of manners. When you welcome guests, you withhold nothing that will please them."

"So how did you save Minik?"

"When I saw Tatterat raising that puppy high to dash his brains out, I jumped right in and caught him. I told the old boy I'd never

152

seen a pair of eyes that blue, and I just had to have a look. He was peeved, but what could he say? Minik followed me around the whole time I was there, and when it was time to go, Sorqaq said I might as well take him because he'd chosen me."

Stig fell silent, swallowing hard and blinking.

"Why don't you just go ahead and cry?" I said.

He shook his head, turning his face away from me.

"Nauja, tell your father what you said about Minik."

She wouldn't, and so I did. "She says Minik is dancing in the sky."

"And always in my memory," he said, his voice breaking.

The next morning when I reached for a pan to fry some of the bear meat, I saw my fingerprint on the grease I never could rub off entirely with the hare skin. It made me sick, and I rushed to the bucket beside the entry. Then I tried to continue with breakfast preparations, but my gorge rose again.

Stig woke and looked at me with concern as I sat down heavily and tried to control myself.

"Did I wake you?" I asked.

"Just by being gone from my side."

"You don't suppose I have what Minik--" I couldn't say the rest.

"I'm sure you don't. As to what you *do* have, we'll have to wait and see."

He was smiling, which enraged me until it occurred to me what that expression meant.

"You don't think--"

"Perhaps hope is a better word." he pushed back the hides and quickly pulled on some clothes, then came to me and held me, kissing the top of my head.

How could it be? I'd brought along enough German contraceptive jelly to last for years, and I'd never forgotten to use it. Had it frozen and thawed, becoming ineffective? I had bemoaned the lack of veterinarians in Greenland, but doctors were just as scarce. What was I going to do?

153

I had nothing but tea for breakfast and then took Nauja with me to consult Semigaq. A number of people were in the store, and she was busy with them, so I went back to the Kaarups' private quarters to wait for her.

It occurred to me that none of the shoppers had looked up and smiled at us when we came in. I didn't know any of them very well, but I was accustomed to that pleasant courtesy.

A long time passed, and even though I heard Semigaq's farewells enough times to account for everyone in the place, she didn't come through the curtains to us. At length, I sent Nauja to find out what was keeping her.

The child returned to me and said, "She says we must go home."

I rose, both puzzled and angry--determined to get to the bottom of this situation. "Semigaq!" I called loudly, parting the curtains and re-entering the store.

She said nothing and kept her eyes down, busying her hands with something on the counter top.

"Why are you acting like this? We're friends, aren't we?"

"We must wait to be friends until the *angakok* tells us why we have had three misfortunes. Perhaps it is not your fault, but until we know, we must be careful."

"What are the three?"

"The child, Patlok's wound, and now Mr. Stig's lead dog. One misfortune would not be enough--or two. But the third makes somebody wonder."

"Why do you think it's my fault? What have I done?"

"You came," she said simply, and she would say no more.

"Come, Nauja. We will not stay where we are not wanted."

I went home seething and flung myself into cleaning the house with raging energy. Coming upon Kullabak's amulet, I threw it against the wall. Nauja went to her pallet and burrowed under her covers to avoid me.

Stig was off bargaining for a new dog or I would have asked him to feed the fire with the chunks of blubber that sickened me now. I longed for the earlier time when we burned heather.

The thought of bearing Stig's child would have thrilled me if we were in Denmark, but living here made it a terrifying prospect. I wasn't up to the stoic strength of the Greenlanders, who took a few hours off to give birth before going about their usual business. *Mor* had almost died giving birth to Frederik. I was five at the time, but I understood the threat of loss.

When Stig came home, he tied a white dog outside. I watched through the wavy glass of the window as the rest of the team strained at their tethers, barking at the stranger.

The dog's name was Miuk, and he seemed to be a fine specimen. Stig told me about the long bargaining process with a man named Odark that resulted in trading the polar bear skin for the dog.

Then I told him about our unfriendly reception at the store, and he said, "That will clear up soon. The *angakok* will hold a seance tomorrow. They're building the big igloo right now."

"I've forgotten what an *angakok* is," I confessed.

"Someone who goes into a trance and discovers things that are hidden. Sigdlu does it best here, but sometimes an old woman can manage it."

"Am I allowed to come? After what happened to me today, I'm not sure I'm welcome anywhere."

"Of course you can come. Everyone does."

Perversely, once I had permission, I wasn't sure I wanted to be present. What if this weird event marked my unborn child?

The igloo built for the gathering was huge. I crawled after Stig and Nauja through the long, low entry and stood up gratefully in the dim light. Blubber burned in stone lamps, and a central fire's flames reached for the vent in the curving dome. Old tent skins lined the walls, and a ledge was built along one wall like a stage. We sat down with the others to wait. Nauja was on Stig's lap.

"Sigdlu comes!" a man shouted.

We all looked toward the entrance, but nothing happened. After the announcement was made twice more, the *angakok* appeared.

The crowd shouted greetings, and he waved his hands and spoke.

Stig translated for me in a whisper. "He says we're all idiots to come here for this sham; that he can't perform what we've come to see."

The people shouted praise and encouragement, and he waved his hands again. He came to stand in front of Stig and me. He spoke and then Stig spoke. Sigdlu turned and went to the ledge.

"He said this is nothing for white people to look at," Stig explained, "and I told him we would like to listen to his wisdom. He said if we're that foolish, so be it."

Sigdlu took off all his clothes, and two men tied his arms to his body and bound his legs together with sealskin lines. They placed a drum and a drumstick and a piece of dried sealskin beside him and extinguished all the lamps but one.

I could scarcely seek Stig's face, and when Sigdlu began to chant, I gripped his arm. The voice seemed to come from different parts of the igloo, and the drumming grew louder, along with the rattling of the sealskin. Soon everybody was chanting, even Stig. I felt someone claw at my sleeve and pulled back in terror. People were flinging off their clothes and swaying where they sat. Somebody howled like a wolf, and the words I was hearing were strange--different from Greenlandic. This was no place for a child, I thought, but Nauja showed no fear.

Sigdlu's voice grew fainter, as if it were coming from outside, and suddenly the lamps were relit. He was gone from the ledge, but the drum and sealskin were still there.

The frenzied singing went on until one of the men shouted an order. The people who had risen to dance sat down again, and when I asked Stig what was happening, he looked at me unseeingly, as if he were in a trance himself. I shook his shoulder, frightened that he could leave me this way, and he came back to me.

"He says Sigdlu is trying to return. He's swimming through the rock under the igloo."

The lights were doused again, and Sigdlu was asked for the secrets he learned in the underworld.

His voice came from the ledge, now, and Stig told me what he said. "The Great Spirits are embarrassed by the presence of white people here and will not tell the reason for the accidents. We are to watch out for huge birds and strange traders, and the women must not eat she-walrus meat for a month. There's always a taboo attached to these revelations."

"And it's always the women who pay?"

Stig laughed. He put his arm around me and pulled me close.

Then the lamps were re-lit, and we saw the *angakok* sitting on the ledge, tightly bound by the sealskin lines. He was exhausted and sweating, foaming at the mouth as if he had run for miles. They untied him, and he fell into a coma for a moment. When he revived, he said, "The wisdom of our ancestors is not in me. This is all lies and tricks!"

The faces of those around us were ecstatic, as if every one of them had seen a vision. Semigaq's eyes were bright and unseeing, and when Harald shook her back to her usual self, she came to me and said, "Somebody is glad you have not been blamed."

"So am I!" I said fervently. Arctic life was difficult enough for the blameless, it seemed to me.

XX

December, the time of deepest darkness, brought calm weather, but the northerly winds were too much for me. I found myself using every excuse to stay indoors.

" I'm going out to a cache of bird eggs. Come along on the sled," Stig said. "You've never ridden behind Miuk, and I think you'll be impressed by him."

To attain the lead dog position, Miuk had to fight Mequsaq, who was certain he had inherited the honor. Fortunately, Mequsaq sensed the white dog's superiority and rolled over to expose his throat before either was seriously injured. I really felt sorry for Mequsaq. Convinced that his life had changed for the better and he would have all the food and bitches he could want, he was suddenly back in the ranks. It was like being exiled to the provinces after the high life of Copenhagen.

I sat down to pull on my hareskin stockings, and as I leaned forward, I felt displaced in my own body. My mid-section seemed to have thickened overnight. I could only hope that Stig would find the manifestations of maternity attractive. At least the morning sickness had passed, and I was free from dealing with menstrual rags for months. What a problem that was! I couldn't put the washed but still stained squares outside to dry because the dogs would devour them, and hanging them above the cooking stove was too disgusting to contemplate. I had tried spreading them out on newspapers under our bed, but the few issues we brought with us were soon used up. Finally, I asked Stig what the Eskimo women did--if he knew--and he said Naika had gathered thistledown, called Arctic cotton, to absorb the menstrual flow and then burned it, or so he thought. She had been intensely private about the whole affair.

"So where can I get some of this thistledown?" I asked.

"Ask Semigaq. I don't know because I have no use for it."

Before I could ask, I didn't need it either. I put on my anorak

159

and tightened the hood cord until the lovely white fox made a perfect oval around my face. Stig had been dressing Nauja while I got ready, and he was so experienced at putting on his outdoor gear that we were outside in no time.

The sledge had been lifted down from its platform, and he quickly hitched the dogs. I sat tailor-fashion with Nauja between my legs, and when Stig gave the command, the dogs leaped forward. He was right about Miuk's impressiveness. He almost flew across the ground, his curled tail held high like a banner, and the others seemed proud to follow him from their own positions in the fanning lines.

In the strange daytime darkness, the sky was clear, and I could see the silhouettes of the mountains and the icebergs. The landscape had an eery beauty, and I was glad I came.

We rode for some time parallel to the fjord. Stig would run behind the sled for awhile, then step on for a brief ride.

"Do you remember where you put the eggs?" I asked.

"I haven't the slightest idea," he teased before telling me he had memorized landmarks and marked the hummock with a pole.

Just when I was becoming unbearably cold and had to work hard to convince myself that I didn't need to urinate, Nauja pointed, and I saw the small black stake lying on the ground beside a rise of ice.

"Ha!" said Stig, "A playful polar bear has knocked it aside. We're lucky it wasn't buried in snow."

I wasn't too sure we were lucky. If blowing snow hadn't covered the stake, the bear must have knocked it over quite recently, and the big beast might be on the prowl nearby at this moment.

Stig had brought a small shovel, and he hacked at the frozen mound until he uncovered some rocks. These he picked up and tossed aside. I got off the sled to come over and watch.

Urine stained the snow near the mound, and I could see claw marks in the side of the hummock still intact.

"Well, I'll be damned!" Stig exploded.

"What's wrong?"

160

"Somebody else got here first."

"They stole your eggs?"

"There's no such thing as stealing here. People take what they need and replace what they can. Whoever got the eggs needed them more than we do."

He thrust his hand among the rocks and brought out four frozen eggs. "At least they left a taste. Try one."

"You first," I said.

Actually, it was Nauja who expertly cracked an egg, brushed away the shell, and popped its frozen contents into her mouth.

Stig ate his and gave me two. "The little mother needs her nourishment," he said.

Clumsy in my mittens, I dealt with the eggs and even enjoyed them. They reminded me of the much bigger hard-boiled eggs Mor had put into a basket with the lunches we took to the shore when I was a child.

"When did you put the eggs there?" I asked.

"A year ago in July. I wasn't here to do it this year."

"You did it before you knew me," I said, marveling that it was possible to eat such an antique egg and at how much our lives had changed since Stig made the cache.

"More, Papa?" Nauja said.

"No more," he said, and I was sorry I hadn't given my second egg to her.

Christmas was approaching, and I was determined to provide as many of the traditional touches as possible. I wondered how Naika had celebrated the season, but I didn't wish to ask.

I carefully cut the white end papers from the few books in the house and looked around for something red. Nothing. Nauja and I went to the store, where I bought some red packets of tea. Dumping the tea leaves into a jar, I smoothed the red bags and cut them into tongues to be woven with the white tongues from the end papers. What was Christmas without woven heart baskets? Nauja turned out to be adept at the weaving, and the size of her fingers allowed her to make tinier baskets than I could manage.

What to do for a Christmas tree was a more difficult proposition. No tree of any description could be found in this region, and after long thought, I commandeered the rack of caribou horns we used for hanging up anoraks.

"But where will we put our clothes?" Stig asked.

"Throw them on the bed. It's only for a little while--Christmas Eve until Twelfth Night."

"What other customs are you bent on?" he asked.

"I'd like a sheaf of wheat for the birds, but all the birds have gone away, I guess."

"Not quite. If you listen carefully, you may hear the chirp of a Horneman's Redpoll. They're whitish finches with rosy breasts."

The thought that all the birds had not abandoned us was tremendously heartening, but now I was worried about finding that sheaf of grain for the door.

"I'll just nail some blubber to a stick and put that up," Stig offered.

Blubber. An ugly word, an ugly thing, but an utter necessity in the Arctic. I smiled ruefully and said, "Blubber, the staff of life!"

Then I had to think of gifts. How lovely it would be if I had a few hours on the Stroget to buy just the right presents for Stig and Nauja. Why hadn't I thought of it before leaving Denmark? I could find some pretty bauble for Nauja among the costume jewelry I'd brought for the "natives," but what about Stig?

Then it occurred to me. Part of a sealskin was outside, frozen stiff on the rack. As a supreme gesture of love, I would chew the wretched thing to make him some new mittens. When the hide was supple, I could sew them myself with the huge darning needle I'd bought at the store.

I could scarcely wait for him to leave the house and let me begin my secret project. As soon as he did, I put on my anorak and dashed outside for the skin. The dogs barked loudly, and I hoped he was far enough away that he wouldn't hear them and wonder what was going on at home. In my haste to get back inside, I jammed the frozen skin in the doorway and had to pound it with my fist to dislodge it while frigid air rushed inside.

Should I start to chew while it was still frozen or let it thaw? I decided time was of the essence, and the taste would not be as rank when it was icy. I put it on the table and took off my outside garments. Nauja watched with wonder as I sat down, took a deep breath, and shoved as much of it as possible into my mouth. I bit down, feeling the ice cold on my teeth. For the first few grinding motions, I held my breath, but that couldn't go on indefinitely. When I exhaled and breathed in, the oily, acrid taste of the skin overwhelmed me. Nauja took up the other end and started to chew, shaming me into going on.

This was true misery, and I was so immersed in it that I didn't hear Stig come in. Not until his shadow fell across us was I aware of his presence.

"Alexandra," he said softly.

I dropped the skin in my lap, covered my face with my hands and began to cry.

He pulled me up into his arms and kissed me, which only made me cry all the harder.

"What is it?" he whispered.

"I--I wanted to surprise you. I was going to make you some--some mittens." I struggled from his arms and picked up the skin, looking at the tiny area I had managed to alter with my teeth. "At the rate I'm going, you'd have them in ten years!"

"I love you for trying," he said, "but there's no need. Old Qinorunna has been chewing skins for me ever since I came. Her teeth may be worn down, but they're still powerful, and she considers it an honor to prepare my hides."

"Even when you have a wife?"

"Even then. Let's have some tea and go to bed."

On Christmas Eve I tied ribbons on the caribou horns and hung a woven heart from each tip. My gifts for Stig and Nauja were insignificant, but I had wrapped them as prettily as possible in the creased tissue paper that had protected my hand mirror on the trip to Greenland and pale blue ribbons pulled from the necklines of two nightgowns. Once the gifts were opened, the ribbons would be re-threaded into the gowns.

When everything was ready, I put on my seal necklace and held out my hands to my family. We couldn't dance around the Christmas tree in the Danish fashion because it was fastened to the wall, but we clasped hands and swayed from side to side in front of it, singing a song we made up as we went along. "Our Christmas tree is ours alone, the only one that's made of bone, we're thankful to the caribou who grew this tree for me and you!"

Stig swung Nauja upward to touch the antlers and said, "I think we've just started a tradition. Aren't we brilliant?"

"Let's open presents!" I said.

Stig set Nauja down and hurried to the chest of drawers beside our bed. He brought back two towel-wrapped objects and placed them under the "tree."

Nauja opened my gift first. It was a short strand of Venetian beads, one of the nicest pieces I had brought. Her eyes shone as she swung the loop back and forth. Stig tried to fasten it around her neck, but she protested, "Somebody wants to look!"

"You're next," I told Stig.

He untied the blue ribbon carefully, and I was terrified that he would be disappointed in what I had managed to find for him, but he smiled broadly upon discovering the small blank book covered in red leather *Fru* Steinsen had given me as a going-away present. "You'll want to record your adventures," she had said.

"Just what I've needed!" Stig said. "Now it's your turn."

He handed me one of the towel-wrapped parcels, and I was surprised by its weight. It was a shell-shaped blubber lamp carved from soapstone with a tiny seal in the lineup of little knobs along the curved side.

"It's beautiful," I said.

"The lamp is the symbol of the home, and I asked the carver to put a seal in it as a symbol of *our* home."

I had some idea of the heavy symbolism of the lamp. Eskimo women measured their importance by how many lamps they tended, and that tending was a tricky proposition. Slanting the lamp and propping the moss wick to get more or less light was something I had yet to master. However, the friendly seal on this one made me believe I could do it. This, it occurred to me, was a flattering gift from a husband who believed I was equal to the challenge. I gave him a lingering kiss of thanks.

Nauja tore the towel from her gift and gave a cry of joy. It was a new doll Stig had made from bear bones and fox fur, drawing its features with his fountain pen.

"Shall we have our Christmas feast now?" I said.

"Nauja has something for you," Stig said.

The child approached and gave me a square of paper folded many times. Inside was the tiniest woven heart I'd ever seen.

"See?" Stig said, "You've won her heart."

My eyes filled with tears as I knelt to kiss her cheek.

Because it was a special occasion, we had coffee instead of tea with our bear meat, and Stig surprised us with a tin of lingonberries he had bought at the store.

He went outside to give the dogs a Christmas treat and hurried back to tell us the Aurora Borealis was putting on a show.

We bundled up and went outside to watch the sheets and curtains of red and green light and listen to the swishing noise that accompanied the amazing sight.

"They say the Aurora is torches held by the dead to help the living see to hunt," Stig said.

We went to bed, but the magnetism in the atmosphere kept us from sleep for a long time. We made love slowly and tenderly, and when I finally did sleep, I dreamed of home--of dancing around the Christmas tree with *Far*, *Mor* and Frederik while the aroma of roasting goose filled the air. I could picture them in celebration, but never in this world would they conjure up our song and dance before the caribou horns. I was now beyond their ken.

XXI

Semigaq and Harald paid us a New Year's call, bringing a jar of pickled herring and a container of *imiak*. When Stig proposed a toast to 1922, I pretended to take a sip, but visions of poor Mel preserved in his barrel made drinking the stuff impossible for me.

The men moved to one side of the room to discuss business; how much stock the fall traders had taken away and which items should be re-ordered when Stig went south to meet the mail boat at Holsteinsborg.

Nauja played contentedly with her new doll, and I took the opportunity to reveal my supposed condition to Semigaq.

"You must eat much fat," she said. When will the baby come?"

"August, I think, but what do I know about such things? At home, the doctor tells you when it will be."

She shrugged. "When babies are ready, they come."

"Semigaq," I can't have this baby by myself. Will you help me?"

She looked away and said, "Somebody is not fortunate in these matters. Two of my babies were born without breath."

"I'm so sorry!"

"You will know what to do."

"No! I can't do it alone!"

Hearing my rising voice, Stig asked, "What is it that you can't do alone?"

"I can't give birth to a child by myself. There's the cord and all that!" Then, because Harald was looking at me as if I had said something unspeakable, I blushed.

"This is not a pressing problem," Stig said, pouring more imiak for Harald and himself. "We'll deal with it later."

Angry, I considered the months of fretting that lay ahead of me. Stig, like the Eskimos, lived in the moment, but I was a careful planner. The only really impulsive thing I'd done in my life was to go off and marry him, and now I would pay the price.

Semigaq and I talked of other things like her new kamiks, their tops brimming with the luxuriant mane hairs of the polar bear Stig had shot. I had suggested that he give that part of the pelt to her because she would appreciate it more than I would, and she had responded to the gift with a dark yellow birdskin shirt for him.

He was overjoyed with the shirt, saying, "It's a wonder Harald hasn't made her too much of a Dane to create one of these."

I told her what a marvel that shirt was. "I can't imagine fitting and sewing so many bird skins together."

"It wasn't so difficult," she said modestly.

I also couldn't understand why anyone would want to wear bird feathers next to their skin, but Stig said they were better insulation that way.

I had made cookies of a sort from melted blubber, flour and sugar, shaping them into animals with my fingers, and I put some on a plate for Nauja to offer our guests. They had baked over-hard.

Semigaq bit off an elephant's trunk with her powerful teeth and asked, "What creature is this?"

I told her, and she said, "We have none of them here."

"True. They live in hot countries where there is no snow and ice."

"Not in Denmark?"

"No," I said, "we have only cattle and horses."

"And pigs," she said. "Harald told me about the pigs you eat there. He misses eating pigs. I told him to send for some, and I would take care of them, but he says it's too cold for pigs here."

I wanted to say, "It's too cold for anything here," but I simply nodded.

When it was time for them to leave, they stood up and said their good-byes briefly, then pulled on their outer garments and went out quickly. At home people often stood in the open door, remembering things they forgot to say, but that was impossible here.

I remarked to Stig, "They say that the people you see on New Year's Day will be a big part of your life all year. We could have

168

done worse."

He laughed and said, "That's why I didn't invite Ugvigsakavsik."

"Who on earth is that?"

"A man whose nose is always running. When he comes to visit, he always offers to chew lumps of caribou tallow to fry the food, and it's considered rude to refuse him." Stig grinned at me as he finished the imiak in his tankard.

I expected to be sick, but the rising gorge re-settled, and I was happy to think the queasy part of my pregnancy might be over.

Stig meant to leave January 15 to catch the mail boat, but first he wanted to do some trapping near Cape York. I was worried about being left alone, but he assured me the meat supply and stove fuel were adequate.

"But what if you get caught in a terrible storm?"

"It won't be the first time. Cape York is the best place to be during a storm. There's a row of caves you can use for shelter."

A gale swept the snow from the ground around our house, and around noon we could see a faint reddish glow to the south. The sun still existed, Stig said, and it would be back.

In the meantime, the people of the settlement were suffering from *perlerorneq*, a kind of depression with a core of anger. Semagaq showed signs of it, and when I asked her about it, she said, "I am sad and sick of life. Others feel worse. They tear their clothes and slash at things with a knife. Some even run into the cold half-naked and eat dog shit."

"I may not be the happiest woman in the world at this moment," I said, "but I certainly can't say I'm sick of life. Mainly, I'm worried about Stig going off with the trappers."

"He has always done that," she reminded me, "and he has come to no harm. It is more dangerous later. A sudden thaw can make clothes wet and melt one's path."

"But what if a terrible snowstorm comes up before they reach those caves?"

"They cover themselves with skins and lie down. If they don't move, they can go without food longer."

"You don't have to worry," I said bitterly. "Harald stays in the store."

"Harald is not somebody's first husband."

Fearing I had said something unforgiveable, I apologized. I yearned to know what happened to the first husband, but I didn't dare to ask.

Stig told me Semigaq's first love had gone through the ice returning from a walrus hunt. Two of his sled dogs chewed through their traces and came home with the unspoken but unmistakeable news.

"Were the two dead babies she told me about his?"

"Only she knows that."

The wind blew fiercely the morning Stig left for Cape York with three Eskimos. I clung to him inside the house as long as I could, and then I hurriedly put on my anorak and went outside for a final farewell.

The dogs were barking, and Miuk was excited to be starting off to somewhere--anywhere. They hadn't been fed for two days, as they didn't run well on full stomachs, but they gulped their food down nearly whole, so it took a long time for it to digest. They couldn't chew efficiently because their teeth had been filed down. I thought this was a barbaric act, but Stig said it was necessary. With their teeth intact, they would eat their traces.

I turned from Stig quickly, adhering to the old superstition about the bad luck involved in watching a departing person until he or she was out of sight, and that's when I saw the two women standing below our house. They waited, holding bedrolls of hide. Stig turned the dogs and headed in their direction. I started to look away again, but curiosity got the better of me.

To my horror, they got on the sled, and off they all went. Stig hadn't mentioned taking women along, necessary as they were on such an expedition. He probably thought I would be jealous, and I was. The Eskimos thought nothing of lending their wives to other men for one reason or another, and since I was next to useless as an

Arctic wife, someone had to take my place.

I remembered the stories he told of men who offered him the favors of their wives and how he could not refuse without insulting them deeply. The women had nothing to say about it.

I couldn't bear it. I shouted Stig's name, and he came back to me.

"Why didn't you tell me about the women?"

He put his arm around me and said, "After I saw you working on my Christmas present, I didn't want to remind you that they can do some things you shouldn't have to attempt."

"Promise me you won't let them into your sleeping bag!"

"Alex, after you there can be no other woman."

"And what if their husbands are offended by your refusal?"

"The husbands know how it is with us. That was not part of the offer."

He kissed me again while the two women sat on the sledge and giggled. Then they were off, Miuk leading the pack with high-hearted energy. Again, I turned away quickly to avoid that ill-fated last look in the daytime dark of January.

While Stig was away, I concentrated on writing a letter to my parents. Knowing the mail boat was months away, I had put it off, and now I was sorry. I should have written a little bit at a time, capturing the excitement of my earliest impressions. Now that I was an old Arctic hand, it was too late for that.

What I wanted to do was unload all my worries and fears on *Mor*, but I couldn't allow myself to distress her. I knew that she prayed for me every day. She always had. I struggled with what I wanted to say for a long time. Writing paper was scarce in Thule, and it never occurred to me to bring some with me. I would decide what I wanted to say before setting anything down. I was writing with a lead pencil, as ink tended to solidify in this part of the world.

Nauja was fascinated by that pencil and wanted me to use it to draw something for her. I found a scrap of wrapping paper and sketched a smiling seal. Then she reached for the pencil and made its twin--almost. Her seal was sleeker and more authentic than mine.

At last I made a start on the letter. "Dear *Mor* and *Far*, This country is like nothing I have ever known. It has beauty, but it also has indifference. At home, I always felt I would be missed if I should die--that I would leave at least a little hole in my world. Here, I think my removal would go unnoticed--except by my husband.

"We are as much in love as newlyweds usually are, and Nauja is accepting me little by little. Her Danish is coming along very well, but I can't say as much for my Greenlandic."

I sighed and put the pencil down. It would be so easy to pour it all out on the paper--my homesickness, my morning sickness, my fear of bringing a helpless child into the hostile cold of this place-- but I simply couldn't distress my family with all that.

If I had known then what I knew now, would I have married Stig? The memory of his embraces, his voice, and the faded blue eyes that warmed when he looked at me told me that I would have had him no matter what.

Part of his charm stemmed from the unknown and unknowable things about him. Like Desdemona, I loved him for the dangers he had passed, but I wanted those dangers to be over. I wanted us warm and safe and together. Why did he have this primitive urge to answer the call of the North?

"Well, Nauja," I said, "are you hungry?"

She nodded, and I mixed some powdered milk with melted snow for her. She wrinkled her nose and refused it, and I felt a surge of impatience. How could a child grow up with strong bones without drinking milk? I was ready to scold when I remembered that generations of her mother's people had lived a milkless existence rather healthily.

We ate our seal meat with some crackers from the store, and then I tried to get her to brush her teeth. She giggled and used the brush on her hair, mashing some of my precious toothpaste into the wisps that flew about her face.

"No, no, Nauja, do it like this." I demonstrated with my own brush.

172

She laughed aloud but showed no willingness to follow my example.

"Well, in that case, I won't waste anymore toothpaste on you!" I tried to say it lightly, but she caught the reproach and the light went out of her eyes.

"I'm sorry!" I said, pulling her to me for a hug. "Since Papa is away, why don't you sleep with me tonight? We'll keep each other warm."

She brightened again and ran to bed, pulling off her anorak as she went. I captured a louse on her tea-colored shoulder, and she watched intently while I undressed more modestly within the tent of my nightgown. Just as I was straightening from preparing the blubber lamp for the night, I felt her small fingers on my back.

"Another louse!" she said triumphantly, grinding it between her front teeth.

"On me?"

"They like you, too."

I gave a startled laugh, and she joined me. Then we snuggled together under the hides. She was as comforting as the towel-wrapped flatirons Frederik and I used to take to bed in the winter.

"You smell nice," she said.

"Thank you." I could scarcely return the compliment. I wondered how long the wherewithal for smelling nice would last? When my cologne and talcum were gone, that would be that. Harald didn't stock such things at the store.

I wondered if I should try to teach Nauja a bedtime prayer, but before I could decide, she was asleep.

XXII

I seldom left the house while Stig was away. A quick trip to the meat racks or a dash to the far reaches of our "yard" to dump the necessary bucket were my only expeditions. I scraped frost from the window to look at the southern sky around noon and saw layers of deep violet, bruised purples and dense blues with a thread of brilliant gold. The days had lengthened since the winter solstice, but they remained dark, at least to my way of thinking. Stig had told me it was not dark as long as a person of normal sight could read print outdoors, and I tested that theory.

The book I picked up for the purpose was Charles Baudouin's book on Dr. Coue's method, *Self-mastery Through Conscious Autosuggestion.* We had talked about the book at our literary evenings, which prompted Claudine to give it to me as a farewell gift. I had been cross with her for burdening me with it at the Hekla sailing party, but now I was glad to have something--anything to read. "Every day in every way I'm getting better and better," I read while a gale blew snow into my face, and I wasn't sure whether I was reading it or just remembering what was there. I wasn't too sure about autosuggestion, either.

Nauja wanted a story, and I found myself telling her Hans Christian Andersen's tale about the shepherdess and the chimney sweep. I tried to define the occupations of the characters for her, and finding Arctic equivalents was impossible. I simply told her that the girl worked safely on the ground and the young man worked on top of houses.

"What does 'worked' mean?" she asked.

Again, I had to search for a definition. I told her, "It means doing things that have to be done. Harald works at the store, selling things to people. Semigaq chews hides to make them soft. That's work."

"Do you work?" she asked.

175

"I used to work in the shop where your papa bought me the seal necklace. Now, I just cook and clean. That's work."

She looked doubtful, and I despaired of making her understand, so I continued with the story. "So the shepherdess followed her chimneysweep to the rooftops, and when she looked out over the city, she said, 'This world is too big. I have followed you into the wide world. Now, if you really love me, you may follow me home again.'"

"So what happened then?"

"We don't really know, but I think he went home with her."

"Then did he work on the ground?"

"I suppose so."

She nodded and asked for my pencil. Then she found a page from an old newspaper and drew an igloo in the margin. She made a small figure far to the left and then drew another atop the curving dome.

"He didn't like it on the ground," she explained.

This story wasn't turning out the way I wanted it to, I thought. Casting Stig and myself in the title roles, I had arranged for him to return to my world with me. His world was too much for me--or too little, perhaps. I longed for civilization.

I got up from the table to feed the fire and cook some seal meat, and as I passed the wavy mirror above the wash stand, I looked at my reflection and said, "Every day in every way, I'm getting better and better!" Then I laughed. Better? My hair was lank, my body was swelling, and my hands were chapped and red. If Stig were here, I wouldn't feel so ugly. His eyes were a kinder mirror. I'd get no sympathy from Semigaq or any of the other women, either. To them, a fat body was an asset--a thing of beauty.

While the meat was boiling, I would sit down and work on my ice glossary. I wanted to surprise Stig with all I had learned about the stuff from listening to him and the others at the store.

"Please listen to me, Nauja, and tell me if I have learned my lessons about ice."

She picked up her doll and climbed onto a chair, fixing her eyes

176

on me gravely.

"Young ice is not strong enough to walk on," I began. "Old ice is from last year or maybe two or three years ago. A floe is a free-floating chunk of ice and lots of them make a pack. Does that sound right?"

She looked away from me and sang to her doll, obviously bored to death with my recitation. I continued doggedly.

"A field is a large mass of pack ice, and a floe is smaller than a field. A cake is smaller than a floe--the size of a piano, maybe."

Nauja's ears were much keener than mine, and I didn't know why she jumped down and ran to the window until I joined her there and saw a bare-chested man running down the path slashing the air with a knife.

"*Perlerorneq*," she said.

"He'll freeze to death out there!" I said, grabbing my anorak and opening the door to run after him. Once outside, I gasped with shock at the temperature and wondered what I could possibly do to help this crazy man. I should have picked up a hide to throw around him. I shouted to him, "Stop! Come inside and be warm!"

He stopped, turned and gave me a dazed look. The knife fell from his hand, and he let me lead him back to the house. In the lamplight, I could see he was a stranger.

"Nauja," I said. "I'll give him some tea, but what else should I do for him?"

"Sleep," she said.

The man began to wail and lament in Greenlandic. I draped a sealskin around his shoulders and offered him tea, which he dashed to the floor.

"What is he saying?"

"Living is no good," she reported, and it was shocking to hear such a message of despair from the lips of a child.

"Put on your anorak and mittens and bring Semigaq or Harald," I told her. "We need help with this man."

She quickly obeyed, and when the door closed after her, I was afraid. What was I doing alone with this maniac? He rolled his eyes, and sweat welled in the hollow of his throat. I wished for sleeping pills to give him, but how could I make him take them? Looking at the clock, I figured it would take at least fifteen minutes for Nauja to arrive at the store and bring the Kaarups back with her. What should I do in the meantime? Without really thinking, I started to sing, "There is a lovely land that proudly spreads her beeches--"

He threw his head back sharply, then focused his eyes on me for the first time. The wild glint faded and he shivered massively, clutching the sealskin around him.

"Would you like to lie down on the bed?" I asked, but he didn't seem to understand Danish.

I brought more tea, which he refused, and so I pulled up a chair and sat down facing him. I said slowly and, I hoped, hypnotically, "Every day in every way I'm getting better and better." He groaned, and I repeated the words over and over, praying that Nauja would hurry back with the Kaarups.

His eyes were starting roll again and I started to hum a tune that came to me from nowhere. It seemed to have a good effect on him, and as I repeated it over and over, I realized what it was--something that Mel had whistled tonelessly while we were shooting film on the ice cap--jerky, jazzy and maddening, now that I knew what it was, but I didn't dare stop.

I wanted to break down and cry. The image of Mel floating in his *imiak*-filled cask would not leave me, and now I was sure that *I* had *perlerorneq*. All the symptoms were there--the core of anger, the deep sadness and the urge to destroy something. I kicked at the shards of the cup the man had broken, and when he started to rise, I pushed him down again. I no longer had a concern for my own safety, and I was furious with him for breaking the cup. It was one of four that matched, and I couldn't replace it.

He stood again, taking quick, rasping breaths. The robe fell from his shoulders as he made a dash for the door.

"Go ahead!" I shouted, "Go out there and kill yourself!" I couldn't believe that I was saying such a thing, but the words came out of my mouth.

He had no chance to take my advice because Harald pushed through the door and caught his arms. Semigaq followed, holding Nauja by the hand.

"Are you all right?" Harald asked.

I burst into tears, and Nauja ran to me, patting me as high as she could reach. Touched by this amazing display of affection, I stopped crying and knelt to lift her.

"Who is this man?" I asked.

"His name is Tulimak," Harald said. "He comes from the far north to trap foxes near the bird cliffs. He and his wife and children are living in Patlok's house while they are here."

"Why didn't his wife come after him?"

"Because he was planning to trade her to Patlok," Harald said, wrapping Tulimak tightly in the sealskin. "I will take him back to her, and perhaps they will change their minds."

Harald bundled Tulimak out the door, and Semigaq stayed to have a cup of tea. I boiled some seal meat to go with it. We ate and drank silently in the soft glow of the blubber lamp, and Mel's jazzy tune played in my head.

"I don't understand how a man can trade his wife away," I finally said.

"Sometimes it is done to let others know what a prize he has."

"But she isn't his anymore, so what does he gain?"

"He is proud."

I clenched my fists and pounded my temples, maddened by this crazy culture, and Semigaq told me to smooth my soul for the sake of my unborn child.

"Sleep," she said, offering the all-purpose prescription of the Arctic.

I took her advice, curling my body around Nauja's for warmth. The fur robes slipped away from me, and I froze. The Greenlanders believe that condition provides the best dreams, and so it did. Stig was holding me, caressing me, speaking to me like a man who would not think of trading his wife.

His breath was warm in my ear as he said, *"Kasuta*

179

mardlulerpugut."

This was no dream. I clung to him, realizing Nauja was no longer in the bed, and when we had kissed until we were breathless, I asked, "What did you say to me?"

"You really must work harder on your Greenlandic," he said with mock severity. I'll say it for you in Danish. "Let us two melt into one."

We did, and my *perlerorneq* was cured immediately. Then we talked in low voices to avoid waking Nauja. His traps were full, he said, and he was fortunate enough to get a white pelt among the many blue skins. A storm had blown up as they approached Cape York, but they made it to one of the caves and waited it out in reasonable comfort. The women sang and told stories, enjoying a bit of leisure before they began to work on the fox skins.

"Did you keep your promise to me?"

"If I hadn't, could I love you this hard? I'm ready again if you are."

It was some time before I got around to telling him about Tulimak and making him promise never to trade me to another man.

"I doubt if I could," he said. "You're not fat enough."

"I'm getting that way very fast."

"But it's only temporary."

XXIII

Stig wanted *Mor* to have the white fox pelt to trim her winter coat, and I packed it in a box from the store wrapped in wrinkled paper and tied with some frayed cord. From the looks of the package, she'd never guess its rare contents. The fur was not snow-white; it was the color of crushed pearls, and I knew how much she would love it. I wrote a note to place inside the package telling her it was a much-belated Christmas gift. This notion necessitated finding something for *Far* and Frederik, and we decided on a knife with a narwhale tusk handle for my father and a pair of seal mittens for Frederik. The spiral of narwhale ivory was beautiful, and if *Far* was much too civilized to put a knife to practical use, he could use it as a letter opener. I could just see him slicing into envelopes with it at his desk in the bank.

I had revised my letter to my parents many times, and now it was ready to go--an energetic account of the months of our marriage that downplayed dangers and discomforts and dwelt on the exotic wonders of my new home. In it I praised Nauja to the skies and neglected to mention the strange times when she retreated within herself and seemed blind and deaf to all else.

Stig did not find these episodes disturbing. He said, "It's probably *qarrtsiluni.*"

I gave him a look of exasperation and asked, "Why do you even use words you know I can't understand?"

"So you'll learn. That word means waiting for something to break--as in the stillness of the artist searching for inspiration."

"What kind of an artist do you think she'll be? She certainly seems to have a flair for drawing."

"It might be that or it might be writing. Greenlanders don't understand fiction. Something is or it isn't. They do make fine poetry, however. They literally take a deep breath to snare inspiration."

"Remember Holger Petersen and his terrible Greenland poem?" I said.

"I should write to him and tell him to take a deep breath--sink into whatever that word is."

"*Qarrtsiluni.* By all means, if you know his address, write to him."

"I don't, but I could send it to Leif. Of course if I do that, I'll have to write a letter to Leif, too. I really don't have anything to say to him."

Stig raised his eyebrows. "Really? He'd be disappointed to know that."

"We were never more than friends."

"Poor fellow!"

I moved from my chair to Stig's lap, aware of my increased bulk but certain of his acceptance. My only concern was sharing him with two children when I was still childish enough to want all of him for myself.

"Take me with you to meet the mail sleds," I said.

"Are you sure you want to go? You'll find it quite uncomfortable."

"I'd rather be uncomfortable with you than comfortable without you," I said, "and I can always call on good, old Dr. Coue. You just keep telling yourself, `It'll soon be over.'"

I collected seal meat, frozen eggs and blubber for the trip, and as I put a box of sulphur matches into the packet, Stig said, "Thank God for those!" The dogs seemed to know they were going on a journey. Instead of sleeping in a ball with their tails over their noses, they were up and barking when we took Nauja to Semigaq and picked up the mail Harald was sending home.

I asked Semigaq about Tulimak, and she said, "He sleeps day and night, and he will soon be himself again."

I gave her a piece of costume jewelry, a *fleur-de-lis* on a neck chain, and she put it on with pleasure. In return, she gave me a new pair of seal mittens so supple that I could grasp things while wearing them.

Stig hugged Nauja and told her to be good for Semigaq, and I knelt to brush her wispy hair from her forehead and kiss it. I remembered that Greenlanders never say good-bye and avoided the word..

"Be careful," Semigaq said. "The ice has not had its sacrifice this year."

I didn't have a chance to ask Stig what she meant for some time. The dogs set up an awful clamor while he harnessed them, and once we were underway, I was preoccupied by the beauty of the mountains in what looked like daytime moonlight. Although we were a mile away, I could hear Harald's greeting to someone entering the store.

"My ears have never been this good before," I told Stig.

"They'll seem even better as we get farther from the settlement. We'll be able to hear dogs barking and an ax on wood ten to twelve miles away."

"Why?"

"No interference. Everything is reduced to the basics up here. Are you cold?"

"I hadn't thought about it, and I don't want to."

"Loosen your hood."

"Then I *will* freeze."

"If you don't, you'll get a ring of hoarfrost around your face."

I sighed and took off my mittens to untie the cord. Steam rose from my hands, dry as they were, and the cold was so biting that I pulled the mittens back on without getting the job done. Stig dealt with the knot for me while I held the dogs' traces, and the heat of his kiss sent a cloud of steam skyward. Steam was everywhere. Each dog left a fog tail, and my own breath obscured my view.

I could no longer feel my feet, so I forced them to move. The brightest light of the day was now gone, and the wind was coming up. I refused to admit, even to myself, that I was miserable. I wouldn't ask Stig how long it would be before we reached the shelter of the cave on Saunders Island, either. I was sure that Naika had never complained to him, and neither would I. *It'll soon be over, it'll soon be over*, I repeated in my mind.

He was trotting beside the sled now, and the exercise probably made him much warmer than I was.

"What was Semigaq saying about the ice's sacrifice?" I asked.

"It's nothing for you to worry about. The Greenlanders believe the ice demands a sacrifice every year, and since no one has broken through and died yet, that unhappy event is yet to come. They're always immensely relieved when it happens--to someone else."

"We're traveling on the bay right now, aren't we?"

"Yes, but you needn't worry. The dogs wouldn't be moving like this if the ice wouldn't hold us. They know. Stop breathing through your nose, Alex. Use your mouth."

I did as he said, and the frigid air hurt my teeth. *It'll be over soon, it'll be over soon.*

My sense of time had deteriorated since I came to Greenland. My watch stopped working shortly after Christmas with no hope of repair, and I had gotten out of the habit of checking the wind-up clock in the house. What did it matter? We ate when we were hungry and slept when we were tired.

My physical misery had put me into a trance by the time we arrived at the cave. It was dark inside, and I stumbled on something that rolled and sent me flying. Once Stig had a blubber fire going, I realized that the floor of the cave was littered with bones former occupants had left behind. I carefully collected them and put them into a pile.

I was ravenous--had been all through my pregnancy--and Stig told me to eat some of the frozen eggs while the seal meat was cooking.

The cave was fairly large. We brought the sled inside and the dogs, as well. Stig had to crack his whip whenever one of them ventured near the seal meat.

At last we were able to eat. It was so cold that the grease from the meat congealed on our faces and fingers, and the wind shifted, whirling snow through the opening into our laps.

"We must leave a piece of meat as an offering to the spirit of

184

the cave," Stig said.

"Do you really believe in that sort of thing?"

He considered, knitting his brow. "I hadn't really thought about it. I guess I believe in good manners."

I shivered and leaned into the warmth of his body. The wind howled, and I thought I saw a dark figure at the mouth of the cave. I nudged Stig and pointed, but he saw nothing.

"Maybe it was a *qivitoq*," he said, "a spirit man. If someone dies under the ice and they don't find the body, that person becomes a *qivitoq* who terrorizes the living. We carry whips to chase them away."

"You *do* believe in all these primitive things!"

"I believe in putting my whole life into the moment. It's impossible to act in the past or the future, so we have to do it now." He pulled off his anorak, his boots and his trousers, climbing into the large hide sleeping sack. "Will you join me, Madame?"

The thought of removing any of my clothing was unbearable, and I couldn't decide what to take off first. Boots, then trousers, I supposed. I could fling the top part of my costume out last. Before I retired, however, I had to urinate, and when I retreated to the far reaches of the cave, I realized others had used it for the same purpose. Our fire had thawed some of the amber ice here and released the stinging odor of ammonia.

Stig had dozed off while I was attending to my necessity, and I marveled at his ability to sleep instantly under any circumstances. My cold feet woke him, and he warmed me in every conceivable way.

It must have been the cold, the bringer of superior dreams. Stig and I were at Kilden in Aalborg on a sunny, summer day sitting at an outdoor table with glasses of wine. A gentle breeze teased the red tablecloths secured with metal clamps. A pram stood next to the table, and I reached out to rock it gently. This was our child, but I could not see its face or know its name.

When we woke, I had a fleeting memory of the dream, and I realized Nauja was not in it. Stig was quick to dress, and without

185

him, the sleeping bag was too cold for me. I shivered massively as I put on my cold clothes and waited for the blubber fire to get a good start.

"Stig, do you think Nauja would be happy in Denmark?"

"Some part of her might be--not all. I'm the same way, you know. I've gone native."

"I realize it's a bit late to be discussing such things, but are we going to spend the rest of our lives here?" Before he could answer, I quickly marshalled some reasons why we should not. "Don't you want a better education for Nauja--and for our other child?"

He looked at me quizzically. "Do you equate education with happiness?"

"Not necessarily, but--"

"We'd better pack up and be on our way. I'd hate to keep the mail sleds waiting." Once the sled and the dogs were outside, he returned to toss a piece of seal meat on the coals of our fire, and we were off.

At long last we came to Cape York, where the sparse houses seemed glued to the boulders along the shore. Smoke rose from the chimneys like signatures of civilization.

"Go up to that first house--the one with the red door--and introduce yourself," Stig said. "I need to talk to some people down at the shoreline."

I did as I was told, removing a mitten to pound on the door with a steaming hand. The woman who answered the door was a Greenlander, and she didn't smile until she heard me say Stig's name. Then she flung the door wide and pulled me inside.

What a blessed relief to come in out of the cold! I pulled off my mittens with fingers that wouldn't bend and gratefully accepted a steaming cup of tea. I was amazed to see a green plant growing in a pot on the window ledge. My hostess had been sewing when I knocked, and now she went on with it, looking up to smile at me occasionally.

We sat like that for some time, and I was feeling almost human when the front door burst open and several men brought Stig inside.

186

His clothes were soaked, and one arm hung uselessly at his side.

Everyone was speaking at once in Greenlandic, and I had no idea what was going on. The woman of the house tore the wet clothing from him and rubbed him vigorously with a towel while one of the men found other clothes for him to put on.

"I slipped on a boulder, came down on my arm and took a little dip in the bay," Stig spoke with effort. "I heard something snap."

"What are we going to do? Is there a doctor here?"

Stig spoke to the woman in Greenlandic, and she disappeared, returning with a soaked sealskin. The bigger of the two men felt Stig's arm carefully, felt his companion's healthy arm, and then set the fracture. Stig groaned as the bones went back in place and the wet sealskin was wrapped tightly around the arm.

"How are we going to meet the mail sleds and get home?" I asked.

"You'll have to drive," Stig said.

We made it to the rendezvous point, and as I watched the mail sleds disappear, I knew my family would never realize what went into the delivery of their packages and letters. I also had a feeling that the self I was sending to them would not be the same the next time they heard from me.

Returning to Cape York, we stayed for a few days--until Stig's arm stopped paining him so severely. Then we retraced our route, spending another night in the cave on Saunders Island. The meat left for the spirit of the cave had been consumed by someone, and new bones had been scattered about for me to clean up.

I had to help Stig with his clothes, and since the broken arm was his right, he even had trouble cutting his food. He made a joke of it, saying, "At least we have food that requires cutting! I've had to eat dog traces and mittens when things were really bad, and you can eat those with *no* hands!"

I forgot about being miserable and muttering Dr. Coue-isms to concentrate on driving the dogs. I spoke to Miuk with what I hoped was authority and cracked the whip for emphasis. He decided to indulge me and took off with an excited bark.

Longing for the relative comforts of home, I couldn't wait to get there. We could hear the voices and foot-stamping in the settlement before we could see the houses, and when our own home came into view, I was puzzled. Smoke was coming from the chimney. Who could be lighting a fire in our absence?

"Look, Stig," I said, "do you think Semigaq came over to warm the place up for us?"

"That would be a kindness," he said, grimacing with pain as he knocked his arm into the sled frame.

I think he knew what was happening, but he didn't want to tell me just then. We both were tired and chilled, and he was in pain.

XXIV

Stig got off the sled and started to unhitch the dogs with his left hand, but I told him to go inside. I would do it. He declined my offer, suggesting that I carry the bedding and the remains of our food supply into the house. Arms piled high, I couldn't manage the latch, and I kicked at the door.

It opened narrowly, and I pushed inside, shocked at coming face-to-face with Tulimak. He smiled broadly. His wife and two small boys sat on our bed, legs stretched out in front of them, and they also smiled.

I dropped my burden in a corner of the room and looked around. The strangest smell imaginable filled the house, and I could see steam rising from a huge kettle on the stove. The contents were a mystery until my eyes fell on the pile of slashed tin cans behind the stove. The almost unbelievable incident Stig had told me about had happened again. Our guests had knifed open all our canned goods, creating a hash of pears, corned beef, mussels, beans, tomatoes, sardines, condensed milk and some unidentifiable meat. The very thought of the mixture was sickening. I pulled up my hood and went out to bring in another load, not saying a word to the unwelcome guests.

"Stig, it's Tulimak, the *perlerorneq* case. He's in there with his family, and they're cooking all our canned stuff."

Stig finished unhooking the last dog and straightened with a grimace. "Poor Alex! I'm afraid we'll have to offer Arctic hospitality whether we like it or not. Strangers who come to the settlement in the winter have the right to move in with anyone they please."

"Why didn't they stay where they were--with Patlok?"

"We may find out--or we may not. Let's go in."

Chilled to the bone and exhausted, I was in no mood to be hospitable, but Stig greeted the interlopers in Greenlandic and smiled at them while I helped him out of his outer garments.

I was wishing I had stayed at home to keep this from happening, but if I had, how would Stig have made it back with his broken arm?

"Alex," he said, "Tulimak's wife is Kasaluk and the boys are Otoniaq and Upik. He has decided not to trade her to Patlok, and that's why they had to move. Since we weren't using our house, they came here."

"Haven't you Arctic types ever heard of door locks?" My voice carried a heavy load of anger, and the visiting quartet regarded me watchfully.

"Up here, an open door might be the difference between life and death," Stig said.

Kasaluk had, at least, melted snow for tea water, and I calmed myself by putting it on to boil and measuring the tea. I was surprised that she hadn't thrown the oolong into the pot as well.

I found plates and dished up the mess in the pot for everyone but myself. Watching them eat with apparent relish, I grew hungrier by the moment, and when Stig said, "Try some of this . It's not bad," I fished out a combination I could bear to contemplate and took a bite. At least it was hot.

Then I considered how long it would be until we could replace the cans of food so profligately pitched into the pot. The baby would be born before a supply ship would reach us. I'd been counting on that condensed milk in case my own was insufficient for the infant. I felt a welling of tears and blinked angrily.

"I'll go over to the Kaarups and pick up Nauja," I offered, eager to escape the invaders.

The wind had come up, shooting icy needles at my face, and I stumbled along behind the shield of my bent arm. Sled dogs barked at me, the fur edge of my hood dampened by my breath chafed my chin, and the short distance to the store seemed like miles. A feeble light shone from the Kaarups' living quarters, and I ran toward it, one hand reaching for the door latch.

Harald looked up from his ledger as I fell inside and stamped my kamiks on the threshold.

"You're back, are you?"

I told him Stig had broken his arm and I had driven the dogs from Cape York.

"Not bad for a city girl from Denmark. I'll call Semigaq."

"Wait--I want to tell you something first.

His brows shot up. "Tulimak, I suppose?"

"Yes. You knew?"

"There isn't much I don't know around here."

"I can't live with those people, Harald. How can we get rid of them?"

"Not much you can do," he said. "Just be patient. Something is about to happen."

"Something already *has* happened. They opened all our cans and cooked up a horrible mess."

"They probably put something back, too. Have you checked your meat rack?"

"No, but it's not a fair trade."

Harald ducked below the counter and brought up two tins of the awful stew Denmark had exported to Germany to feed the troops early in the war. "You're welcome to these," he said.

"You're very kind, but no thank you. I hope Nauja wasn't too much trouble for Semigaq."

"She's never any trouble, but about four days ago she got real restless. She ran to look out the window every few minutes and whispered to her doll about Papa, Semigaq said."

"Four days? That was when we got to Cape York and Stig fell. Do you think she had some way of knowing?"

Harald shook his head. "You never know about these people. I'll get her for you now."

Nauja came racing from the living quarters, followed by Semigaq. Her face fell when she saw it was me rather than her papa, but still she came to me and let me help her into her anorak.

Somehow I couldn't talk about my unwelcome guests to Semigaq. It would be an insult to her people. Instead, I gave her the details of Stig's accident and bragged about how well I handled the dogs.

I hated to leave the store and the Kaarups, but Nauja and I faced into the wind and trudged home. Perversely, the wind had shifted, attacking my face both coming and going.

"We have company, Nauja," I said. "Visitors with two little boys."

"Otoniaq and Upik?"

"Yes. How did you know?"

"They came to the store, and we played with bull-roarers."

"What's a bull-roarer?"

"A piece of bone with little teeth. It has a string, and it makes a big noise when you do like this--" she swung her hand rapidly above her head.

As soon as we got in the house, the boys ran to greet Nauja, whirling their bull-roarers with great enthusiasm. I had to admit the humming sound was quite pleasant, if anything could be pleasant under the circumstances. Stig kissed his daughter and returned to a Greenlandic conversation with Tulimak. He looked exhausted, and I wondered how we would manage to retire with Kasaluk sitting on our bed. When other women came to visit, they were hot in our house and stripped down to little more than foxskin panties. This one's face gleamed with sweat, but she still wore her anorak.

Nauja shrieked as the bull-roarer flew from Upik's hand and struck her in the temple. The sharp, little teeth drew blood, and as I rushed to her aid, I thought how dangerously close the projectile had come to her eye. Just one more reason to resent these people.

Kasaluk turned a mild gaze on her son, offering no reproof, and the boy's father was ignoring the whole matter. Nauja didn't cry, but her lip quivered as her small fingers felt the wound and smeared blood. Stig opened his arms to her and went on with his conversation.

I turned abruptly and went to the kitchen, pushing the disastrous mixture on the stove away from the hottest burners. Tulimak's family would have to stay all winter to eat it up, but I couldn't bring

192

myself to throw it out.

Just then I heard three heavy sounds like drumbeats and went to the window. The light was too dim for indentification, but a man stood on our path holding a drum and a large bone for beating it.

"Stig," I said. "Someone is out there. Shall I ask him in?"

"Patlok," Tulimak said, and it seemed to me that he looked frightened.

"Yes, Alex, tell him to come in and bring his *ayayut*."

"His what?"

"It's a drum made of wood and caribou stomach. He'll have people with him, so invite them in, too."

"Maybe you'd better do it. I don't know what's going on, and I might be misunderstood."

Stig went to the door and motioned with his left hand. Patlok entered, shaking his hood off and firmly grasping the drum by its handle. Eight other men from the settlement followed him, which meant that the door stayed open a long time. The room chilled quickly. Even so, Patlok and several of the others bared their bodies to the waist and sat down on the floor. The only place for me was on the bed beside Kasaluk, and I quickly sat down.

Patlok gave the drum to another man, who struck it three times before Patlok began to sing and sway, keeping the continuing three-beat rhythm. Stig came to sit beside me and translate.

"He says Tulimak makes promises he won't keep."

After several repetitions of that wording, the whole group joined in a refrain, "Ay-ay-ay-aya!" Then Tulimak sang and danced, using even more motion to the drumbeat. Stig told me Tulimak accused Patlok of borrowing his wife without invitation, forcing her husband to beat her.

Patlok scowled at the accusation, and he refused to join in the refrain, saving his energy for his next salvo. By this time, I was singing the refrain in my head, "Ay-ay-ay-aya!"

Patlok's eyes glittered as he hopped up and down and made another singing accusation--if it could be called singing. The tune had a three-note range, and the tempo was slow and monotonous.

"He says Tulimak copulates with dogs," Stig reported.

"What does Kasaluk think of all this?" I whispered. "And the children?"

Stig's answer was drowned in the refrain, and I was amazed to see the whole family join in the "Ay-ay-ay-aya!"

Tulimak's answering insult concerned Patlok's neglect of his young son. Stig explained, "He says Patlok knows all about loving dogs and loves them better than he loved his dead wife."

The drum beats became more insistent, the men removed more clothing, and the pitch of the singing rose higher and higher. Finally Patlok grabbed the bone drumstick and shook it in Tulimak's face, and whatever he said ended in a shriek. The men made low sounds of amusement that built into guffaws, and Tulimak had the look of a man who has been doused with a bucket of cold water. He grabbed his anorak, spoke sharply to his wife, and ran outside, leaving her to follow with the children.

When they were gone, Patlok and his friends continued to laugh and slap each other on the back. Stig brought out some tobacco he kept for guests and some cheap Dutch pipes. He didn't join them in the smoke, and I remembered him saying he'd rather not have a habit that was sometimes impossible to indulge in the Arctic.

I served them bowls of the awful mess in the kitchen, which they seemed to appreciate. Eventually, they went home, leaving us in a state of exhaustion.

"Why did Tulimak go?" I asked.

"Because they laughed at him. No Greenlander can stand that."

"What was so funny?

"Patlok said Tulimak was afraid to trade his wife and have his secret known."

"And what secret is that?"

"She may look beautifully plump, but it's really wadded-up sweaters under her clothes, and she holds lumps of blubber in her cheeks to make them puff out. Patlok says he knows all this and it doesn't matter; he needs a woman only to chew skins and tend the fox traps, but he says Tulimak married for lust, and he was fooled."

"Where do you think they've gone?"

"Someplace where no one knows them, and it won't be easy. Stories like this travel fast."

I began to feel sorry about turning them out in the night. They could have departed in the morning more comfortably. But what Greenlander knew anything about comfort? They simply rose above misery. I wondered if Dr. Coué's techniques could have reached this wilderness before me?

We got ready for bed, and I told Stig I regretted his broken arm for many reasons, among them the curtailment of lovemaking.

"Why should that be?" He stretched out on his back and pulled me over him with his strong left arm.

I started to wonder if he had made love this way with Naika and then was so taken out of myself that I wondered about nothing.

"Even when your arm heals, let's keep this in our repertory," I said. "Someday when they ask me how I was able to endure the Far North, I'll have a quick, easy answer."

"Such as?"

"Sex."

As I drifted to sleep, I re-lived the sense of power I felt while driving the dogs and the marvel of escaping what Claudine called "the missionary position." It occurred to me that I was very close to being a real New Woman.

XXV

We had a calendar on the wall next to our bed, and I marked off the days of January. I was waiting for the sun, waiting for some measure of comfort, waiting for the more remote birth of our child. I had one book that I hadn't read before, Rafael Sabatini's *Scaramouche,* which came out just before we left, and I rationed myself to three pages a day--scarcely enough to let me immerse myself in Brittany.

I found that I was hungry for landscape, something I'd never relished in literature before, and Sabatini scarcely mentioned it in his rush to get on with the adventure. And when I read the line, "My dear ingenuous Philippe, dog doesn't eat dog," I snorted.

Stig looked up from his own reading with a raised eyebrow, and I read the line aloud, adding, "That's what *he* thinks."

Stig said, "Maybe I tell you too much about life up here--more than you can bear. I know you think it's barbaric that a crippled dog is killed and fed to the others--or even to the humans, if necessary, but we all do what we must to survive."

"Survival would be much easier almost anywhere else in the world. Why do you stay here?"

"Something pulls me northward. There's a touch of eternity here--don't you feel it?

"I'll worry about eternity later. Right now, I'd just like to fill a bathtub to the brim and have a long, warm soak. Stig, will we ever go back to Denmark?"

"Of course we will. Your parents will want to see their grandchild."

He never spoke of his own family, except for the ancestor who adventured with Bering, and I had been reluctant to ask about his relatives. Now I felt that I must. "Stig, do you have anyone--I mean, you never--"

He sighed deeply and said, "I knew it was too good to be true."

"What do you mean?"

" I thought I was complete just as I stand as far as you were concerned, but I guess not. When I came to Greenland, I was accepted as I was. Nobody expected me to be anything else. When I go back to Denmark, I remember that my parents died disappointed in me. I never had a chance to prove that I was doing someing important--mapping the ice cap, adding to the information we have about the world. They wanted me to be a doctor, and I tried, but I just couldn't do it--not after what happened to Hans Bronlund."

"Who was he?"

"A poor devil who got drunk and fell down on the streetcar tracks. I was an interne at the time, and he was the bloodiest mess I'd ever seen. We patched him up as well as we could, and after two months in the hospital, he was ready to go home. We even had a little farewell party for him. He thanked us, walked out the door and got hit by another streetcar. Died instantly."

"How horrible!"

"How senseless, was my thought. No matter how hard you try, life is a game of Russian roulette. I went down to the docks and signed on as a stoker on an old tub sailing for Greenland."

I dropped the book I had been holding and went to embrace Stig, taking care not to touch his broken arm. Knowing about his medical training gave me a great lift. When my time came, surely he could help with the birth. I was almost afraid to ask if he had helped Naika give birth to Nauja, but I got the words out.

"She refused my help," he said. "I could see that she was in labor, but she told me to go down and visit with Harald. She wanted to be alone, and she was quite fierce about it. She had dug a hole in that space beside the stove where we have a dirt floor and put boxes on either side to support her arms. I looked through the window and saw her kneeling above the hole. I managed to stay away for an hour, and when I came back, Nauja was in her arms."

Hearing her name, the child looked at us expectantly. Stig smiled at her and said, "We were talking about you, not to you,

Sweetheart."

Nauja went back to her dolls, which had increased in number since her stay with Semigaq, and the soft light of the blubber lamp played over our charming domestic scene.

I had a burning desire to go to the kitchen and search for the spot where Naika had deposited her child, but I sat still, clasping my hands tightly. No child of mine would be born into a hole.

"Have your parents been gone for a long time?" I asked Stig.

"They died within a week of each other in 1918--Spanish influenza."

I was speechless with pity. Everyone Stig loved best had been taken by the same enemy--one the profession he had rejected was powerless against. At least he had no cause for guilt. He couldn't have saved them.

"No brothers or sisters?"

He shook his head. "All their hopes were in me."

"Did they know about Nauja?"

"The mail came too late." He rose and looked out the window. "The aurora is putting on quite a show out there. Shall we have a look?"

Nauja ran for her anorak and mittens while I helped Stig into his coat and put on my own outdoor gear. The dogs barked loudly, thinking we planned to take the sled, and Stig shouted for them to be still. Miuk's distinctive bark was the last one silenced.

My nostrils seemed to close against the intense cold, and I breathed through my mouth, watching the spectacle in the sky through a gauze of steaming breath.

Pale green and rose curtains of light undulated, folding back on themselves in huge S-curves. They made the whistling, crackling sound of a flag waving in a high wind. Unborn children at play, the Eskimos believed. I could almost feel this evanescent beauty moving in my body.

When we came inside and sat drinking tea, I did feel it. The child in my womb moved. My eyes widened, and my almost-doctor husband knew. He put down his cup and came to kneel beside my chair, pressing his cheek against my belly.

"I love you so much, Alex--both of you."

"Does this tell you when it will be?" I asked, "I haven't known."

"Sometime in May."

"That's when we met--sometime in May."

February brought raging gales, and the intense cold yielded to hot spells that thawed igloos and opened stretches of water on North Star Bay. Stig pointed out the water sky--black fog high in the air indicating open water.

Animals were too lean to be worth hunting, and we were glad for the seal meat Tulimak had left on the racks to replace the late, lamented canned goods. The dogs had a sexual awakening, and Stig allowed Miuk to service any bitch in heat before the other males had a chance. One of the oldest dogs died trying to copulate, and Stig cut up the carcass to feed to the others. He was nearly ambidextrous, but still it was a hard job for a man with one good arm, and I couldn't bring myself to help.

Watching this grim feast, I muttered, "So much for you, Andre-Louis Moreau!"

On the seventeenth day of February, we climbed up the mountain overlooking North Star Bay and prepared to welcome the return of the sun. The whole settlement was there, gathered around a blubber fire, and several lookouts were posted to shout the news of the first rays of light.

"Here we go!" Stig said.

We hurried to the summit, where we caught the full force of the wind, and I was astounded to see the Eskimos pull their hoods from their heads, throw down their mittens and raise their hands to the sky. Stig and Nauja did the same.

"Are you all crazy?" I said. "It must be forty below zero!"

"This is the traditional welcome to the sun," Stig said. "It only takes a minute."

I sighed in exasperation and threw back my hood, then struggled out of my mittens and raised my arms like some strange, prehistoric creature. To my surprise, I didn't feel the cold. I was too busy marveling at the rosy-mauve shades of the ice and snow. They didn't look cold. Then I shivered massively and the baby moved in response. I grabbed Stig's bare hand and positioned it to let him share the moment.

"He likes the first sunrise of the year," Stig said.

"He?"

"Whoever," he amended. "This will be Nauja's fifth sun ritual." He smoothed his daughter's hair and replaced her hood, handing her her mittens.

"How long do we stay up here?" I asked.

"Not long. The first day of sunlight is just a few minutes long. In fact, it's almost sunset right now."

I laughed and said, "Stop the clock! My life is going by too fast!"

When we got home, I fastened the silver seals around my neck and opened the throat of my shirt to let them show.

"What's the occasion?" Stig asked.

"I'm celebrating light--light and life."

XXVI

On the first day of March I felt an intense longing for my homeland that surprised me. Recalling the hummocks of rust-colored heather and the woods that were blue-gray masses in the distance, I remembered how melancholy they seemed when we walked along a sandy road edged with moss, Frederik and I. What did I know of bleakness then?

The Arctic had its own signs of life. Polar bears were giving birth, and the males would eat their young, given half a chance. The ferocious mothers fought off such cannibalism--almost always.

"Do you suppose the mother bear ever forgives her mate for eating their child?" I asked Stig.

"They're not terribly emotional. They live together only as long as she's in heat, which is about a month. After that, who knows? They may not remember each other at all."

"I'm glad we're not bears."

Stig laughed and picked up the blubber lamp. "Enjoy this while you can. The lamps are put away March 21."

"Whatever for?"

"To conserve oil. We'll soon have a two-hour twilight, and we won't need lamps."

"What other rites of Spring should I know about?" I asked sarcastically.

"The whales will be starting north, the lemmings are giving birth, and the ptarmigan will soon arrive."

"Semigaq says ptarmigan tastes terrible."

"When you're hungry, you can't be choosy," he said, "and they're relatively easy to catch. I'm going to bring Miuk in and work on his feet."

The lead dog started to pant almost the moment he came through the door, and he whined when Stig held his paw while I rubbed grease on the cracked pads. We worked through all the dogs, and Stig said, "If I had two good arms, I could have dug the snow

203

out of their toes, but they had to do it themselves, and they're gnawed bloody."

It was time to change the bait in the fox traps, and since Stig couldn't manage it alone, I had to go with him. Nauja would stay with the Kaarups. We set out in a terrible gale that blew the snow into high drifts and carried a canvas tent for shelter.

The first cluster of traps had one missing, and Stig said a bear probably was wearing it as a bracelet. He baited the others with rotten seal meat and went on. By now, Stig's arm was past the painful stage, and he drove one-handed, warning me to be ready to take over when he asked.

Seeing a smoking patch of open water near the shore of North Star Bay, he stopped and baited a fish hook. The dogs, who seemed to smell a thaw, wouldn't go close to the bay, and Stig left me holding them while he lowered his hook. I watched him from a distance and knew I would recognize him anywhere and at any distance by the way he held the body that was so dear to me. His hood came forward to hide his face and his garments were shapeless, but the thrust of a thigh as he went down on one knee and the tilt of his torso were distinctive. He had learned how to live in the moment, and it showed.

The dogs sent up foggy balloons of breath, and even though it was overcast, the light was strong enough to make me wish for my sunglasses of slit bone. Stig had told me about snowblindness--first the sensation of grains of sand in your eyes, then shooting pains. What if I went snowblind and had to tie a scarf over my eyes for three days? I closed my eyes and waited for what seemed like forever.

"Ha! Got one!" Stig yelled.

"Congratulations!" I yelled back, eyes still closed.

When he got back to me, he assured me that I was not going snowblind and started to gut the fish.

"I love it when we switch from rotten to fresh," he said.

Having refused all rotten fish, I was glad to have any at all, and when he got a blubber fire going, I relished the sizzle and aroma

204

from the small iron spider. I was sure I could eat the whole thing by myself.

We sat down on the sled and fended the dogs off while we ate, then set off for the next bunch of traps. The snow was wet enough to pack in the dogs' paws, and it was my job to dislodge it with the handle of an old fork. It occurred to me that I was much braver about these beasts than I had been in the beginning. Things might have been different if we still had Minik with his wild, blue eyes. I had the feeling that he had been more than a dog--a human of other than good intentions transformed into a canine. Such a thought warned me that I was going native in this place, but maybe one had to do that to survive.

At the next traps we found two dead foxes. They had been there for some time, frozen in their death agony, and Stig said they could stay like that for years without deteriorating "like the dead explorers they've found. They may have died more than a century ago, but to look at them, you'd think it happened this morning. See what I mean about eternity?"

"What about `dust to dust' and `ashes to ashes'?"

"We have precious little of either up here." He removed the trap from the neck of one fox and started to free the other one, then winced and said, "Can you get this one out? The arm is acting up."

I looked down at the poor beast and was sickened. The fox had nearly chewed off its own leg in the struggle to be free. I took a deep breath and grasped the jaws of the trap, but I couldn't move them.

Stig pulled out his hunting knife and hacked at the leg clumsily with his left hand until it was severed. He put the carcasses on the sled, and I wondered how I could bear to ride with them. Seeing my reluctance, he covered them with a hide.

My fur trousers were now so tight that I had trouble lowering and pulling them up in time of need. I put off my necessities as long as I could, but finally I would have to steel myself and expose my body to the frigid air while Stig kept the dogs from rushing at me and knocking me over. As I took care of this dreadful business, I thought of the restroom in Copenhagen's Hotel Terminus--roomy and warm with a huge towel roller. The baby gave me a sharp poke, as if to protest a draft.

I returned to the sled with watering eyes and a runny nose and told Stig, "If you can love me after watching that, the gates of hell can't part us!"

"I can and I will."

We pitched our tent with the slope to the east, and Stig explained, "If the rising sun hits the canvas broadside, we won't be showered with hoarfroast when we wake up in the morning."

I shivered massively, saying, "I thought tents were for summer."

"They are, but I'm in no shape to build an igloo, so canvas will have to do."

We had just settled in and were making good use of the heat produced by passion when we heard shouts of greeting. We hastily adjusted our clothing and opened the tent flap to see a dog team and three Greenlanders approaching.

"Is it anyone you know?" I asked.

"It's someone we both know. Kullabak and two of her boys."

I ran toward her, calling her name joyously, and she held out her arms to me. When we broke the embrace to look at each other with delight, she opened the neck of her anorak to show me the amber pendant I'd given her. I pointed to my belly to indicate what her amulet had done for me, and even in the excitement of the moment, I realized my thought had been *for* me rather than *to* me.

"One is happy to see you again," she said. "These are my sons, Awala and Krisuk."

I smiled and nodded, not knowing how much Danish--if any-- they spoke. Our dogs and their dogs were barking in conversation, and I couldn't hear what the young men were saying to Stig.

Kullabak said, "Your man has a bad arm?"

"Yes, he fell and broke it in Cape York."

"My sons will build an igloo big enough for all of us," she said, "and I will cook seal meat."

I suppressed a sigh at the thought of more seal meat, but

Kullabak caught my expression.

"Soon the walruses will come back," she said. "Then we will have something else to eat."

I watched her start a blubber fire and fill an iron pot with snow. Her hands were cracked and darkened, but they moved with a speed and efficiency that put my Arctic housekeeping efforts to shame.

"What brings you this way?" I asked. "You are very far from home, aren't you?"

A look of deep sadness crossed her face like a cloud obscuring the sun. "The *angakok* had a vision about my brother. He saw Pualu pulled down under the water with the whales, and they would not let him come up. We came to see."

I questioned her with my eyes, unwilling to do so with words, and she gave me an answer in a dulled voice.

"No one was alive to tell what happened," she said. "Pualu must have gone seal hunting and broken through the ice. His wife and children waited many weeks. When the food was gone, they ate mittens and kamiks, and finally there was nothing. We found them holding each other in death."

I put my arms around her in wordless sympathy. How could such a thing happen in modern times?

Finally, I said, "Kullabak, don't you sometimes wish you were back in Denmark? No one ever starves there."

"The body may not starve, but somebody's self is not the same there. This is one's place, and this is where one should be."

Hearing this, I felt a rush of tears. I knew I could never be at home in Greenland, and Stig could never be at home anyplace else.

Stig was helping Awala and Krisuk as much as he could, but he couldn't manage the snow knife, a broad-bladed saw used to cut the wedge-shaped blocks of snow.

I offered to help, but he told me this was a man's job. A woman built an igloo only to save her life.

They worked fast. The fifteen foundation blocks were set in the base circle in no time at all, and then they cut smaller blocks for the rising walls. Awala climbed over the base circle to the inside, and

Krisuk handed him the blocks, which he set up to the last circle of five. Stig was taller, so he hoisted the block for the top hole with his strong left arm. A hole was bored in it to let the warm air out.

Kullabak motioned to me and showed me how to tighten the cracks between the blocks with snow. In the meantime, Awala cut a low arch for an entrance hole and came out to help his brother build an entrance tunnel. Finally, all of us threw snow over the whole structure. The whole process had taken about an hour.

I remembered my first night in Copenhagen; checking into the Terminus Hotel until I could find a place to stay. The room was huge, and the bath towel was the size of a bed sheet. At the time, I never dreamed I would be building my own hotel in a frozen wasteland like this.

Kullabak took skins and cooking equipment from their sled and went inside to set up housekeeping. I crawled after her, still dreaming of a Copenhagen bathroom where one could fill the tub with hot water and enjoy a luxurious soak.

She started a blubber fire inside with moss, and because the melted snow already was hot from the outside fire, the pot was soon ready for the seal meat.

She asked me what happened to the sick boy after we took him back to Holsteinsborg.

"He died of pneumonia, and they sent him home in a cask of *imiak*. I have nightmares about that even yet!"

"Somebody will make a song for him, and then he will leave your dreams," she said.

She sat very still, and I remembered Stig's explanation of *qarrtsiluni*, the stillness while waiting for something to burst. Finally, she took an empty cooking pot into her lap and beat out a rhythm.

"Eyya-eya!
"The boy was blameless as the blue sky,
"He fell, he cried,
"He could not breathe,
"But he will never thirst

208

"In the lights in the sky,
"Where he is happy.
"Eyya-eya!"

She sang it again, and I joined in at the refrain, feeling comforted. I wished Mel's mother could hear Kullabak's song and know he was happy in the brilliant heart of the aurora, but she probably couldn't believe it. I was amazed to discover that I did. What kind of a pagan was I becoming?

Stig and I abandoned our tent to join our friends in the igloo, and I was amazed at how cozy an ice palace could be. Hides on the platform and attached to one wall kept us from sitting and leaning on hard snow and ice, and smoke from the blubber fire went straight up and out the hole in the center block. Soon it was warm enough for the others to take some clothes off, but I kept mine on.

We ate our seal meat and talked. Stig commiserated with them about the fate of Pualu and his family, and Kullabak said the *angagok* had said something more, but it had not yet come to pass.

"Surely your family doesn't deserve more sorrow," Stig said.

"One does not think it is for us," Kullabak said. "He saw a big bird--bigger than any he had ever seen. It fell from the sky and spit out men."

"An airplane?" I whispered to Stig.

"Perhaps," he said. "I've never seen one."

"I have," I said proudly. "Leif took me to a flying field, and we watched one go up and come down. It had double wings of cloth and looked like a big, clumsy moth. He said we'd have a Danish airline sometime in 1922, and he needed to be up on such things. The pilot offered to take us up, but I wouldn't go, and Leif made fun of me."

Stig laughed and said, "Too bad he can't see you now. I think you're as brave as a woman ever needs to be."

That remark obscurely offended me, but I shrugged it off. Kullabak had scooped some soot from the outside of the cooking pot and was rubbing it under my eyes, on my lids and on each side of my nose.

"What's that for?" I asked.

"It protects you from snowblindness," Stig said.

"Wish I had a mirror."

"I'll be your mirror," he said. "It gives you a gamin look."

Something else it gave me was a warm feeling of being mothered. Kullabak's touch, despite her roughened hands, was so much like *Mor's*.

We slept chastely that night, being in company, but Stig said our friends would have thought nothing of it if we had chosen to make love.

In the morning, we packed up and took turns using the igloo for a latrine before abandoning it. I was the first, and it was a lovely luxury to attend to this necessity out of the wind and away from the dogs.

Both parties headed for home, and when I turned to look at Kullabak and her sons for the last time, I had to avert my eyes quickly to avoid watching them out of sight. Their dogs were racing, carrying them away so quickly that they were tiny specks on the horizon all too soon.

Stig was quiet for many miles, and when I asked him what he was thinking about, he said, "Kullabak's *angakok*. It's good to have a little warning, even if you don't know what it's all about."

"You don't really believe in such things, do you?"

He shrugged and yelled, "Pick it up, Miuk! We need a cup of tea."

When we finally did get home, he didn't come into the house. He was off for the store, carrying the sad news about Pualu's family to the settlement. For the hundredth time, I thought how wonderful it would be to have a telephone.

XXVII

April was the month of courtship in the Arctic. The eider-drake pursued the duck, swimming after her with his head thrust up and back. "Ah-oo," he called, and she answered with a low, hoarse, "Orr-orr." As we watched them, Stig mimicked the call of the drake, and I answered as well as I could. Nauja laughed.

The seabirds were returning to the bird cliff on Saunders Island, auks and gulls creating a snowstorm of feathers, and the walruses sunned themselves on ice thin enough to discourage human pursuit--most of the time. Patlok had regained a lost confidence when he banished Tulimak, and he slithered onto the dangerous surface on his belly, rising from that awkward position to throw a deadly harpoon. Holding the rope fastened to his weapon, he made his way toward safety in the same manner, but the ice gave way. The immense weight of the walrus kept him from sinking, and the men at the shoreline pulled him out.

He helped pull the huge carcass in, not even noticing that he was soaked until the others threw him down and rolled him in the snow to absorb the moisture. The women had come down with their flensing knives, and they went to work immediately on the bleeding beast with tusks as long as a man's arm.

"Should I be helping?" I asked Stig.

"They don't really expect it."

"You helped them pull it in, even with a broken arm."

"That's different."

I would have welcomed some activity to warm myself, but I didn't want to bloody the wonderful mittens Semigaq had given me, and I certainly didn't want to carry chunks of meat and blubber with my bare hands. Some--but not all--of my fastidiousness had deserted me.

Stig nudged me and nodded toward Patlok. Ice had formed on the man's eyebrows, and he looked like a creature from ancient mythology, but he was glowing with the thrill of his accomplishment and trying to catch the eye of a girl named Magdalerak. She was bending to the walrus, exposing that band of skin that turned so leathery as women aged. In her case, it was tea-colored and supple, and she seemed to know that Patlok was admiring it.

Young girls like Magdalerak were not well dressed in the settlement. Their fathers were waiting for a husband to outfit them. Her trousers were too small, and her anorak was ratty-looking. Only her beaded kamiks were worthy of her ideal Greenland beauty--fat cheeks, narrow eyes, tiny nose and ample body. All the men had thrown spears at the walrus before it was hauled in, staking their claim to some of the meat, and Magdalerak had the job of returning them to their owners. She saved Patlok's harpoon for last. I would have had trouble picking it up, as it was long and heavy, but she offered it to him effortlessiy with one hand, and their eyes locked.

"Something will come of that," Stig said, and he was right.

That night Patlok visited Magdalerak's house. He talked with her father and ate with the family. The next day, he brought a fine fox skin to her door. I saw the hand that reached out and took it as I was walking to the store. When I returned from my errand, Patlok was standing outside the closed door looking anxious..

"What's going on?" I asked Stig when I got home.

"He's waiting to see what she will do with his gift. She might throw it out and say, `Something was forgotten. This is too good for a poor woman to use.'"

"She wants something less?"

Stig laughed. "What a literalist you are! It means her feelings for him are cool."

"What if she can't stand him?"

"She'll cut up his fur and throw it outside. Then he'll know his love is hopeless. When you came past, Patlok was waiting to see if she would do that."

"And how does she encourage him?"

"By using his gift conspicuously."

212

Later that day Magdalerak did exactly that. Either she or her mother had sewn the fur around her hood, and she strolled down all the paths of the settlement to show it off. At this fortunate sign, Patlok hurried back to her father's house for a conference, and before the day was done, he took Magdalerak home with him.

Thinking about this whirlwind romance, I fastened my seal necklace around my throat. Without even realizing it, I had given Greenlandic encouragement to a man who understood such things. I thought Stig's wooing was speedy, but it was snail-like compared to this love affair.

"How old is that girl?" I asked.

"Twelve, I think."

"That's barbaric! She's just a child. At that rate, Nauja will be married in seven years, and what will you think of that?"

"If I'm here, I'll accept it. At home, I probably couldn't."

Patlok and his bride were not seen for several days, and then Magdalerak took up her new duties in full view of the community. She fetched chunks of walrus from the meat rack, chewed hides, and shopped at the store. But she still had time to play with the other children, as she always had done.

"Mala is almost as old as his stepmother," I observed. "What if he falls in love with her?"

"What if he does?"

"You make me feel like Alice in Wonderland," I fumed. "Sometimes I don't know who or where I am anymore."

"You're my wife, and you're at the top of the world. Any more questions?"

"Not at the moment."

Patlok invited the whole settlement to his house to celebrate his marriage, and when we all were wedged tightly inside, Magdalerak dipped walrus meat from the cooking pot with a caribou antler. She licked it before handing it to her husband to keep the soup and blood from dripping on his fingers, and I shuddered.

Patlok shoved the meat into his mouth as far as it would go, then cut off the rest with his knife and passed it along. Magdalerak

213

watched closely to see how far it got and offered a new piece as needed. Stig and Nauja partook of this hospitality, but I simply could not.

Instead, I tried to talk to Mala about his "new mother." All he would say was, "I can run faster than she can."

After the meal, the men and children went outside to play football with a seal head stuffed with grass. The object was to kick it from one end of the settlement to the other, and Stig said it would take the rest of the day.

I sat with the women, understanding more Greenlandic than I had when I came but still not enough for intimate conversation. Most of them were shy about their Danish and would not speak it but undoubtedly understood more of it than they would admit. In any gathering of women who had known Naika I wondered if they were comparing me to her.

One of the women had a new baby who bore Naika's name, and I watched her closely because I had to figure out how to clothe and care for an infant in this climate. The child was naked inside her mother's garment, warm against her bare back. She simply slid her around to the front to nurse her, loosing her hair to wipe the small face when necessary.

The mother saw and felt my interest, seeing the reason for it in my swollen belly. She smiled and held out the child to me. I took her reluctantly and clumsily, tucking the tiny Naika inside my own clothing to keep her from the cold. Then she did what I knew she would. The pooling urine was hot on my skin and it felt good, much to my surprise. Even so, I vowed I would find something somewhere to use for diapers. Maybe Harald had a tablecloth at the store that I could cut into squares.

Magdalerak's mother seemed happy about her daughter's marriage, and Stig had told me she had absolutely nothing to say about the arrangement, but she had been active behind the scenes.

Magdalerak and I had something in common. Both of us were second wives. I watched the girl serve the guests, whisper to Patlok and put on her anorak to go outside with the children. They had

214

been trying to play hopscotch in the crowded room, and when they were gone, the adult guests could spread out more comfortably.

Only the toddlers were left, and I was amazed to see a three-year-old uncover his mother's breast and nurse contentedly. I asked Semigaq if this was common.

She laughed and said, "This is nothing! I have seen a boy of fourteen at his mother's breast. He climbed out of his kayak to refresh himself."

Patlok was poor-mouthing his hospitality in a most disgusting manner, saying his wretched wife knew nothing about cooking and it was unfortunate that the walrus meat had fallen into dog dung. He begged his guests to leave him alone with his shame, and I heartily wished that I could, but Stig showed no signs of being ready to leave.

With great difficulty, I got to my feet and looked out the door. The children were sliding down the smooth side of a big, slanting rock.

"Nauja," I called. "You're wearing the fur off your pants. Don't do that."

She picked herself up at the bottom of the rock, gave me a long look and got in line for the next slide.

Furious, I closed the door and knelt beside Stig to tell him what she had done. He took my hand and kissed it before he spoke.

"You're being too Danish, Alex. Nauja will ruin her pants without giving it a thought, but one day she'll think of how difficult it is to trap and chew and sew the skins for a new pair. On that day, her childhood will be over."

"But she defied me. It's disrespectful."

"No, it's just young. We believe in progressive education here, my love."

Thinking of what would have happened to me if I had behaved that way when I was Najua's age, I shook my head.

The guests were breaking wind and belching to show their appreciation of Patlok's fare. Some would sleep, then wake to eat

215

more. When Patlok called his bride inside to put more meat into the pot, she whispered to him urgently, and another hunter took that as a signal to issue his invitation.

"Come and see what my poor house has to offer."

I groaned inwardly, knowing that this progressive house party could go on indefinitely.

A small boy rushed into the house to say a sled was approaching, and since everyone in the settlement was accounted for, the curious hurriedly put on their outer garments to learn who was coming.

I stayed inside with Naika and her mother until Stig returned. He had a gleam in his eye that worried me.

"What is it?" I asked.

"The *angagok's* big bird has fallen. A plane is down on the ice cap. I'm going home to harness the dogs."

"Don't go," I begged.

He gave me an incredulous look and said, "I *have* to go."

XXVIII

The wedding celebration ended abruptly as all the men hurried away to harness their dogs. Sleds were loaded with skins and frozen meat, and when they lined up to depart in a tumult of barking, more than fifty dogs were chafing at the leads.

I tried to talk to Stig, but it was almost impossible for us to hear each other. He threw back his hood and motioned for me to shout directly in his ear.

"How long do you think you will be gone?" I shrieked, baring my own ear for an answer.

"I can't imagine where they were going," he said, misunderstanding me completely.

I repeated my question, and he said, "I don't know. It's unfortunate that we fed the dogs at the wedding party. We won't be able to make good time until they're hungry again."

Nauja hooked her arm around her father's knee until he picked her up and hugged her, speaking into her ear. Watching Patlok and Magdalerak touching noses in a tender farewell, I awaited my turn.

Finally Stig took me in his arms, but he was so preoccupied with the rescue mission that I was hurt. How could he leave me like this? What if the baby should come early? What if his arm gave out?

His words vibrated against my temple. "If it *is* a plane, where did it come from? How could it get this far? How could it carry enough fuel?"

"I don't know," I yelled, adding silently, *and I don't care!*

Sigdlu, the *angakok*, was to lead the expedition, and now he gave the signal to depart. Stig gave me a deep, rough kiss and sprang to his sled. I reached for Nauja's hand as the loud caravan moved out in a route that zig-zagged to avoid the bare expanses the wind had swept free of snow.

I turned away while I could still see Stig's red anorak. The other women stayed until their men were out of sight, as they did not share my superstition. I always had considered myself to be more civilized than they were, but that certainty was weakening. I was beginning to fear the spirits in this place more than they did, or perhaps it just seemed that way because I looked ahead and worried. They took life a day at a time.

With no men to feed and care for, the women got together and sewed tents, laughing and gossipping as they worked. I tried to help at first, but my stitches with thread made of narwhal sinew were clumsy. I gave it up, sparing them the embarrassment of asking me to desist.

I read the last page of *Scaramouche* with regret, as I had nothing else to read. "M. de Kercadiou, emerging a moment later from the library window, beheld them holding hands and staring each at the other, beautifically, as if each saw Paradise in the other's face." The tortuous love affair of Aline and Andre had come to its happy ending. What happened to them after the book closed? Ordinary things, probably. Things more ordinary than what I was experiencing in this place where the ordinary was bizarre.

Harald was the only man in the settlement who didn't join the expedition, and I went to the store daily just to speak my own language and stay human. Not that I didn't talk to Nauja, but I could scarcely burden her with my fears.

"Stig can take care of himself," Harald said.

"I know," I said. "It's just that I want him to be here taking care of me."

I was so heavily pregnant that I had trouble sleeping at night, and the dazzling white light of early May was a further deterrent to sleep. Staring at the ceiling, I replayed the first time I saw Stig in the *Rigsdag* chamber. I didn't know my rival then, but I might have guessed when his eyes focused on something no one else could see and he said, "All who love Greenland are lost."

Somehow I knew that when--not if, but when--he came back, something would have to change. I wasn't exactly sure what I wanted, but something had to be different. Maybe I needed a promised return to Denmark for the child's sake and my own. As I

218

thought of this, the baby moved vigorously in my womb.

Since I couldn't sleep, I got up and turned back to the beginning of *Scaramouche*. Mor's check for five thousand *kroner* had been my bookmark, and I fingered it reflectively as I read, "He was born with a gift of laughter and a sense that the world was mad." Then I tossed the book aside and got up to put the check in a safe place. In all the months I had lived here, I had spent a ridiculously small amount of money, and I no longer responded to money in the old way. How strange it was for a banker's daughter to treat a check for a sizeable amount of money like any other scrap of paper, but I would put it in a safe place. It would be useful if we went home. If? Why didn't I say when?

As I passed Nauja's pallet, she cried out in her sleep, and I knelt to comfort her. "What is it? A bad dream?"

"Papa!" she whimpered.

With great difficulty I managed to sit on the floor and pull her onto my lap. I stroked her hair and crooned to her, but she refused to be comforted, and that made me afraid. Greenlanders had ways of knowing things, and I didn't want to hear what she knew.

It seemed strange to have all the dogs in the settlement gone. I was so used to their barking clamor that the silence was eery. With the approach of May, they had stopped covering their noses with their tails, about the only sign of spring that was apparent to me. Stig had told me the loss of a tail could mean death to a dog, leaving it with no protection from the elements.

The long, bright days seemed endless as we waited for news of the rescue party. The *angakok* had agreed to send word back to us with one of the boys when they found what they were seeking. Each day I put on my bone sunglasses and stared in the direction the sleds had taken, seeing nothing but the empty frozen landscape.

Nauja and I walked to the shore of North Star Bay to watch the seals on the ice. We were separated from them by a widening strip of open water, and they seemed to know they were safe as long as the men were gone. No woman would ever throw a spear at them. The males were doing a courtship dance, a pattern of somersaults and vertical leaps in their swimming that eventually excited the females to the point of joining them in the water.

Nauja laughed and shouted, "*Kasuta mardlulerpugut!*"

I was mildly shocked that a five-year-old child would know the meaning of "Let us two melt into one," but I just smiled and nodded. It occurred to me that I did not know when her birthday was. We should have had a celebration when she turned five. She probably didn't miss it because Greenlanders paid little attention to such milestones. Many of them had no idea how old they were, I gathered. My own birthday was in June, and it occurred to me that it might be appropriate to add two years rather than one. Under Arctic conditions, it wouldn't be long until I resembled those youngish "hags" we met in Holsteinsborg. It didn't bear thinking about.

Harald had said the lemmings would soon be upon us, and I was eager to see the strange, little puff balls that migrated every four years, eating everything in their path and finally throwing themselves into the sea. Would it be possible to capture one and keep it as a pet? Harald said no one ever had thought of doing that.

Everything in the Arctic had its use, and there was no comprehension of being friendly with animals. Dogs were for transportation and the untameable creatures were for food. Copulation with dogs was not unheard of, but it had to happen out of doors, Stig said, and that lessened the attraction of the practice.

I did long for a pet now. Wistfully, I remembered the kitten of my childhood, a tawny tiger with topaz eyes named Kaja. I was forbidden to sleep with the cat, but I often sneaked her under my covers, where she purred and kneaded ecstatically. Was there any warmer sound than a cat's purr? Those were the days when I was cozy in my feather *dyne* and didn't have the sense to appreciate a warm bath. It occurred to me that I hadn't been wet all over since I came to Greenland. Like Kaja, I cleaned myself a bit at a time.

I didn't like to cast a pall over the happy memories by thinking of Kaja's fate, but I couldn't help it. She was a tiny cat, and after a marauding black tom impregnated her, she did not survive the birthing. At first, *Mor* told me she ran away, but *Far* forced her to tell me the truth, saying, "What kind of a story is that from a pastor's daughter?"

"What about the kittens?" I asked through my tears.

Far, who believed in the bald truth, said, "Into the fjord. They couldn't live without their mother."

Why did I have to think of that now? I watched the amorous play of the seals with a growing sense of dread. What if I died in childbirth? Who would care for my baby? The physical pang that accompanied the thought terrified me. I never had felt such a strong pain.

"Come, Nauja," I gasped, breaking into a waddling run toward home.

Before we reached the door, a warm, liquid gush between my thighs frightened me even more. "Bring Semigaq!"

I pulled off my fur pants and dried myself, searching for something else to put on as I bit my lips at another swelling pain. "Oh, Stig!" I wailed. I paced and prayed and yearned for my mother.

Then Nauja was back--alone.

"Where's Semigaq?"

"She says she can't come. It would be bad for you."

"Why? In the name of God, why?"

"Bad spirits are with her when babies come."

Nauja went to the kitchen and brought me a chunk of blubber. I shook my head violently, and she bit into it herself, chewing solemnly while she watched me stiffen with a new pain.

Because my kamiks were wet, I was walking barefoot, and the floor was frigid. I asked Nauja to put dry grass in the soles of my kamiks. I sat heavily on the bed and swung my feet up with great effort, covering them with a sealskin. Minutes later, I was up again, pacing and moaning.

My situation seemed unbelievable. Here I was at the ends of the earth, chilled to the bone, in terrible pain, without a husband, in the hands of a five-year-old midwife. I started to laugh hysterically. Considering past experience, if Stig *were* here, he would expect me to produce the child, rest for an hour or so, and rise to prepare his dinner.

I found the seal necklace and fastened it around my throat with shaking hands. It was cold on my skin, but I needed an amulet to bring Stig closer. If Semigaq was sending someone to help me, why didn't she come?

Nauja talked and sang to her doll in Greenlandic, seemingly unconcerned about my travail. This whole process was unnatural only to me, it seemed. Time passed slowly, and just when I would relax with relief at the cessation of pain,a huge fist would squeeze me again.

At last she came. Alakrasina was the mother of the infant I had held at the marriage celebration, and she brought little Naika with her. I wondered what kind of an omen that was--giving birth in the presence of a baby named for Stig's first wife? Was the spirit of that Naika hovering here? Did she wish me well or ill?

Alakrasina placed firm hands on my belly and smiled. She spoke little Danish, but I gathered that my ordeal would go on for some time. She made tea, which I drank without enthusiasm. I considered not drinking it at all because I had no wish to use the latrine bucket in the entry. What if the baby should mistake it for the customary hole in the floor? That notion was insane, I realized immediately. Stig and I were Danes. Our child would not expect a Greenlandic entry to life.

Alakrasina fed Nauja, ate some seal meat herself, and sat down to nurse little Naika, watching me with calm eyes.. I couldn't bear the thought of eating.

"Do you think Nauja should see this?" I asked, and Alakrasina didn't understand. Finally, by pointing and gesturing, I made it clear, and she laughed.

Nothing was kept from children here. They watched their parents make love and imitated the act with their young friends, much to the fond amusement of those parents. They watched dogs copulate, and sometimes they served as guards armed with sticks to keep the dogs at bay while others evacuated. No wonder Alakrasina

222

found my delicacy so amusing.

I had not yet learned to tell the time of day by the light that was so unnatural to me, and the wind-up clock I had relied upon had stopped running weeks earlier. How would I ever know the hour of our child's birth? I tried to express this to Alakrasina, but it was hopeless.

The pains came in quicker succession, and I gnawed at my knuckles to keep from screaming. Alakrasina put the baby inside her clothes against her back to free her hands for stitching the sleeve of a sealskin jacket. From time to time she would look at me, shake her head and return to her work.

Did she know what she was doing? What I wouldn't have given to place myself in the hands of a doctor in Aalborg or Copenhagen right now.

After what seemed an eternity, she put down her sewing, placed her naked baby on Nauja's pallet and took my arm. "Down," she said.

"Down?"

She got on her knees to demonstrate, and it was my turn to shake my head. "People have babies in beds," I said.

Alakrasina continued to insist, and I begged Nauja to make her understand what I was saying. They had a vehement interchange, and Nauja told me, "You must do what she says. Baby comes this way," she stabbed her hand toward the floor, "and not this way," the hand shot out horizontally.

I moaned, knowing I had to do things Alakrasina's way if I expected her to help me. I knelt with great difficulty, and she pressed down on my belly. Overwhelmed by pain, I tried to push, but nothing happened. Alakrasina muttered in Greenlandic.

"What is she saying, Nauja?"

"The baby won't come until the *angagok* is here to put its soul in a safe place. She told me to get the blubber lamp. If he doesn't come, she will hide it there."

Nauja brought one of the lamps we had stored away at the beginning of the endless light season, and Alakrasina looked happier. I was so weary and wracked with pain that I didn't understand any of this and didn't care. Alakrasina bodily moved my knees farther apart, and our child was born on the floor, slimey with blood and mucus and entangled in the umbilical cord. She cut the cord with a flensing knife, and that pang was lost in a host of others as I dropped on my hands to look at the child. We had a son.

He gave a lusty cry as Alakrasina wiped him with a piece of skin, passed her hand before his face as if collecting something and placed that invisible something under the blubber lamp. "Now he is safe," she said in halting Danish.

I rose from my knees with difficulty and fell on the bed, opening my arms to receive the baby. His mass of dark hair, wet as a swimming seal, was his legacy from Stig. What he had from me was not yet apparent. Alakrasina pushed his seeking mouth to my breast, and he seemed outraged by what I had to offer. I questioned her with my eyes, and she said, "Milk will come."

""Soon, I hope. We have nothing else to give him."

Her eyes crinkled with amusement. "*Ayorama,*" she said.

"That's how it goes?" I started to laugh, realizing I wouldn't have known how to have a baby any better in Denmark than I did here. I had experienced the mystery of life's beginning, and already that reality was receding. But the pain was over, the child seemed healthy, and I had given Stig a son. All I needed now was Stig's arms around the two of us.

Having done her duty, Alakrasina thrust Naika into her coat, collected her sewing and headed for the door.

"Don't leave me!" I cried in panic. At home, I would be in the hospital for at least ten days with nurses carrying my baby to me to be fed.

"Now Semigaq will come," Nauja said.

And so she did. When she arrived, she touched the baby's cheek with an expression of sad longing and explained we couldn't come near him until his soul was hidden under the blubber lamp, the one place where it was safe. The evil spirits who had taken her own babies swirled around her when she even thought of an infant.

"It's too bad the *angagok* wasn't here to hide the baby's soul," she said, "but Alakrasina said she went into a small trance and called him to her before she coaxed it out and put it under the lamp. He was there, she said."

The baby, exhausted from the exertion of being born, slept soundly in the curve of my arm, covered by a blue fox skin.

"Where is the skin she wiped him with?" Semigaq asked. "You must always keep that as an amulet to ward off evil."

"I don't know," I said, feeling sudden panic. "I didn't see what she did with it, did you, Nauja?"

Nauja hadn't noticed, and she helped Semigaq conduct a frantic search for the blood-stained skin. They finally found it, accidentally kicked under the bed, and were profoundly relieved. So, unaccountably, was I.

"What is the baby's name?" Semigaq asked.

"I don't know. We decided to wait until we saw him--or her. When Stig gets back, we'll choose." I didn't tell her I was calling him Christopher in my mind.

What seemed like minutes later, I felt the sudden emptiness of my arms and cried out. Semigaq touched my hand and said, "I have him. You may rest now."

XXIX

At long last the messenger came. The rescue party had found the big bird and the men who had fallen from the sky. They were Danes, and one was dead, he said. The rescuers were returning as quickly as possible.

Semigaq brought me the news in the morning as I was nursing Christopher, but I sensed that she was not telling me all she knew.

"Is Stig all right?"

"One does not know everything," she said evasively.

I fought anxiety as the hours of the day crept past. The last thing I wanted to do was dry up the milk in my breasts. I repeated the incantations of Dr. Coue, told fairytales to Nauja, and sang lullabies to the baby.

Toward evening I heard a shout at the door, "Someone comes!"

I opened the door and gasped at the sight of two men carrying Stig on a stretcher of skins.

"Alex!" he said weakly.

"Put him on the bed," I said.

He groaned as they rolled him off the stretcher, and I embraced him fearfully.

"What happened?"

"My leg. I went into a crevasse after the pilot and the ice caved in before I reached him. They had to chop me loose."

I started to pull off one kamik and he screamed with pain. One of the men stepped forward to cut the leather, and I was sickened by the blue, swollen flesh beneath it. While I was trying to decide what to do, Nauja came to the bed with the baby in her arms.

"Look, Papa!"

Agonized as he was, Stig smiled and reached for Christopher. "Alex, I should have been here--" Then he fainted.

The leg had been crushed, and I nearly fainted myself as I tried to wipe it clean and cover it with some of the diapers I had torn from tablecloths.

The knock on the door startled me. Greenlanders simply announced themselves, saying, "Someone comes visiting."

I opened the door and stared in disbelief at Leif Skovgard.

"Aren't you going to ask me in, Alex?" Leif said with a crooked grin.

"*You* were on that plane?"

"I like to make news as well as report it. Hey, it's cold out here!"

"Come in, then," I said, distracted to the point of tears.

Leif entered and looked around, saying, "Fairly cozy for Polar quarters."

"Just tell me what happened. I'd like to understand why my husband had to hurt himself so terribly trying to rescue a fool like you!"

Leif took off his anorak and made himself at home, lighting a cigarette before he began his tale. The very fact that he had a cigarette meant he hadn't been in the Arctic long.

He was taking his time getting to it, which gave me the opportunity to berate myself for watching him out of sight and bringing this rotten luck upon us.

"Well, are you going to tell me about this expedition?" I said, crossing my arms over my chest. My breasts were swelling with milk, and I hoped to hear Leif's recital before I had to nurse Christopher.

"As you probably know--" he broke off, laughing. "How could you know anything up here?"

I gave him a filthy look, and he threw his hands up in apology, saying, "Well, we have a new Danish airline, and this little jaunt was an experiment. It would be much easier to supply the settlements and outposts by air than by ship and dogsled--if it were possible at all--and I convinced the powers that be that I should be in on it to tell the world about this pioneering enterprise. Unfortunately, it didn't work according to plan."

"I can't imagine how it could work at all," I said. "Those little canvas things can't carry enough fuel to get anywhere."

"We thought we had that part worked out. We took the disassembled plane to Iceland by ship, put it together, and got as far as the ice cap before we ran out of fuel."

"The pilot died, they say. How did you manage to survive?"

"The impact threw both of us out of the plane, and he was just unlucky. He fell into a crevasse, and and I fell into deep, powdery snow. I tried to throw some supplies down to the pilot, but he wasn't showing any signs of life down there. I had enough supplies to keep going for awhile, and I had enough sense to sit tight until somebody came for me."

"What made you think they ever would? This is the wilderness."

"This is also the place where heroes never count the cost."

"That's for certain," I said bitterly, glancing at the unconscious Stig. "Why couldn't you just stay home where you belonged--both of you?"

"Because I love you. The mere fact that you married someone else is of no importance to me."

"Oh, go to Hell!" I shouted, turning my back on him. I picked up Christopher from the limp curve of his father's arm and went into the kitchen to nurse him. My emotions must have curdled the milk because he played with the nipple peevishly.

I thought of my pastor grandfather and was glad he couldn't hear me consigning someone to Hell. I re-lived the moment when I watched Leif out of sight in Copenhagen and yearned to change it.

"Alex?"

Leif's voice startled me, and I covered the baby's head and my breast. "What is it?"

"I really think we'll have to get Brand somewhere for medical attention. I don't like the looks of that leg."

I started to cry, and Leif put his arms around me and the baby. For want of any other comfort, I allowed this.

Then Harald came, the *angagok* arrived with Patlok, and the men held a small seance. I huddled in the kitchen with the children while this was going on, but I could see Leif's rapt expression and begrudged him the scoop he would wring from this occasion.

Stig had regained consciousness and was participating, his eyes glittering with fever. I longed to go to him, but I couldn't while this was going on.

When it was over, they had a plan. We would eat a hearty meal of seal meat, then pack three sleds to move along the ice cap as rapidly as possible to a port where we could find a doctor and/or a ship bound for Denmark.

This mode of travel for a newborn and a seriously injured man seemed unthinkable to Leif, but Harald convinced him it was the only way.

"The ice is broken up nearer the shore, so they'll have to take an inside route," Harald said.

I packed everything I owned, which wasn't much, but I left *Scaramouche* for Harald to read and told him he could have Dr. Coue as well, but he said he didn't believe in that nonsense.

I gave what was left of the costume jewelry to Semigaq, and both of us were teary in a farewell embrace. Then I climbed onto a sled with Christopher and Nauja, took one last long look at the house and turned my face into the wind.

The first night out Patlok and his friend Otoniaq quickly constructed an igloo to shield us from the high winds, and we made tea over a small blubber fire. I climbed carefully into Stig's sleeping bag of skins, trying not to touch his bad leg, and we warmed the baby between our naked bodies. This was true parenthood, I thought.

"He's a good child," Stig observed.

"Yes, he seldom cries."

"Did you think of me when he was born?"

"I called your name."

"And I called yours when the ice fell on me."

"Leif isn't worth what happened to you," I said.

He laughed and said, "The pilot might have been."

"I wonder if he had a wife and children? That one---" I nodded toward Leif, who was playing solitaire in the faint glow of the blubber lamp, "he wouldn't know about anything human like that."

"You're too hard on him, Alex. Now listen to me. I have enough medical training to know how serious my condition is. If I don't make it--"

I put my hand over his mouth. "Don't even say it!"

The dogs were hungry enough to make good time, and when we would stop to rest, Leif would pull out a nub of a pencil and scribble on a small pad he carried.

"I love this country where necessity is the reason for everything!" he said.

"Even cannibalism," Stig said, telling a story of surgical butchery in an expedition that ran out of supplies during a storm of record duration.

Leif looked queasy, but he took some quick notes.

The trip seemed endless, and Christopher cried a lot, picking up on my anxiety. Would we reach Holsteinsborg in time to stem the infection in Stig's leg? Would the baby stay well? I never could tell if we were making progress in the trackless white landscape.

Stig slept most of the time, and I was too angry about the grief Leif had caused us to take any pleasure in his company.

At last Patlok shouted up ahead, and I glimpsed the spire of the Holsteinsborg church. Thank God!

We went immediately to the doctor's house, and he was just sitting down to his supper. *Hr.* Beck was dining with the Petersens, and he greeted us cordially before returning to his rapidly cooling soup.

Holding Christopher close, I watched the examination with dread. Dr. Petersen shook his head and said, "This calls for amputation, I'm afraid, and I hate to tackle that."

"Oh no!" I cried.

"The Polaris sails tomorrow for Copenhagen," the doctor said. "I think you'd do better to take a chance on getting there than trying to deal with this in Greenland."

Hr. Beck offered to make the sailing arrangements, and we

231

went to the Rasmussens to spend the night. On our way there, we said good-bye to Patlok and Otoniaq. I even felt a pang at leaving the dogs, particularly Miuk who had responded to me so well when I was forced to drive after Stig broke his arm.

Frue Rasmussen was welcoming and sympathetic, and after she fed us the best meal I had eaten since our last stay in her home, she took the children off to another room, leaving Stig and me to ourselves.

He was in constant pain, I knew, but he tried not to show it. I told him he didn't have to be brave on my account.

He sighed and said, "I never thought it would turn out like this. When we were here last summer, I felt immortal--probably because I was drunk on love."

"And now?" I asked fearfully.

"The love part is the same, but I'm not so sure about the immortality."

"Please don't say that."

Leaning heavily on me, he hobbled to the window, and we looked out together. The Aurora was putting on a spectacular show with quivering curtains of rose and green, the pulsing light making huge S-curves.

"What a lovely farewell," I said.

"Farewell forever."

"We can come back," I said.

"A man needs two legs in the Arctic."

"What *I* need is you. One leg will be enough."

When the Polaris set sail, I thought of our voyage to Greenland aboard the Hekla when we were dizzy with love and full of hope for the future. Now I was full of foreboding and exhausted by caring for two children. For Stig's sake, I tried not to show it, but he knew. He would hold me carefully, trying not to touch the leg. He was silent much of the time, staring off into the distance and making a mighty effort not to complain about his terrible injury. Dr. Petersen had given him some pills for pain, but they didn't seem to help much.

"Somebody in Copenhagen can save your leg, Stig," I told him.

He looked at the discolored flesh I was bathing so carefully and shook his head. Bits of broken bone made malevolent hills under the skin, and he couldn't bear to put weight on the leg. He was using a makeshift crutch one of the sailors had found for him when it was absolutely necessary for him to move. Most of the time, he stayed in the berth, and I would sit beside him holding Christopher and trying to make cheerful conversation.

Leif turned out to be a godsend in one way, at least. He took charge of Nauja during most of her waking hours. She loved running around the decks, poking her head through the rails dangerously.

Christopher had turned peevish, probably because my milk was affected by my emotional state, and I would jounce him up and down, singing to him and wishing with all my heart that he could age miraculously and take care of himself just long enough for me to get the sleep I craved so desperately.

Stig said, "I was just remembering the day we met in the *Riksdag* chamber. You were so lovely--but if I could have foreseen all of this, I might have had the strength to look the other way and spare you."

"Oh, no, Stig! I would never give up the good times we have had to avoid the bad times. Besides, you warned me. You said, `All

233

who love Greenland are lost.' Remember?

He nodded morosely. "I still have the longing, but now I can't answer the call."

"Stig Brand, I can't believe that you would give up the dream in the blood, as you called it. And what's more, I have it, too. I caught it from you."

He reached for my hand and squeezed it, sighing deeply. "What's to become of us, Alexandra?"

"When your leg heals, we'll go back."

"Alexandra, this leg will never heal."

"How can you know that? We'll find a wonderful doctor who can save it." Even as I spoke, I wasn't sure I believed what I was saying, but I couldn't let him give up.

The night before we came into port, Leif came to our cabin and offered to take charge of our belongings when we landed.

"Alex, you can have my apartment," he said. "I can bunk somewhere else for awhile. I'll take your things there, and I'd offer to take the children, too, but I think Christopher needs you rather frequently."

"Just help us get ashore and call a taxi," I told him. "I want to get to a hospital as soon as possible."

I had no time to revel in the joy of homecoming. I had expected to be thrilled by the bustle of Copenhagen after the long silences of the North, but now I cursed the traffic that slowed our cab. We finally arrived, and I practically threw some *kroner* at the driver. Balancing Christopher on one hip, I reached for Nauja's hand. She was terrified by the cars, never having seen such things, and clutched my knees. How in the world would I be able to help Stig into the hospital?

In the end, the driver helped. Stig's forehead was beaded with sweat as he leaned on the man and hobbled toward the entrance.

Inside, I explained our situation to a nurse at the desk. She hit a bell with the palm of her hand, and two orderlies came to lift Stig onto a gurney. I walked beside him, carrying a crying Christopher and dragging a terrified Nauja.

A doctor was found, and when he slashed the leg of Stig's trousers to look at the injury, he said, "My God! When did this happen."

"Last month. The doctor in Holsteinsborg said it was beyond him."

"Well, Sir, you're lucky to be alive," the doctor said. "Let's get to the operating room."

"You'll save the leg, won't you?" I said.

"I'll do my best."

I stooped quickly and kissed the angry-looking flesh of Stig's leg in a kind of farewell should that be necessary. At the swinging doors of the operating room, I kissed his lips and said, "I love you. I'll love you forever."

"And I'll love you with whatever is left of me," he promised.

Then the doors closed behind him, and I stood staring at them with tears running down my cheeks. Nauja observed this and pulled my hand to her lips. I was overwhelmed by this uncharacteristic gesture of affection.

Pulling myself together, I went to find a telephone. I wanted my mother and prayed she would be at home to answer my call. She was. At the sound of her dear   voice, the tears started again. "*Mor?" I said. "*It's Alexandra."

When she recovered from shock, she asked where I was, and I told her the whole sad story. She said, "*Far* and I will be there as soon as we can."

I told her we had a baby--Christopher--and she asked if I was all right and if he was healthy, sighing with relief when I said yes to both questions.

I asked if they would be taking the next train to the city, and she said she couldn't speak for *Far*, actually, but if he couldn't get away, she'd bring Frederik. She also told me that Frederik thought he was in love.

I hung up hugely relieved. My mother was on her way to make things right for me as she had always done. I was feeling much too warm in my Arctic clothing, but Leif had taken everything else to the apartment, and I would just have to suffer. Nauja was hot, too. Perhaps we could go to the apartment and change, returning before Stig's operation was over. I told the nurse at the desk where I was going, found the key Leif had given me and hailed a taxi.

I had been in the apartment when Leif entertained the poetry group, and I found his stereoptican glasses for Nauja to play with. I deposited Christopher on the bed where I had thrown my coat on so many bohemian evenings.

Our belongings were stacked in the hallway, and I found a waist and skirt that would do for me and a shirt of mine Nauja could wear until we could find something more suitable. Then I stripped off the hot anorak and decided a sponge bath would be a good idea.

Naked to the waist in the bathroom, I heard noises at the front door. Before I could cover myself, Leif was in the doorway looking at me.

"Beautiful!" he said. "As beautiful as I had imagined."

I folded my arms across my chest and told him to get out.

"You're throwing me out of my own home?"

"The rent is too high," I said, slamming the door in his face. I dressed hastily and started to drag our possessions out of the apartment. Christopher was crying in the bedroom, and Nauja ran and hid behind a chair.

"Come on, Alex," Leif said, "What kind of a life can you have with Brand? All he knows is the far North, and that's scarcely a place for a one-legged man."

"His place is with me, and my place is with him. I met him thanks to you, but our friendship is over, Leif."

I picked up Christopher, grabbed a suitcase and told Nauja to carry what she could. A sullen Leif decided to help, and soon we were on the sidewalk waiting for another cab. When one arrived, I threw the apartment key at Leif and started the loading process.

At the hospital, the doctor was looking for me. He introduced himself, something there had been no time for earlier. "I'm Ivar Westergaard. I'm afraid the leg was too badly crushed to save."

"Does he know?

"Not yet. He's still under the anesthetic. He's a very strong man. The infection he had would have finished most people. He should heal well, and then we can fit a prosthesis."

"May I go to him now?"

"Certainly. He's in the recovery room."

We sat beside him for a long time, and I averted my eyes from the flat place under the sheet where a leg should be. A nurse brought some food for me and Nauja on a tray. I was too devastated to eat, but Nauja relished the bread, cheese and fruit. She didn't understand what had happened.

At long last, Stig's eyelids fluttered, and I leaned close to say, "I'm here."

"The leg is gone, isn't it?"

I nodded, fighting tears. "The doctor says you will heal well, and then they can fit a new leg."

He closed his eyes and turned his face from me.

"Stig, look at me," I said. "I kissed the old leg good-bye, and when you get the new one, I'll kiss it hello." I bent down to kiss his lips.

My parents arrived in the late afternoon, and *Far* immediately offered Stig a job in the bank.

"That's very kind,*Herr* Lund," Stig said without enthusiasm.

Mor was enchanted with her grandson, who stared up at her with the dark blue gaze of infancy and almost seemed to smile. Nauja loved her, too, and soon both children were on her lap.

I moved back to *Frue* Steinsen's house, and the children loved her, as well. She cared for them while I went to the hospital to see Stig.

One day I went to the Strøget and looked in the window of the Georg Jensen shop. Hr. Supercilious was serving a customer, and he looked up, almost into my eyes, but he didn't recognize me. I decided not to go inside. Why look at beautiful but useless things? The trading post stocked with goods necessary to maintain life made far more sense.

Another day I strolled in Tivoli after leaving the hospital and passed the wine bar where I spent so many late afternoons with Leif. We had left the place to go to the workers' café where Stig joined us and took me home after that crazy poet knocked Leif unconscious--the night he kissed me lightly and left me wanting much more.

I stopped for coffee at a sidewalk café, remembering how I had longed to do that when I was in Greenland, and it didn't come up to my expectations despite the excellent brew and the warm sun. It seemed that I could not live in the moment in Copenhagen. I was either in the past or pushing at the future, demanding to know what would happen next.

Claudine heard I was back and invited me to a literary evening. I told her I had no wish to encounter Leif, and she said he was out of the country on an assignment. I went and discovered that sitting on cushions listening to bad poetry didn't have the charm it once had for me. When they started talking about the New Woman, I recalled my female friends in Greenland--Kullabak and Semigaq in particular. I told the group about them, saying, "They are the closest thing to the New Woman I've ever met."

"But they're primitive," Claudine said.

"That may be so, but they are independent, wise and loving. And they know how to be happy." Saying this, I yearned for my friends.

Stig's leg had been amputated just above the knee. He learned to walk quite well with its artificial replacement. We moved to Aalborg and lived with my parents temporarily. This was a happy arrangement, for the most part, but Frederik brought his girlfriend home far too often to please me. Her name was Thea, and she treated Nauja coldly, embarrassed by the introduction of this "foreign" child into the family.

"How can you love such a girl?" I asked Frederik.

And Frederik, who adored Nauja, said, "I'm beginning to wonder."

That conversation took place while we were weekending at the shore, and this time, I didn't find the water so cold. I plunged right n with my brother.

Stig became a banker, wearing suits and neckties, and he said, 'You might as well get rid of all that Arctic gear we brought back. We'll never use it again."

But I kept it. Now I was the one with the dream in the blood, the love of Greenland that draws one back. Although we learned to make three-legged love in a Danish featherbed quite satisfactorily, I missed the sleeping bags of the far North. I missed the wild beauty of the Arctic landscape, and I missed my friends.

"Are you happy here?" I asked Stig.

"I would be happier if we had our own house."

I took his hand in both of mine and said, "We do--in North Star Bay. Oh Stig, let's go back. I used to think Greenland was north of the heart, but now I know better."

His eyes lit up, and he said, " But you realize that I won't be able to jump around on the ice floes anymore."

"Good! Then you'll spend more time with me, and I'm sure Harald will be glad to have you in the trading post more, too."

And so it was that we booked passage on the Hekla, the same ship that took us to Greenland the first time. The captain who married us was still at the helm.

Our spirits rose with each northward nautical mile, and once more the engines throbbed,"Greenland, Greenland, Greenland." We were going home.

Cape Farewell looked fierce with its foaming, beating sea, but we took the crash of the waters as a welcome. We had returned to a place where we would live in the moment because each moment required one's whole being. And that was happiness--using it all.

THE END

ABOUT THE AUTHOR

Julie McDonad has published ten novels, including two back-of-the-book novels in Redbook Magazine, and her pure Danish ancestry inspired the choice of Scandinavian subjects for half of them.

She is a graduate of the University of Iowa and attended the Iowa Writers Workshop. A working journalist (feature writer and columnist), she also is a lecturer in journalism at St. Ambrose University and has taught in the Iowa Summer Writing Festival. She is a former chair of the Iowa Arts Council and a long-time participant in its Writers-in-the-Schools/Communities program

She lives in Davenport, Iowa, with her attorney husband and a Scottish Deerhound named Lochinvar.

Printed in the United States
1690